Dirty Sexy Knitting

CHRISTIE RIDGWAY

BERKLEY BOOKS, NEW YORK

THE BERKLEY PUBLISHING GROUP
Published by the Penguin Group
Penguin Group (USA) Inc.
375 Hudson Street, New York, New York 10014, USA
Penguin Group (Canada), 90 Eglinton Avenue East, Suite 700, Toronto, Ontario M4P 2Y3, Canada
(a division of Pearson Penguin Canada Inc.)
Penguin Books Ltd., 80 Strand, London WC2R 0RL, England
Penguin Group Ireland, 25 St. Stephen's Green, Dublin 2, Ireland (a division of Penguin Books Ltd.)
Penguin Group (Australia), 250 Camberwell Road, Camberwell, Victoria 3124, Australia
(a division of Pearson Australia Group Pty. Ltd.)
Penguin Books India Pvt. Ltd., 11 Community Centre, Panchsheel Park, New Delhi—110 017, India
Penguin Group (NZ), 67 Apollo Drive, Rosedale, North Shore 0632, New Zealand
(a division of Pearson New Zealand Ltd.)
Penguin Books (South Africa) (Pty.) Ltd., 24 Sturdee Avenue, Rosebank, Johannesburg 2196,
South Africa

Penguin Books Ltd., Registered Offices: 80 Strand, London WC2R 0RL, England

This is a work of fiction. Names, characters, places, and incidents either are the product of the author's imagination or are used fictitiously, and any resemblance to actual persons, living or dead, business establishments, events, or locales is entirely coincidental. The publisher does not have any control over and does not assume any responsibility for author or third-party websites or their content.

DIRTY SEXY KNITTING

A Berkley Book / published by arrangement with the author

PRINTING HISTORY
Berkley edition / June 2009

Copyright © 2009 by Christie Ridgway.
Cover illustration and hand lettering by Ben Perini.
Cover design by Rita Frangie.
Interior text design by Laura K. Corless.

ISBN: 978-0-425-22829-6

BERKLEY®
Berkley Books are published by The Berkley Publishing Group,
a division of Penguin Group (USA) Inc.,
375 Hudson Street, New York, New York 10014.
BERKLEY® is a registered trademark of Penguin Group (USA) Inc.
The "B" design is a trademark of Penguin Group (USA) Inc.

PRINTED IN THE UNITED STATES OF AMERICA

10 9 8 7 6 5 4 3 2 1

One

"It's my party," Cassandra Riley told her companions as she wiped a tear from her cheek with the back of her hand. "I'll cry if I want to."

The pair on her couch didn't look up, and the one near the overstuffed chair in her living room continued toying with a small ball of soft yarn. It was left over from the dress Cassandra had made to wear to the celebration-that-wasn't, and she fingered the mohair-nylon-wool of the crocheted skirt, wishing the April sky would take its cue from the blue color. Stanching another tear, she pressed her nose to the sliding glass door that led to her backyard. Beyond the small pool with its graceful, arching footbridge, the green of the surrounding banana trees, sword ferns, and tropical shrubs looked lush against the dark storm clouds.

The rain hadn't let up.

And neither had Cassandra's low mood.

Thirty years old, she thought, feeling more wetness drip off her jaw, and she was all dressed up with no place to go.

That wasn't strictly true. Three miles away on the Pacific Coast Highway, at her little yarn shop, Malibu & Ewe, the ingredients for a birthday bash were ready and waiting. But a spring deluge had hit overnight and before her landline phone connection had died she'd been informed that the road at the end of her secluded lane was washed out. The narrow driveway beyond her place led to only one other residence.

She wouldn't be partying over there, even if the owner would let her through the doors. Even if he was inside his bat cave.

Though they'd been lovers for four weeks, he'd dumped her yesterday, hard. She suspected that following their public scene he'd immediately headed for someplace where he could indulge in another of his self-destructive benders without anyone's interference.

"That means we're alone, kids," she said over her shoulder. "Isolated."

All she'd never wanted by thirty.

She'd made contact with her donor sibling sisters because she wanted the family ties her sperm-inseminated, single mother had always eschewed. Cassandra had forged a real relationship with Nikki and Juliet now, but there was trouble on that front, too.

So here she was, all by herself again. Lonely.

The rain picked up, drumming harder against the roof and all three "kids" jumped. She'd taken them in last year during a torrential storm and they probably remembered what it was like to be wet and muddy and barely clinging to life.

She couldn't blame the cats for being spooked. Besides being brokenhearted, Cassandra felt a little twitchy herself. She wiggled her toes in her warm down slippers and rubbed her arms to smooth away her chills. Dark was approaching, the weather wasn't abating, and with the road gone already, she had to be on the lookout for more evidence of mud slides.

Blinking back another round of self-pity, she scrutinized the backyard once more. At the rear was the first of the narrow flights of steps that led to the other house farther up the Malibu canyon. A creek ran through the northern end of the property, very picturesque, but if its banks overflowed, then water would come gushing down those stairs, just like—

Oh, God.

Just like it was doing right now.

She stared at the widening wash of muddy runoff tumbling Slinky-like down the cement steps. This wasn't good.

This wasn't supposed to happen on her birthday.

Or ever, for that matter.

Thumping sounds from the direction of her front porch caused her head to jerk around. Floodwaters behind her and what—who was on her porch? Her heart slammed against her chest. The cats jumped to their feet and rushed toward the front door.

Surely only one person could get them moving with such haste. They loved him, though he pretended not to care.

Could it be . . . ?

She crossed the room, almost beating the kids in the impromptu footrace. Their tails swished impatiently as she grasped the doorknob, twisted, and pulled.

In the deepening dusk, the visitor was just a dark figure in a sodden raincoat, a wide-brimmed safari-style hat shadowing his face and leaking water at the edges like she'd been leaking tears a few minutes before.

Cassandra's heart smacked in an erratic, painful rhythm against her breastbone. Yesterday he'd walked away from her and she'd doubted if she'd ever see him again.

The figure pushed aside the open edges of his long coat. The sleeve slid up, reminding her of the bandage he'd wound around his cut wrist just a few weeks before. She knew the skin was healed there now.

His hand appeared pale against the blackness of his clothes. She saw the gleam of something metallic shoved into the waistband of dark jeans.

Oh, God.

She'd known he was in a bleak mood yesterday.

I was thinking about Maddie. I've been thinking about Maddie all day.

But even after the many times she'd rescued him off barroom floors, even after the numerous occasions he'd gone missing for days at a stretch, even after the skydiving and the hang gliding and the dangerous solo kayak ocean voyages, not to mention that walk down the middle of a dark, rainy highway just two nights before, her mind couldn't fathom . . .

"Gabe?" she whispered, her gaze lifting to the face beneath the hat's brim. "A gun?"

Six weeks earlier . . . The ring of the bedside phone jolted Cassandra from a fitful sleep. She jackknifed up, disturbing the snoozing cats. Her hand snatched the receiver from its base as adrenaline sluiced through her veins. "Gabe?" It was either him, or about him. Her two A.M. calls were like that.

It was of the second variety. She assured the caller she was on her way, then dressed, her movements made choppy by the adrenaline hit she'd taken. In cropped sweatpants, T-shirt, and her yoga slip-ons, she let herself out of the house.

She didn't feel the chill in the spring night air.

She didn't feel the rough gravel under her thin-soled shoes.

She only felt relief.

After three days without any sign of him, he'd turned up. This wasn't his longest stay away and this wasn't the most worried she'd ever been, but still she had to take deep breaths to calm her heartbeat on the short drive to the Beach Shack, notable for only two things: In Malibu terms it was quite far from the beach, and the owner kept Cassandra's number pinned on the corkboard next to the bar's house phone.

Gabe's been found, she told herself, pulling into the small, potholed parking lot. *We have another chance.*

There wasn't any "we," she knew that, but she used the word anyway, as if by doing so she could make him an active partner in this endeavor to keep him engaged in the world around him.

Come on, Cassandra. She knew where her insidious inner voice was going, and she wished she could block it out as she pushed open the Beach Shack's door. *Don't you really mean in this endeavor to keep him alive?*

He looked half-dead, she had to admit. In jeans and a long-sleeved shirt, Gabe sat with his butt on the sticky floor, his back against the battered bar, his head down. Black hair obscured his face as a little man wearing stained khakis and a greasy-looking Dodgers cap swept around his long, outstretched legs.

The baseball fan looked up. "Closed," he said, his Spanish accent thick.

She pointed her forefinger at the ragdoll figure. "I'm here for him."

Another man bustled through a swinging door behind the bar. "That's becoming a bad habit, Cassandra," he said. His cap proclaimed him a Lakers devotee.

Shrugging, she smiled. "Hi, Mr. Mueller." She'd gone to middle school with his daughter and he'd never failed to attend the annual father-daughter luncheon. In seventh grade, she'd been assigned the seat next to his and she'd pretended for forty-two blissful minutes that the potbellied man who smelled like Marlboros and deli pickles was her daddy.

Mr. Mueller wiped his hands on a dingy rag and then made his way around the bar to stand beside her. They both gazed down at Gabe.

"He showed up about eleven," the older man said.

"You could have called me then," she replied, frowning. "I would have—"

"He was with a woman."

The quick breath she took hurt her lungs. "Oh." Her face burned, and she pretended not to notice the sympathetic look he sent her. Malibu was like any other small town in the way that everyone thought they knew everyone else's business.

Mr. Mueller grimaced. "If it helps any—"

"It doesn't matter," she interjected.

"—she looked like a two-bit . . ." His voice drifted off as the man on the floor stirred.

"I stink," Gabe mumbled.

"His, uh, friend threw up on him," the bar owner said to Cassandra. "After that, I called her a cab." He reached down to grab Gabe's arm. "Let's go, buddy. Your ride's here."

"Don' call her," Gabe said, his head swinging up to pin the other man with bloodshot eyes. "Don' wan' her here."

"It's okay, fella," Mr. Mueller said, helping him to his feet. "A taxi took your date away."

Cassandra stepped forward to slide her arm around the drunk's lean waist. "Gabe means me."

To prove her true, he let out a long, low groan. "C'ssandra." When he shook his head, he stirred the air around him, his disgusting smell wafting closer.

An odor she could blame on some other woman.

Gabe's date.

She looked like a two-bit . . . Cassandra suspected Gabe hadn't had to pay his evening's companion a thing. The dark spaces inside of him acted like a magnet for all kinds of women.

The wrong kind.

Even the smart kind.

Especially the kind who seemed to be lacking self-protective instincts.

"Let's go," she said, trying not to breathe through her nose as she led him outside the bar.

She spread an old beach towel she found in her trunk on the passenger seat then helped Mr. Mueller insert Gabe into the car. She buckled him in as his head lolled on the cushion and then blessed the donut-and-chow-mein scent that rose in the air as she started the motor. Gabe always gave her grief about the odor of the used vegetable oil she put in the gas tank of her converted 1980 Mercedes, but it smelled a heck of a lot better than he did.

She glanced over at him several times on the trip home. He'd passed out again, she decided, and that was a relief in its own way. After parking in the circular drive by his front entrance, she jogged around to open his door. Then it was up to her to search his pockets for his house keys. Better to get the front door open before trying to drag him up the steps and inside.

No need to instruct him to lift off the seat. Gabe carried his wallet and keys in his right front pocket. Leaning in, she inserted her fingers between layers of tight denim.

She shrieked when a hard hand clamped around her wrist. "Darlin'," Gabe said, apparently conscious again. "We fin'ly gonna do it?"

Rolling her eyes, she yanked on her hand, but he wouldn't release her. "Let go. Let go, you idiot."

"Liked where you were head'n."

Cassandra rolled her eyes again. There were twelve steps to self-recovery, so it shouldn't surprise her that there were steps to self-destruction, too. For Gabe, those tended to go like this: 1) a short-to-long disappearance 2) followed by a scene of public drunkenness 3) ending with demands for sex with Cassandra.

He never remembered them after he sobered up.

He never seemed interested in her that way after he sobered up either.

She yanked again, freeing her hand, then patted his thigh to check out the pocket from the outside. It seemed empty. "Gabe, where are your keys?"

"Dunno." Frowning, he managed to get his feet out of the car and then he stood, swaying as he held on to the open door. His hands searched all four of his pockets. "C'ssandra. Do you have m'keys?"

"No." Thinking fast, she decided the best way to deal was to run to her house and get the spare set. She'd dash through his front yard to the steps leading to her back area. He'd be better off waiting here in the fresh air until she returned. "Stay," she told him, then made for her place.

It was the big splash that told her he hadn't followed orders. At her back door, she whipped around to discover he'd fallen into her small pool. So small that she could lean over the side and grab his arm and tow his body to the side. "What are you doing, you fool?"

"Can't leave a girl 'lone in the dark." He grasped her waist to hoist himself up, lost his grip, then slipped back underwater. "Watchin' after you," he added wetly, as he broke the surface again. This time he dug his fingers into her hips and with her help managed to exit the pool. Standing up, he shook himself like a dog.

Dodging the spray, she decided that thanks to her good deeds there must be a cloud in heaven with her name already inscribed on it. And she hoped it was plenty fluffy, because handling Gabe was making her old before her time. She left him on her back patio and scurried for towels before he could get into any more trouble.

Scurry proved useless, however, because when she returned from the linen closet he was standing in her small living area, stark naked.

Cassandra focused on his face. "What are you doing now?" she demanded.

He lifted his arms away from his lean, muscled body. The benders didn't seem to affect his fitness level. "Shortcut. I'm naked. Now you."

She threw the towel at his chest, but his reflexes were off and it fell to the floor after briefly catching on the impressive erection he was sporting. "I thought too much booze made that impossible," she muttered.

He looked down at himself, palmed the thick flesh, then sent her a grin. "Hung like 'n elephant. Did I tell you that?"

"Only every time you've been drinking." Except this was the first time she'd seen the evidence for herself. Oh, and he had a nice ass, too, she noticed, as he turned and headed down the short hallway that led to a half bath on the left and her bedroom on the right. She trailed his slow-moving figure, then had to yell out, "Left, left! You want to go left," as he veered into her bedroom.

Oh, fine. There was an attached bathroom there, too, complete with a shower.

But he didn't make it that far. Instead, he found her queen-sized mattress and fell on it, faceup. One of the cats tiptoed over and settled on the pillow around his head, just like a coonskin hat.

"My comatose Davy Crockett," she said, aware he'd sunk into drunken dreamland again. Resigned to an unexpected overnight visitor, she reached for the covers to pull them over his nakedness. Her gaze snagged on a thin strip of fabric tied with a clumsy knot around his left wrist. Watery bloodstains marred the white material.

Her stomach flipped. A high whine rang in her ears and her spongy knees had her sinking to the mattress. She lifted his hand into her lap. His fingers were curled in relaxation, the skin warm, the callused palm scratchy under her thumbs. The bandage—

"Wha'?"

Her gaze jumped to Gabe's face. He was awake again, and staring at her.

"Your wrist," she said. "How did you get hurt?"

His gaze flicked down to the bandage and he looked at it, obviously bemused. Not alarmed. Alarmed was her.

"Accident." It was the first nonslurred word he'd spoken that evening.

Her alarm level rose. "What kind of 'accident'?" When

he didn't respond, she shook his hand. "What kind of accident, Gabe?"

The same kind of "accident" that had led her to find one of his cars with a garden hose trailing from tailpipe to window? The same kind of "accident" that had led him to take a hunk of rope and coil it into a noose that she'd caught him tying from a beam of his backyard gazebo? She swallowed.

What kind of accident?

He frowned, as if thinking back. "Box cutter."

Box cutter. *Box cutter.*

"Gabe." She wanted to shake him, slap him, scream for mercy, but all she could do was say his name and hold tight to his hand. "Gabe."

He smiled, as charming as any angel seeking entrance into hell. It was obvious the discussion of the bandage and the box cutter was already forgotten. "Is so true, Froo' Loop. I so want to do you." Then he slipped his hand from hers so he could roll to his side and drop back into sleep.

Cassandra came to a hasty stand, then stepped back, putting space between herself and the man she'd been trying to save for the past two years. *I so don't want to do this anymore. I so* can't *do this anymore.* Because there was no longer a way to fool herself that there wouldn't come a day when she couldn't rescue him.

Backing up, she kept her eyes on his sleeping form sprawled across her bed. The cat at his head was snuggled against the nape of his neck now. The other two were draped across his limbs—one on his arm, one over his thigh—keeping him close like she'd always wanted to. Gabe was where she'd always imagined him in her deepest, darkest, most secret fantasies, but it was going to be a one-time, no-touch night.

It had taken her two years to grasp the truth, but now she knew that if she let him any closer to her heart his self-destructive bent was going to make her collateral damage.

Meaning it was past time for Cassandra Riley to rescue herself.

Two

The family you come from isn't as important as the family you're going to have.

—RING LARDNER

The couch was lumpy and the cats disloyal, so Cassandra woke up early and alone. She suppressed the urge to call her sisters. Juliet was in Hawaii on her honeymoon with Noah and early in California was even earlier on the island of Kauai. Her other sister, Nikki, claimed she wasn't a stay-in-bed person, but Cassandra imagined her snuggled next to her fiancé, Jay, at their Malibu beach house and decided against disturbing their morning.

She sat up, already fidgety. With her sisters happily happy-ever-aftering and with herself sworn off Gabe-detail, she lacked something to focus on. Someone.

Cassandra was the kind of person who needed a project.

From the basket beside the small coffee table, she picked up a sock she was knitting, but found herself staring at the four needles instead of manipulating them. With a sigh, she put the piece aside and headed for the kitchen, refusing to give in to instinct and check on the still-slumbering Gabe.

He was fine. And his status was no longer her concern anyway.

A steaming pot of herbal tea was on the countertop when the first of the bedroom's occupants made an appearance. Gray-striped Moosewood.

Each of her cats had picked its own name. Moosewood, because that was the title of the vegetarian cookbook he'd settled on after she'd gotten him warm and dry. Breathe had found her spot on top of the reminder printed on Cassandra's lavender-colored yoga mat. Ed had marched in circles then landed on one of the odd missives mailed to her from an ex-boyfriend, the once nice-enough yet now apparent deep-end-diver Edward Malcolm IV.

Cassandra opened the back door to let out the cat for a short, supervised wander. Warm air wafted across her face and she could already smell the sunshine in the air. It was going to be one of *those* days. May had its gray, June had its gloom, and April could be iffy in SoCal, but the rest of the year made up for it in summerish splendor.

December 25 was notorious for the kind of temperatures that made new sweaters and plush robes impossible to wear. And there were many other glorious moments in "winter" that could seduce anyone into swallowing whole the California dream. This March morning was clearly one of those.

Her phone rang. She crossed the room to snatch up the cordless receiver. The number on the display was unfamiliar. The voice calling out "Hello? Hello?" wasn't.

"Judith!" Cassandra exclaimed, greeting her mother, who had always insisted on being called by her first name. Her mother, who though she might not be the warmest of parental units—despite the fact that she was Cassandra's only parental unit—must today have tuned in to her maternal radar. "Judith, where are you?"

Static made several long syllables unrecognizable. ". . . on a sat phone," Judith Riley concluded.

"Great," Cassandra said, though the location could be somewhere in South America or in Somalia as far as she knew. The older woman had been bouncing around the world for over a year and there didn't seem to be any particular logic to her route. "And you're well?"

More static cut in again, obscuring her mother's reply.

"Terrific." Cassandra crossed to the sliding glass door to let the cat back in, hoping she hadn't just expressed approval for an invasion of intestinal parasites or the appearance of a scaly rash. Her gaze caught on the wet clothes piled in a heap on the patio deck a few feet from the door.

Damn. Gabe's stuff. Last night, she'd forgotten to rescue it—but she was finished with taking care of the man and that included his clothes, too. Still . . .

Stepping outside, she tucked the phone between her ear and shoulder to pick up his wet shirt. A quick toss landed it on one of the painted metal garden chairs to dry.

"And how are you?" Cassandra's mother's voice suddenly sounded so clear that she started, turning to see if somehow the woman had been magically transported from Timbuktu or Turkistan.

She laughed a little at herself and turned back to bend down and retrieve the crumpled pair of sodden jeans. "I'm okay. But Gabe . . ." She swallowed the rest of the story.

Judith Riley had chosen to conceive a baby without even using a willing bed partner in the process, because it was important to her to prove that women did not need men. Not to make a baby. Not to raise a child. Not to lead a fulfilling life.

She was right, of course. Cassandra would never say it wasn't so. But she had to wonder why biology compelled people to partner up if there wasn't some advantage to it.

Her mother's thoughts never wandered in such a direction, however. So her daughter didn't share with Judith about the man in her bed—even though Cassandra had decided that once she booted him out of it she was turning her back on him, too.

Instead, she changed the subject as she threw his jeans over another chair. "Do you have your arrival date set for next month?"

She thought the silence on the other end was due to the shaky connection. But then she heard her mother's slow "Weeell . . ."

The space under Cassandra's heart hollowed. "You're not coming back for my birthday." No question mark necessary.

"I have an opportunity to get into Tibet. I met someone who . . . It doesn't matter. I'm sure you understand that it's a once-in-a-lifetime opportunity, Cassie."

Her mother hadn't called her Cassie since she was in kindergarten. She tilted her head toward the blue, blue sky. "I'm only going to turn thirty once in this lifetime, too."

"Yes, yes. But the Dalai Lama—"

"Judith, the Dalai Lama isn't even in Tibet. He lives in exile in India."

"Well, of course you're right about that. But you don't really need me there, do you? You've met those two new friends of yours, Nancy and Jenna—"

"Nikki and Juliet. And they're my half sisters, remember? The sperm donor whose specimen was used to impregnate you was the same their mothers used to conceive."

"Even more to my point. You'll have family on your big day."

Family. What Cassandra had always wanted, though her mother had never before conceded the benefit of one until given the chance to visit the place where the Dalai Lama wasn't. "I was looking forward to you meeting them, Judith."

"And I will," her mother declared. "Not next year, but maybe the one after that—"

"What? I thought you were coming back for my birthday, then coming back for good in six months."

"Plans change, Cassandra. You should learn to be more flexible."

Blinking against the sudden brightness of the sun, Cassandra lowered her head. Gabe's soggy boxers were in her line of sight and she nudged at the cotton with her toe, revealing something beneath them. With another nudge she uncovered what they'd been hiding. There, the leather water-stained, was his wallet. She reached for it.

"So when shall I expect to see you again, Judith?" she asked, straightening.

"I'm not sure. There's Tibet, and then maybe a quick trip to Hong Kong, followed by visiting some new friends in South Africa . . ."

"I see." She squeezed Gabe's wallet in her hand, noticing the heft. He carried more than a debit card and his driver's license.

"I'll pick you up some lovely gifts. How does that sound?"

Like a piss-poor substitute for her mother's presence on

her thirtieth birthday, but Judith Riley had never been one to worry about someone else's expectations or needs.

"What are you going to do to celebrate?" Judith's voice came through loud and clear again, and lighter, too, presumably because she'd broken the bad news.

"I don't know now," Cassandra said. "I had been hoping we'd have a few days together. You know, stroll along the beach, hang out at the shop, maybe lunch with my sisters on the actual day."

"You should do something special for yourself. Buy something you've always wanted. Have an experience you've been dreaming about."

Cassandra's thoughts shifted instantly to Gabe. Gabe in her bed. Without curbing the impulse this time, she strolled back into the house and took the short hallway to look at him through her half-open bedroom door. He was belly-down on her sheets, his head buried in the pillow, the covers riding low along the edge of his hips.

Above them she glimpsed the upper curve of his taut butt, the long valley of his spine, the tangle of his too-long black hair. It was always either too long or too short. He'd let it go until it brushed the tops of his shoulders, then he'd visit some mysterious barber he called "Sammy" who left nicks on his scalp from the brutal clip of a razor.

She suspected he liked the pain.

And yet she still wanted him.

"Do you have something like that in mind, Cassie?" her mom said in her ear.

Cassandra had had Gabe in her mind and in her fantasies since he'd walked into Malibu & Ewe one day two years before and told her he'd bought the building that housed her little yarn shop. He'd bought the café/fish market across the parking lot, too. There were other properties in the Malibu area that were now his. He hadn't been particularly friendly, but that hadn't mattered to her.

In the succeeding months, she'd refused to let him get away with his short responses and his stiff attitude. She'd wheedled, she'd charmed, she'd outright lied about needing the occasional repair so that she could get him into her shop and out of whatever black hole had sucked him down.

They were friends now. She was convinced of it when he told her about this funky little place on his property that she was welcome to rent when the apartment building she lived in went condo. He gave her a deal on the monthly cost and she cooked him as many healthy dinners as she could coax him into accepting.

Friendship wasn't all she wanted, though. She'd always known that on some level.

Could joining him in that bed be the birthday gift her mother was suggesting she should give herself? They'd never kissed. They'd never really touched, except for those drunken times he didn't remember, when she scooped his sorry ass from some seedy place and dragged him home.

And yet every inch of her flesh ached to be stroked by him. She wanted his hard mouth on hers, even though 99 percent of the time she'd be risking whisker burn from his five-o'clock shadow that was from the five o'clock three days before.

Yearning rushed like heat across her skin.

"Cassandra?"

She'd forgotten all about her mother, and she started at the sound of her voice. "Yes, yes, I'm here." It came out so loud, she saw Gabe twitch, and then begin to stir.

Cassandra stumbled back from the doorway, and she bobbled the wallet she was carrying. It flew out of her hands to land on the floor, the two edges opening. Inside, in one of those protective sleeves, was a photograph.

"Are you thinking about your celebration?" her mother asked.

"Yes," Cassandra said slowly. "Right." She retrieved the wallet from the floor, staring at the small, plastic-covered rectangle the whole while. Two people were pictured. A slender dark-haired woman with a sleek, short bob. There was a child leaning against her leg, her long hair just as dark as her mother's—and Gabe's.

Funny, she'd never pictured them in her head. Cassandra had never imagined what Lynn—his wife—had looked like, or Maddie, his five-year-old daughter either. Maybe he had trouble keeping their looks in mind, too. The plastic over their faces was worn away, as if he'd run his thumb over their features countless times, trying to memorize them.

Or trying to bring them back.

Closing her eyes, she snapped shut the edges of the damp leather. She could never compete with that. She could never snag his romantic attention, not when he was so devoted to the ghosts of his wife and daughter who had died at the hands of a drunk driver three years before.

She'd always known that at some level, too, which is why she'd settled for being his friend. But it wasn't working for her anymore. It wasn't enough.

So she *had* to turn away from him.

She had to turn toward her future.

"I'm going to throw myself a big bash, Judith," Cassandra said, making a sudden decision. "I'm going to open the shop and have the best damn thirtieth birthday celebration I can put together."

"Good idea," her mother enthused. "Invite everyone. You know they'll all come."

"Right," she agreed. Except one someone. But that wouldn't matter. While she might include Gabe on the guest list, she promised herself it wasn't going to break her heart if he didn't attend.

Gabe Kincaid woke to the familiar: the Death Valley dryness of his mouth and tongue, the pounding at his temples as the hangover goblins used their mallets to knock nine-inch nails into his brain, the last wisps of a sexual dream that left his body hot and his cock erect.

He shifted his legs, noting a warm weight across one ankle. Opening his eyes, he stared, astonished, at the creature draped over his lower limb. It blinked back at him, its yellow eyes wide.

Not the pussy he'd been fantasizing about.

Shutting his eyes again, he breathed deep and tried regrouping. In the last three years, he'd come to consciousness in a variety of places under a range of circumstances. Once, he'd found himself on the beach at Zuma, surrounded by surfers who'd paid him no attention as he'd rolled over and yakked up ninety-proof who-knew-what. Another time, he'd come awake inside a yellow cab parked in the lot of a local bar. Apparently he'd told the driver to leave him in the backseat with the motor running until the meter ran up to the four-hundred bucks he had in his pocket.

In the last year it had been relatively better. He'd wake up with a raging hangover, in his own bed or on his own couch, a note left nearby informing him of his car's location. Yet one aspect of his benders had always remained the same. He never remembered getting drunk and he never remembered how he got to the beach or to his bed—for which he'd always been grateful.

It was the whole damn point, after all. To forget.

But this morning he didn't feel so full of gratitude, because he had a bad feeling, a very bad feeling, about where he'd spent last night.

Steeling himself, he took a quick inventory. All right, he was naked. And, yep, he was in between rumpled sheets. Opening his eyes the merest slit, he checked out the animal at the end of the bed.

Damn it, he hadn't made a mistake. The yellow-orbed pet was none other than one of Cassandra's cats.

Which meant he was naked in Cassandra's bed.

Of course, Gabe didn't really need the visual clues. Now that his brain was getting into gear, he registered it was her scent that was surrounding him, the lemony freshness of the lotion she used on her skin and the sweeter, more flowery fragrance of her shampoo that often drifted through the air as her waterfall of rippling brown hair moved.

The stuff was a mystery to him—its perfect waves and its silky-looking length that, when she was naked, would flirt with the crease at the top of her round ass. Not that he'd ever seen her naked.

He'd just thought about it a lot.

Groaning, he threw his forearm over his eyes to hold back the image in his mind. This was *Cassandra* he was thinking of, who was kind of like a nun, and kind of like a sister, and the closest thing to a friend he had in his whole, fucked-up little world.

Because he honored all that—a half-dead man like himself had to honor *something*—not once had he come on to her like his libido always urged him to.

Except now he was naked in her bed.

And as usual, he had a big gaping hole in his memory. How many days did it go back? Two? Five? It wasn't something he usually bothered to calculate, other than to be glad that time had passed.

Still, it didn't mean he'd actually made another entry in the long list of his life's mistakes, did it?

The sudden sound of rushing water caused his arm to drop and his eyes to pop open. A shower noise, but he knew this place, owned it as a matter of fact, and the shower was in the attached bathroom. The door to it was ajar, the light inside was off, and he'd know if Cassandra was that close.

Then, in the periphery of his vision, something moved.

Oh, no. Oh, God.

There *was* another shower; he knew that, too, because he'd installed its rainwater showerhead with his very own hands last summer. It was situated outside, against the side of the house a few steps from the pool, and that's where his hostess was making her morning ablutions.

Probably so she wouldn't wake him; Cassandra was courteous like that.

And if he had an iota of her good manners, he wouldn't be using the angle afforded by the half-opened mirrored closet door to gawk at her wet body through the bedroom window.

She was naked now, too.

With her head thrown back, her eyes closed as she wet that length of spectacular hair, there was nothing to hide the most amazing pair of breasts he'd been trying not to think about for two long years. It wasn't as if anyone could ignore them—and her sisters teased her about nature's bounty all the time—but on only a very few occasions had Gabe allowed himself to even glance at the abundance of female flesh below her clavicle.

And now here that flesh was, for his secret, private

viewing, the pale globes that would spill out of his palms and the hard, pink nipples that pointed toward him in invitation. There was all the rest, too: the taut sweep of her abdomen, the tight swirl of her belly button, the cluster of soft brown curls that matched the warm brown on the top of her head.

There was liquid soap in the cups of her palms. Where would she take those lucky bubbles first? Gabe moved a hand in the direction of his hard-on, ready to—

He groaned, fisting the top sheet in his wandering fingers and rolling away from the reflection in the mirror.

What the hell was he doing? This was *Cassandra* he was a minute from masturbating over. Cassandra, who, it bore repeating, was kind of like a nun, and kind of like a sister, and the closest thing to a friend he had in his whole, fucked-up little world.

And yet with all that in his head, he rolled to look at her reflection again. His heart slammed once, then stopped. Shit.

She'd turned. Now it was her wet back and ass he was offered, and on either side of her waist, he saw four bruises, each the size of a fingerprint, standing out on the creamy skin of her hips. Fingerprints right in that place where the back of a man's hands would be tickled by the ends of her lustrous hair. Right where a man would grip a woman when he was holding her steady for hard, eager thrusts.

He looked down at his fingers, then groaning again, once more turned away from the image of the woman who he feared he'd plundered in this very bed. Had he really?

The hangover goblins went after his brain with more wicked glee and he welcomed the brutal pain.

Still, over their manic nail-pounding, he knew when

Cassandra came into the bedroom. Obeying his first, cowardly instinct, he faked sleep. But then one of her damn cats, the yellow-eyed devil that had been at his feet, pounced on his naked back with force, claws unsheathed.

"Yaaah!" He shook the damn thing free of his skin, twisting and sitting up at the same time, so that when he was finally de-felined he was left facing another pair of big eyes.

Blue.

Cassandra's big, blue eyes, the surrounding dark lashes still spiky from her shower. A short flowered robe was belted around her waist. In the vee of the lapels was the deep cleavage of her centerfold-worthy rack.

He jerked his gaze back to her face. It was flushed, but that might be due to the mug she carried, its steam curling in the air. "You're awake," she said.

"Just now," he replied, his voice sounding as if he'd swallowed gravel. He made sure he kept his body angled away from the closet door so she wouldn't notice that she'd unintentionally provided him with a peepshow.

"Sorry about Ed," she said, nodding to the cat that was sitting on his haunches, one leg rising as straight as a middle finger while he tongue-washed his black-and-white fur. "It's just that he loves you, you know."

"Yeah. The free acupuncture session sends just that message."

She didn't laugh. Instead, she approached the bed, not getting too close, but close enough to set down the mug on a paperback sitting on the bedside table. The book was titled *Veggie Cooking for Carnivores*. The contents of the mug emitted a stench one degree off crap.

"That's for you," she said, quickly backing off.

She wasn't acting like herself, which made him even more jittery. But her beverage habit was her usual. He sneered at it.

"I'm not drinking some tuber you dug up in the backyard and then steeped in hot cat piss," he said. "Instead, when I come over to your shop for the usual break time this morning, I'll double the size of my latté we both pretend you don't drink down every time I turn my back, Froot Loop."

That lit the fire in her eye. She looked like the old Cassandra when she slammed her arms over her chest. "You know I detest that nickname."

"Since when has that stopped me?"

"I thought after last night . . ."

Oh damn, oh damn, oh damn. He cleared his throat. "Last night . . ."

"Admit you owe me now, Gabe."

For the bruises he'd put on her backside? For the sexing he couldn't recall?

"What, uh, what is it you want, Cassandra?"

She looked away. She *never* looked away from him. For as long as he'd known her, she'd been in-his-face, on-her-toes, up-in-his-business. When he was in the blackest of black moods, she'd call him over to fix her refrigerator or help eat her dinner or, once, zip up the back of an incredibly slinky cocktail dress.

He'd pinched the metal tab between his thumb and forefinger, keeping her an arm's length away as he nudged it upward. Still, he'd breathed in a new perfume he'd never smelled on her before. He'd told her he hated it.

When what he'd hated was that she was wearing it for some man other than him.

"About that 'usual break time' thing we've gotten in the

habit of sharing. I think . . . I think starting today I'd like a little distance, Gabe."

He stiffened. That was his line! No matter how many times she called, no matter how many meals they shared, he was always careful to keep a certain reserve. Cassandra was too damn nice to be saddled with the walking black shadow that he knew he was 99 percent of the time. But what had he done to put her off a simple, uncomplicated coffee break?

Those bruises lit up like neon in his mind's eye. "Froot Loop." His throat felt strangled. "Did I . . . somehow hurt you?"

She shook her head. "No. Of course not. It's just . . . things are different for me now."

Now? Different *now*? He closed his eyes. That meant they'd done it, right? Inhibitions annihilated by too much alcohol, he'd gone ahead and seduced Cassandra, who had been on a self-selected celibacy kick as long as he'd known her.

It was the only thing that had stopped him from refusing to let her leave the house that night she'd worn the tight dress and the new perfume.

"Cassandra. I'm sorry—"

"There's nothing to be sorry for." One of her hands fluttered. "But last night . . ."

"You came and got me. You've done that before." He knew that, of course. Those times he'd been left in his place with the handwritten notes telling him where to find his car—those notes had been written by Cassandra. Yet neither one of them had ever acknowledged her past good deeds.

She smiled now. On the right side of her full lips was just the tiniest of dimples. It flickered. "Those other times didn't end quite like this time."

"Right." He wanted to talk about exactly how "this time" had ended. And begun. The middle part, too. He definitely wanted to have her tell him all about the middle part. But wouldn't that be worse than the seduction itself? Wouldn't admitting that he didn't recall a moment of their time together only add insult to injury? He thought of those eight bruises on her perfect ass and wondered what that flesh had felt like against his palms.

"So . . ." Her brows lifted over those beautiful eyes of hers.

"So . . ." he repeated stupidly, then remembered that she'd asked for distance. It was the least he could do for her.

It was something he should be eager for himself. He should be eager to go back to his house, to his solitude, to the darkness that he'd fall into with a bottle of booze when the pain got to be too much. Still, he lingered between Cassandra's sheets, frustrated by the perplexing holes in his memory.

Ironic, wasn't it? After all the drinking to forget, he was finally wishing he could remember everything.

Three

The great advantage of living in a large family is that early lesson of life's essential unfairness.

—NANCY MITFORD

It was as if fate had put its stamp of approval on her fresh life plan, Cassandra decided, when she turned into the parking lot of Malibu & Ewe and saw her sister Nikki standing outside the shop. Besides the birthday party, there was another item on her new agenda, one that required her younger sister's cooperation.

A paper cup of coffee in hand, Nikki waited for Cassandra to unlock the door and then followed her inside, proceeding directly to the sliding back doors where she rolled up the sunshades that were lowered each night. Cassandra stowed her purse in the back storeroom, then joined the other woman as she stared out the glass at the wide view of the blue-gray Pacific, the light from the summer-warm sun carving gold discs in its breeze-roughened surface.

Her yarn shop, perched on a bluff above one of Malibu's south-facing beaches, had a wide back deck that held chairs convenient for knitters who liked to work with the open air on their faces. For those who wished for more shelter, a grouping of sand-colored couches was placed at the center of the store. The walls were stacked with bins holding yarns and lined with racks displaying needles and other knitting and crocheting accessories.

Cassandra turned to Nikki. "Do you want to finish your coffee outside? Or I can brew some organic herbal tea—" She broke off as her sister mimed poison by arsenic, free hand clutching her throat, her tongue lolling, her expression tortured.

Rolling her eyes, she shook her finger at her sister. "Be careful, your face might get stuck that way. And wouldn't that make for some lovely wedding memories."

Nikki instantly prettied up, and a smile sparked in her bicolored eyes, the trait she shared with their older sister, Juliet. "Which reminds me. Jay and I finally found a photographer we can agree on. So what's your vote: Should we risk bad luck and take pictures of us dressed for the ceremony before the 'I dos' or should we go old-school and make everybody wait for the reception to start while we do one of those interminable photo shoots?"

"Don't buck tradition," Cassandra said. "But serve some tasty hors d'oeuvres for your guests to nibble on until you're ready to join the party."

Nikki beamed. "Excellent suggestion. Since I'm on such close terms with the chef planning the menu—"

"Since you *are* the chef planning the menu, you mean."

"Yeah, and since this chef-slash-bride isn't doing anything but wedding junk until we're back from the honeymoon at the end of June, I think I can figure out just what will keep the complaints down." Then Nikki looked out the window, glanced over at Cassandra, turned oceanward again.

Frowning, Cassandra put her hand over the anxiety starting a little flutter in her middle. "Everything okay? Are you and Jay . . ."

"Blissful," Nikki said, "with the exception of us both nearly regretting this whole-hog wedding thing. What was I thinking?"

"That you couldn't say no to Jay, who decided he wanted the traditional June tie-the-knot date as well as all the attending hoopla and over-the-top trimmings."

"Show-off," Nikki agreed with affection.

"Which might describe you, too, having bagged the biggest bachelor in the greater Los Angeles area."

"Oh, and there's that." Nikki grinned. "Go me."

But Cassandra knew her sister better than she would have thought possible when she'd taken the first step on the journey to find her family several months ago. "There *is* something wrong, though."

Nikki's gaze slid sideways again and she bit her bottom lip. "Jay and I heard about last night at the Beach Shack."

As if killed by a clean shot, the flutter in Cassandra's belly died, leaving her insides cold and empty. Ignoring her sister's worried look, she hurried away from the back doors to busy herself at the register. She had to flip it on, didn't she, and straighten pencils and . . . and . . .

"The woman was Sammy Dennison," Nikki said. "Jay heard that the two of them ran into each other at that bar on Ocean Boulevard, and then they moved on to the Beach Shack."

"Oh." So Sammy was a woman. Cassandra shrugged her stiff shoulders. "She's his barber."

"How long had he been missing this time? Two days? Three?"

She gave another shrug, unwilling to admit she'd calculated it to the minute.

Nikki looked as if her older sister didn't fool her, however. "Well, the point is, Cassandra, that it doesn't seem as if he was holed up with the barber all that time. Word is that none of his lost days include him doing anything more than bending elbows with a female companion."

There was no reason to feel relief. Especially when it was embarrassing that anyone thought she might be hurt or even the least bit bothered by the idea of Gabe sleeping with some other woman. "What he does is none of my business."

Nikki gaped. "Huh? Who the heck do you think you're talking to? I've been along on at least two of your let's-get-Gabe's-drunken-ass-home adventures. I think you've earned a place in his business."

"Not anymore. I'm done with that. I'm done with being his Mother Teresa and his Florence Nightingale and his . . . his . . ."

"What exactly *are* you to Gabe, Cassandra?"

"Nothing."

Nikki shook her head. "What exactly do you *want* him to be to you, Cassandra?"

"Nothing."

"Froot Loop—"

"Don't call me that!" It was a stupid nickname that Gabe had given her and she'd vowed to put him out of her life. But from the stubborn expression on Nikki's face, Cassandra knew she was going to have to come up with a powerful distraction.

Lucky for her, she had one.

"Nik," she said. "I've got something to tell you as well."

"Don't think you're going to get out of—"

"I want to meet our father," Cassandra said quickly. "Dr. Frank Tucker. I want to meet him as soon as possible."

Her sister's jaw dropped. With careful movements, she balanced her coffee cup on the register's counter, then looked over to meet Cassandra's gaze. "We discussed this before," she said, her voice tight.

"I know. But let's recap. At first you said 'no,' and then at Thanksgiving you agreed to let Juliet approach him."

"But then Juliet's bitch of a stepdaughter, Marlys, spilled the story to the tabloids. 'Celebrity Plastic Surgeon Fathers Three Malibu Babes.' We figured he hated the publicity just as much as we did, because we didn't hear from him following the media blitz. And then we all agreed to table making contact until some unspecified future date."

"Check your calendar," Cassandra said. "It's some unspecified future date."

Nikki was quiet a moment, then her eyes narrowed. "What did you do to Gabe last night? Not that I'd blame you or anything, but after you yanked him out of that bar, did you rearrange his face or something? Do you need dear old dad's help to fix his broken—again, not that I'd blame you—nose?"

"I could never hurt Gabe," Cassandra scoffed.

"There's the whole damn problem in a nutshell," Nikki muttered. "The guy needs a serious wake-up call and I can think of several soft spots of his anatomy that might benefit from a swift blow or two."

"This has nothing to do with Gabe." Or everything. No, it had everything to do with *her*, with Cassandra, who wasn't involved with Gabe any longer and who wanted to have at least one-half of her parental DNA at her upcoming birthday celebration. Then she wouldn't feel so . . . so rootless when contemplating the next decades of her life. "I know you're leery of men—"

"I'm not—" Nikki halted as the bells on the shop's door

rang out. Her head jerked toward the man strolling over the threshold. "Tell her," she called out to him. "You tell her."

Jay Buchanan's golden eyebrows rose as he made his way toward his fiancée. In designer trousers, a silky shirt, and Italian loafers, he looked as über-cool as the über-bachelor he'd always been. But now he wore a heavy gold "engagement" band on his left hand that looked completely at home next to the hulking diamond he'd slid on Nikki's finger three and a half seconds after she'd agreed to marry him.

He took hold of that finger now, and rubbed his thumb over the beautiful ring. To this day he said without shame that he'd chosen all four carats in an effort to weigh her down. That he'd do anything it took to make it hard for her to ever run from him and what they had together.

How hard the mighty fall, Cassandra thought. Jay had never known what love was like, while Nikki had been distrustful of too-close connections. Depending upon others had disappointed her before, and she still had a tendency to claim she could take care of herself under any circumstances.

But Jay was wearing her down, Cassandra realized, if she was looking to her fiancé to explain her position.

"Tell her," Nikki said again now. "Tell my sister I am not leery of men. I'm just leery of contacting a man who gave some samples thirty-plus years ago and then promptly forgot about them."

"You don't know that," Cassandra refuted. "I told you, it was common at that time, in the early years of artificial insemination, for medical students like our father to be donors. And infertility itself was rarely addressed publicly by anyone. He did nothing wrong."

Jay ran his fingers through Nikki's tangle of gold-streaked

brown hair. "Cookie, remember that some months ago he registered at that site that connects donors to offspring. He's expressed curiosity, too."

"And then nothing," Nikki pointed out. "Though he knows where to find us, thanks to that queen-of-mean, Marlys the motormouth."

Jay looked over at Cassandra, his left eyebrow winging up. "Cookie's right."

"But—"

"But what's the big hurry anyway?" Nikki asked. "We agreed to do this Three Musketeer style if we did it at all. You, me, and Juliet. Why not wait until she and Noah get back from their two weeks of nudie-nudie in nookie-nookie town?"

Jay winced. "Nudie-nudie in nookie-nookie town. Always the romantic with you."

His fiancée turned to him with a tender smile. "Just so you know, I'm saving up rose petals to scatter on the bedsheets during *our* honeymoon."

"You are not," Jay started, a laugh in his voice, then it died away. "You are?" He yanked her close and kissed her, sweet and long.

Cassandra watched the show out of the corner of her eye. She'd tell them, she thought. She'd tell them when they came up for air that with her sisters occupied otherwise—though she didn't begrudge them their happiness—she needed to see this family thing through for herself.

With no Gabe to distract her—

The bells on Malibu & Ewe's doors rang out again. Jay and Nikki broke their kiss and all three of them watched the newcomer enter the shop. A glance at the clock showed it to be the usual time—the exact hour she'd come to expect her landlord's daily visit. Gabe would drop by with a large latté and then idly shoot the breeze or silently brood sourly, depending upon his mood. She'd pretend she wasn't drinking the beverage down and he'd pretend he didn't see her enjoy the caffeinated, non-soy beverage that she'd deny imbibing to her dying breath.

The man striding over the threshold carried the coffee all right, though whether it was indeed her landlord she wasn't entirely certain. Because this man had shaved. And his hair appeared to be combed and was slicked back in damp waves. The post-bender, green-around-the-gills part was familiar, though, as well as the grim set to his mouth.

It turned even grimmer when Nikki announced in a perky voice, "Check out what the jaws of hell have barfed up."

Jay winced again. "Bad Cookie," he murmured, then cleared his throat. "How's it going, Gabe?"

"Fine," the other man answered absently, his gaze shifting to Cassandra's face.

That flutter was stirring back to life in the pit of her belly. She watched him set his cup beside Nikki's on the counter. Why was he here? Hadn't she made it clear she wanted him to stay away?

"Did you forget—"

"Yeah," he answered, skirting the cash register to join her on the other side of the counter. "Yeah, I forgot something this morning."

He stepped closer, invading her personal space. Gabe *never* got this close, unless he was reeking of booze and crowing over his elephantine endowments.

She swallowed. "You forgot what?"

"To thank you." He smelled like sandalwood soap, the bars she'd bought for him herself at the organic festival in Ojai last summer. Cool fingertips, *Gabe's* cool fingertips, burrowed beneath her hair to touch her nape.

Startled, her muscles froze. "Oh. You're, um, welcome."

His fingertips applied pressure to the back of her neck, and she found herself forced into stepping closer. "Not that kind of thank you," he murmured, and she could taste the hot-cinnamon toothpaste on his breath. "This kind."

And then he kissed her.

Cassandra's mouth. It was soft and warm and Gabe had surprised her into a little "oh" that gave his tongue the perfect opportunity to glide—

Pain poked his lower leg. "Ah!" He jerked from the kiss, his gaze shooting down to catch Nikki rising from a crouch, a knitting needle in her hand.

She'd learned an innocent eyelash flutter from her big sister, and she used it on him now, pretending a quasi-apology. "I dropped my needle, and then . . ." She shrugged. "Did I hurt you?"

"Not really." But she'd given Cassandra time to back-pedal. The yarn shop owner had retreated a good five feet away and was staring at the wall to the right of his shoulder, her expression dumbstruck.

"Too bad," Nikki murmured, her eyes narrowed. "Because—"

"Because then she'd have to make it up to you by baking a batch of her vanilla-cherry cookies," Jay interrupted. "And with all the wedding planning, she really doesn't have the spare time. As a matter of fact, maybe we should—"

"Stay right here," Nikki said sweetly, doing her own interrupting. "I need Cassandra's help on the naughty little number I'm knitting to wear on our wedding night."

Jay's eyebrows rose, obviously derailed by the words "naughty little number." A smile quirked the corner of his mouth, proof that his bride-to-be had given a definite tug to his libido.

Gabe could relate. His own libido had been held fast like a fish on a line from the moment he'd woken in Cassandra's bed. The damn thing wasn't going to stop jerking him around until he figured out exactly what had happened between those sheets.

He'd thought a kiss might stir his memory.

That wasn't exactly the part of him that felt stirred up right now, though. He slid Cassandra another glance, but she was still staring at a two-by-two section of plaster behind his back. Truth to tell, he was a touch poleaxed himself, which was just damn crazy.

The kiss had been brief. Broken off by a needle jab.

And, as far as he could tell, completely unfamiliar.

He'd swear he'd never before tasted such soft, sweet heat.

Shoving his hands through his hair, he crossed to the back of the shop. There, he stared out the back doors and considered the drop from the balcony to the ocean. He'd thought about it before, but at low tide a leap would land a man on soft sand. At high tide it would be nothing more lethal than a jump from a high dive.

Neither idea was the least bit tempting now, not even if they'd been more daring, not when the mystery of last night wouldn't let him go. He just could not believe that he'd gone to bed with Cassandra. If he had, how could he have blocked out such a thing? It was hard to imagine, just as it was hard to imagine that he would have let himself go that far. For months he'd worked so hard at being so damn cautious around her, never letting on that he was fascinated with her mouth, her rippling hair, her spectacular breasts and ass.

Not once had he ever let her know he'd sell his black soul—that not even the devil seemed to consider worth buying—for the chance to bury himself between her thighs. He hadn't done that to Cassandra—who was like a nun, and a little sister, and the closest to a friend he had—because she deserved a whole man, a bright-white love, a passion un-besmirched by the ashes that were the only thing left of Gabe's heart.

The air stirred around him. He glanced over, seeing Jay beside him and noting the other man's perfectly layered hair and his impeccable shave. A wave of odd embarrassment moved through Gabe, and he smoothed a self-conscious hand over his scruffy hair. He remembered the cut on his chin from the dull razor he'd scraped over his face before coming to the yarn shop.

"Cookie didn't injure you, did she?"

"No." He hesitated. "But I'm picking up on the fact that I might not be her favorite person."

Jay glanced over his shoulder, and then Gabe did, too. A couple of women had come into the shop and Nikki was chatting them up. Cassandra still wore that spacey expression, but she was moving toward the customers.

"Look," Jay said, "I'm going to be honest, Gabe."

He braced himself. Though he'd not gone looking to make friends in Malibu, thanks to Cassandra and her relent-lessness, he'd spent time with her sisters and the men in their lives. He respected Juliet's Noah as well as Nikki's fiancé, Jay. "Go ahead and get it off your chest."

"Here's the deal. We all worry about her going out at night."

To collect Gabe from bars, the other man meant. "Hey, I never expected—"

"The first couple of times you did some drunk-dialing. After that, the barkeeps have gone ahead and called her themselves when your situation turns south. I don't know how many seedy joints she's visited after last call the past year or so."

"It's not all that often." As a matter of fact, his "lost weekends" had tapered off considerably in the last few months.

"It's enough," Jay answered flatly. "And not every drunk she meets in those places is harmless."

Shit. Gabe jerked left to stare at the other man, his stomach suddenly churning. For a second he worried it might be like Zuma, when he'd upchucked three days' worth of booze and just about all of his dignity. He hauled in a deep breath to calm his gut. "I hadn't thought . . ."

"Yeah? Well, maybe you should start. Maybe you should start thinking about what you put her through."

Shit! He pushed his fingers through his hair and another sick sense of shame twisted his gut. He turned again to stare unseeing at the Pacific view.

"Has someone hurt her?" he asked. Though surely everyone from the beach at Zuma to the pier in Santa Monica would have raised holy hell if Malibu's favorite local girl had run into trouble. Gabe swallowed down another bubble of bile. "Has someone . . . has someone come on to her or something?"

"I know of one man who propositions her every time she goes out on a two A.M. pickup."

It wasn't bile, but anger that spiked inside Gabe now. Someone was harassing his Froot Loop? Some dumbass drunk thought he could come on to beautiful, untouchable, celibate Cassandra? He pivoted toward Jay again, his fingers curled into fists. "Who the hell is he? I'll—"

"It's you, Gabe."

His fingers went slack. "No. No, I don't."

"Yep, you do."

He shook his head in confusion. "I can't believe . . ."

Jay lifted an eyebrow. "Does this ring a bell? Your first order of business is to tell her you're hung like an elephant."

Unable to take it in, he stared at the other man. *Oh, God.* "She called me Dumbo once when she was really mad at me. I didn't get it."

"We all wanted to make a habit of that, but she put her foot down and we promised we wouldn't speak of it. We know why you do what you do, Gabe."

He dismissed that with a gesture. It wasn't the important point right now. "So I tell her what I have to . . . to . . . offer and then I . . . and then I . . . what?"

Jay shrugged. "Varies. And I haven't been there on every occasion, of course. But you make it pretty clear what you want from her. That you want her."

Gabe groaned. So much for his hard work at keeping his lust for her a secret. "Why hasn't she just hauled my stupid ass to the road and then run over it to put me out of my misery?"

"Interesting question, that. Maybe because she thinks that's exactly what you're looking for, or maybe because . . . ?"

Maybe, maybe, maybe, he thought, staring out the glass doors at the ocean. So many maybes, and then the one certainty that yes, despite all his caution when he was sober, last night he could very well have let her haul his stupid ass home and then ended up seducing her between her lemony-scented sheets.

Turning away from the view, he spun toward the shop's interior, thinking he had to get out of the place, that he had to get away from what he'd just learned. But his gaze caught on Cassandra—and he was caught up by the sight of her.

A woman he didn't recognize was sitting on one of the couches and Cassandra was leaning over its back to inspect a piece of knitting. She held her spill of hair behind her shoulders, which gave him an eyeful of her bountiful breasts—the same ones that he'd spied wet this morning. He forced his attention from the soft, sexy sight, only to have his gaze catch hers.

The line that had hooked his libido snapped tight. And then something was reeling him forward. Without a second thought, he walked toward her with single-minded purpose.

Want. Have. Touch. Taste.

The woman on the couch was still talking to Cassandra, her focus on the scrap of pink knitted yarn in her hands. "It was an 'ooops,' plain and simple. We have a nine-month-old! Scott said, 'How could this possibly have happened?' Only a man would ask such a dumb question."

Some concern tickled the back of Gabe's mind, a worry that scented the air almost like smoke, but he ignored it as he drew closer to Cassandra. She straightened, stepping away from the couch that held the oops lady, but held her ground as he came to a stop a foot from her.

Her tongue made a nervous pass across her bottom lip, yanking him another inch closer. "Gabe . . . Gabe, what do you want?"

But she already knew, didn't she? She'd known for months, and last night he'd finally acted upon the desire.

And if Cassandra hadn't desired in return, he wouldn't have ended up among her pillows. She wasn't *that* nice.

And not really like a nun either, apparently.

He reached out and touched her hot cheek with the tip of

his forefinger. He felt hot, too. They both were burning—no wonder he could smell that smoke again. Stronger.

Bells rang out. More customers for Cassandra, damn it, but he kept her attention on him by running his thumb along her bottom lip.

Then a sharp voice cried out. "People! Parking lot. Flames."

The mention of fire acted like an overturned bucket of ice water. Cassandra spun, Gabe leaped, they both ran for the front door with Nikki and Jay right behind them. Outside, a few feet from the shop's solid side door, the one that led directly to the smaller of the building's storerooms, they found a petite, dark-haired young woman stomping on some charred cardboard.

From behind Gabe, Nikki spoke first. "Marlys? What the hell are you doing?"

"A public service," the woman spit out. She shot them all an angry look. "I was just . . . just walking around and saw some kids playing Matchbook Bonfire. They ran off when I yelled."

Gabe pulled Marlys away from the ashes so that he could make sure the fire was extinguished himself. It was out, and the dark, papery remains were already lifting into a cinder tornado stirred up by the ocean breeze.

"Kids?" Nikki questioned, her voice sharp. "I don't see any kids."

"Nik . . ." Cassandra warned.

Color shot up Marlys's face. "They ran off. I told you."

"But—"

"I'm no arsonist!"

"Yeah?" Nikki sneered. "Maybe not, though we know for certain you're a bitchy snitch."

Jay made a sound that could have been a choked-off

laugh. "Cookie, let's go. We're late to . . . something. Everything okay, Gabe?"

He nodded. "I'll call the sheriff, though. And keep an eye out. You do the same, Froot Loop."

Cassandra nodded, too, though her gaze was trained on the brunette. A frown turned down her pretty, full mouth. "Are you all right, Marlys?"

"I'm fine." Without another word, she stomped off.

Nikki muttered something under her breath, but soon she and Jay were on their way as well.

Gabe trailed Cassandra back into Malibu & Ewe, less concerned about some delinquent kids with matches than he was about why Marlys Weston was hanging around Malibu. The daughter of Juliet's late husband, she'd stirred up trouble by seeding the tabloids with ugly rumors about Juliet. When she'd found out that the three donor sibling sisters were fathered by the same famous Hollywood plastic surgeon, she hadn't hesitated to pass that info along as well. Bitchy snitch pretty much summed it up.

Inside the yarn shop, the oops lady hovered by the door. "Was there a problem?" Her hand covered her belly, and he recognized the protective gesture. His wife, Lynn, had caressed Maddie's growing body just that way when she was in the womb.

Then it all came together for him. The pink piece of knitting, the mention of the nine-month-old, the "plain and simple" oops. The lady was pregnant. Apparently she and her husband hadn't used any—

Gabe froze.

—protection.

Protection!

Had he and Cassandra used any last night? He didn't carry condoms. She'd claimed to be celibate.

Oh, hell.

Hell.

If Cassandra Riley was pregnant with his child, he was already smack-dab in the middle of the underworld's flames.

Four

Happiness is having a large, loving, caring, close-knit family in another city.

—GEORGE BURNS

" 'Bitchy snitch,' " Marlys muttered, glancing over at her dog, Blackie, who was grinning out the passenger window of her Miata. "I don't know why you think that's funny. If you ask me, I'm a hero."

Her conscience gave her a pinch, but she ignored it and raised her voice. "I'm serious, Blackie. Those little surf rats could have caused a major problem. Think of all the wool and stuff in the shop that might burn. My evil stepmother's sisters should have thanked me."

Okay, maybe looking for gratitude was too high an expectation. Marlys might be unabashedly selfish, but she was a realist, too. Nobody liked their secrets revealed, and it was true that she'd spoon-fed information to a tabloid stringer of her acquaintance a few times. When her father's wife, the too-good Juliet, had been at a spa during her husband's final hours on earth, Marlys had made sure the info got out.

Yeah, it was true that Juliet couldn't have known Marlys's

terminally ill father would die that day. And it had come to light that General Wayne Weston himself had arranged it so that neither Juliet nor Marlys took on deathbed watch. But still!

"I admit it, Blackie," she told her dog. "I have a few issues. I'm not exactly rational when it comes to men leaving me."

The dog looked over at her.

She met his big brown eyes. You couldn't lie to a dog. "When it comes to men. Period."

On automatic pilot, she took a right-hand turn, beginning the climb into the hills that separated the Malibu beaches from the rest of Los Angeles. Still stewing over the suspicion she'd encountered at the yarn shop, it wasn't until she'd driven past a familiar driveway and spotted a familiar vehicle parked in it that she became aware of where she'd driven.

It was a harsh wake-up. Her stomach leaped, slamming into her plunging heart. Somewhere in her torso the two met with the pounding power of elk antlers. Truly. It felt like a moment you'd see documented on a TV network— one that was a weird hybrid of Animal Planet and Discovery Health. No wonder her foot stomped on the brake pedal as she jerked to the curb outside Juliet and Noah's house.

The couple was on their honeymoon! There was no good explanation for why there was a motorcycle parked in the driveway.

A cold sweat rolled over her skin even as her flesh flushed hot. Especially *that* motorcycle. The one that belonged to Dean Long.

He'd left months ago.

He was a soldier, on tour in Afghanistan.

He was the man she'd thought she'd loved.

Blackie looked over at her again.

"All right, yes," she admitted to her pet. Dean was also the man she'd betrayed. And it was thoughts of him that kept sending her back to wander Malibu where they'd met.

No way was he here though, she thought, even if he was on leave from the army. After what she'd done to him, surely he'd crossed the entire state of California off his mental world map.

Blackie whined. Thanks to the man who'd had a motorcycle very much like the one in the driveway—really, it just *couldn't* be the same one in that driveway—the dog had once experienced a drastic behavior change. Her canine terror had turned into a tame pussycat.

Blackie whined again. "Sorry for the metaphor, dude," she said. "But facts are facts." The dog had gone back to his old, look-out-for-number-one ways the minute Dean had left town. And Dean was still gone . . . wasn't he?

When her pet emitted another high-pitched noise, she finally figured out what he wanted. Obviously Blackie had some pressing doggie business that would be best addressed at the empty lot across the street. But Marlys had learned a thing or two since she'd last been in this vicinity. Reaching behind her, she snagged Blackie's leash and clipped it to the ring on his collar.

She cracked open the driver's-side door, and undisciplined Blackie, intent on his me-first agenda, pawed across her lap and then leaped onto the street. Marlys's fingers snatched for the fluttering end of the leash, but things hadn't gone her way since she was twelve years old.

Her animal dashed away, apparently intent on relieving himself on Juliet and Noah's flowering front shrubs instead of on the weeds across the street. Bad dog.

She followed him, not letting her gaze linger on the motorcycle.

Blackie didn't linger at the flowering bushes.

Instead, he raced for the side gate and nosed it open, just like those working dogs they'd seen on that *National Geographic* special Friday night. "We've been watching too much television, Blackie," she called out, hurrying after him. Oxygen wasn't making it into her lungs, but that was because she was jogging after the dog, she told herself. Anxiety, anticipation, plain old fear, none of those had anything to do with that tight feeling in her chest.

Because surely Dean wasn't in Malibu.

Because surely Dean wasn't staying in the guesthouse on the other side of Juliet and Noah's pool.

Because surely that couldn't be him standing in the doorway of the aforementioned guesthouse, staring down at her dog in bemusement. Then, the-person-who-couldn't-be-Dean looked up. Marlys tripped. She stumbled forward, almost pitching herself into the pool.

"Are you all right?" the-man-who-wasn't-Dean asked.

At the voice—*his* voice—she stumbled again. Her right foot missed the cement deck, found air, found water, then landed on the first plaster pool step. She gasped.

And there he was—*Dean*—reaching for her. "Ma'am . . ."

Ma'am? Her head jerked up even as she yanked her foot from the pool to jolt away from his big hand. "Don't touch me!"

His long arm dropped. Marlys backed up another step, her drenched shoe squelching, the very sound she figured her leaking heart was making inside her chest with each hard beat. Her gaze couldn't leave his face, and she noted that his chiseled features looked leaner, his tan shades lighter than it had been in November. His silver eyes were the same, so piercing she was certain they were boring inside her and finding her every weakness.

Her only weakness.

Him.

"What . . ." She had to swallow, her mouth as dry as her Adidas running shoe was wet. "What are you doing here?"

"Noah said I could use the guesthouse while he's on his honeymoon."

Marlys retreated another foot as Blackie pranced between them. Could it . . . Could it really be Dean?

The big man looked down at the dancing dog. "Sit," he ordered.

Blackie did.

That clinched it. "It's really you," she said.

His head tilted. A lock of his straight black hair fell away from his forehead, revealing an ugly, half-healed wound at his hairline. She couldn't breathe again.

"What happened?" It came out as a whisper so she gestured at the scar. "How were you hurt?"

He gave a little shrug. "Soldier stuff."

Soldier stuff. He'd always been a man of few words, damn him. But it was the potential for "soldier stuff" like that injury that had made her push him away last autumn. Her hand stole up to her chest and she pressed her palm against the silver tear pendant containing her father's ashes that she'd worn every day since Dean had left. With her notion of hell being the long—and maybe unending—wait for a man to come back from war, she'd tried to save herself the pain of it by driving Dean away.

But now he was back. And she couldn't read from his cool expression why.

Or how he felt about her.

"Are you going to be okay?" she asked, eyeing the scar again.

He shrugged again. "I am okay."

Pretty hard to disagree with that. He was six two to Marlys's five one. The scales would give him a hundred pounds on her, all of that muscle. No one was saying he wasn't a beautiful man and if anyone besides him knew what she'd done to kick him out of her life, they'd say she was nuts.

Right now she felt a little crazy. Staring down at her wet shoe, she tried to pull her whirling thoughts into some semblance of order. What now? What should she do? Why was he just standing there, when by rights he should be giving her the cold shoulder or turning his back or—

"I'm completely okay," he said, "with the exception of a little memory loss."

Her gaze jumped to his. "Memory loss?" she repeated, her voice squeaking.

"Yeah. The explosion in Afghanistan's a blank page. And before that . . ."

"You don't remember . . ."

"Other stuff. I lost a chunk of time. Nobody knows whether it's for good or not."

Marlys swallowed. "And Malibu?"

"Well, I remember being on my way here. To visit my friend Noah."

And then? A voice inside her screamed. *What do you remember after that?* But she couldn't bring herself to ask the questions, not when he was unsettling her with that intense regard. Was he recalling that flare of attraction they'd had at their first meeting?

The air had crackled with sparks from the instant their eyes had met. And when he'd touched her palm the sensation had seared her to her elbow. "Wow," he'd said, and something had told her to run. She had, but then she'd found herself coming back to him. Too bad she hadn't listened to that sensible inner voice.

Marlys wiped her right palm against her jeans as if she could rub away the memory of that burning touch, aware that Dean continued to stare at her. She stole a glance at him through her lashes.

His expression remained unreadable. She supposed he was reliving their last moments together. That night, at her front door, her ex, Phil, had spilled the beans about how she'd been leaking gossip to his tabloid-stringer little brother. Dean had appeared pretty disgusted by that.

But what he'd learned moments before had been oh-so-much worse. She wiped both palms on her thighs now, because it made her feel dirty just thinking about it. Suppressing a shudder, she glanced over at silent Dean again. Her gaze caught on his left hand. She stared, watching him worry a worn-looking business card. He turned it over and over between his long fingers.

He must have noticed her intense regard. His hand stilled and he cleared his throat. "My good luck charm. Strange, huh? Lots of the guys have them, though. On each and every mission they bring their granddad's old dog tags or their baby's ultrasound image or their local library card. I know a soldier whose talisman is a receipt from Gordo's Taco Stop in Texarkana, Texas, showing he consumed sixteen bean burritos in one sitting."

"I'm glad I didn't have to share his barracks that night."

Dean laughed. "Now this," he said, waving the business card that advertised the Ms. M boutique in Santa Monica, "is mine. My buddies tell me I carried it with me all the time in Afghanistan. It was beside me in the hospital, too.

Every day. Every hour. Call me superstitious—or maybe it's my Cherokee forefathers telling me something—but I'm still carrying it."

Now she understood. "Though you don't recall how it came into your possession, do you?" Because he couldn't possibly remember her and their time together. If he did know that it was a card from her boutique, if he did know that *she* was Ms. M, then he wouldn't still be calling it a good luck charm. The likely reason he'd been carting it all over Afghanistan was to find some godforsaken place to burn the thing. She looked up to meet his eyes. "And you don't know me."

"Uh." He hesitated. "No."

At the confirmation, Marlys went light-headed. She actually swayed on her feet and he stepped forward, catching her elbow to steady her.

This time, the electric burn zipped down to her fingertips and then up again, crackling from the top of her head to the filed edges of her French pedicure. It was heat and sweet and so damn scary that tears pricked the corners of her eyes.

"How could I have forgotten this?" he murmured, staring down at her.

How indeed. But it had happened. Dean Long had lost months of his life, meaning he didn't remember that ugly, dirty, desperate night when she'd ruthlessly arranged for him to find her post-coital with some other man.

For a person who'd spent more than his fair share of time playing kissy-face with beer-stained and grime-gummed barroom floors, Gabe figured going through garbage wouldn't cause him a quiver. And he was right; it was nothing to delve through the little bag of trash that Cassandra left in a can inside the single-sized carport attached to her house. Fact was, because Cassandra put her vegetable parings and fruit scraps in a compost heap and separated for recycling her plastic, glass, paper, and aluminum, what she actually threw away was little more than a flattened tube of toothpaste.

There wasn't any sign of a condom. Not the thing itself. Not the foil wrapper either. Could you recycle those? Shit.

Headlights appeared at the end of the lane, bobbing a little as the old Mercedes hit the ruts in the blacktop. They caught him in their yellow-white gaze, but he didn't flinch or fade away into the shadows. Instead, he twisted the end of the bag to tie it off and waited while Cassandra stopped her car.

She didn't seem surprised to see him either. Part of their deal was that he took care of trash disposal. They didn't get garbage service out here in the secluded canyon and so he drove their bags into town once a week and deposited them in the big commercial bins behind his fish market.

No, he didn't have a real reason to feel bad about being caught with her garbage, not at all. As a matter of fact, he'd planned to be found right here, right now, just in case he didn't discover the reassuring evidence of a rubber among Cassandra's detritus.

"Good evening," he called to her, smiling as she stepped out of the car.

In the glow from the security lights he'd installed along the eaves of the narrow carport he saw her send him a startled look. "Hi," she answered, and ducked into the car to pull out a couple of her reusable grocery sacks, both filled with foodstuff.

Perfect. He dropped the bag he held and hurried over. "Let me take those for you."

Gripping them tighter against her body, she drew back a little as if surprised. "I've got them."

Gabe tried to figure out the cause of her odd reactions. Did he never smile at her? When he found her with groceries, did he never offer to ease her load?

Apparently he didn't.

A moment from his past reared up. Lynn, that funny, triangular smile of hers tugging up the corners of her mouth. He'd been playing tea party with Maddie, bowing over her hand and kissing her fingers before settling cross-legged on the floor behind the dainty teacups and pretend petit fours she'd set out. "You're such a gentleman, Gabe," his wife had said. "Be careful, you'll spoil our daughter and make her unprepared for the men who'll come along and break her heart."

It turned out that Maddie had never lived to have her heart broken.

It turned out that Gabe was a piss-poor gentleman.

He stomped toward Cassandra and slid his arms under the grocery bags. "Give me those, damn it," he said, his voice brusque. "What kind of asshole do you think I am?"

She resisted for a moment, allowing him time to breathe in that incredible Cassandra scent and for the back of his hands to register the warmth of her skin radiating through the soft knit of her sweater. Then he wrenched the groceries from her grasp and marched up her porch steps to her front door.

This had been the second part of his plan, after all—that

if he didn't find evidence in the garbage, then he'd get into her house and do a little sleuthing around. If he discovered an opened box of condoms or packet of birth control pills, he could breathe easy again.

Such a gentleman, Gabe.

Okay, fine, now he truly felt like a slimy Dumpster diver. Because, of course, "sleuthing" was just a euphemism for "snooping." Still, he just couldn't see himself confessing to his neighborly nun/sister/friend that he didn't recall boinking her and oh, since it was so unmemorable, could she please assure him they'd actually taken steps to prevent a pregnancy? Which meant looking around on the sly was necessary, damn it.

He shuffled aside to let her unlock her front door. She slipped inside the house first, then barred the way, holding out her arms for the bags. "Thanks," she said. "I'll take it from here."

Astonished, he stared at her. She seemed to be guarding her gate. Cassandra never guarded her gate. Cassandra was open and generous and she was always trying to coax him inside so she could cook a meal for him. Except not tonight.

"I'm . . . hungry," he said, frowning at her.

"It's that time of day," she responded. "Let me have the groceries."

It was his turn to tighten his grip. "Do you . . . Do you have a date or something?" What was the name of that asshat for whom she'd donned the slinky dress and new perfume? "Are you seeing, uh . . . Darryl again?"

"Dante."

"Dante." Yeah, there was a name. He was either a wannabe soap actor or some androgynous dude who did hair up in Hollywood. "Are you entirely certain he likes women?"

Her reusable bags had woven handles. Cassandra grabbed them up and then yanked the groceries away from him. "He likes me," she said. "Why do you care anyway, Gabe?"

Well, he didn't care. Not about Dante. He didn't give a hoot whether someone liked acting or styling or sexing it up with a member of the same gender. It's just that when it came to Cassandra . . . she was like a nun/sister/friend and he was required to look out for her. Particularly because there might be unintended consequences from the other night.

So when she spun and kicked the door with her foot, trying to shut it in Gabe's face, he cared enough to kick back. The thick wood reversed direction and he followed her flouncing hair across the threshold and into the living room.

Over her shoulder, she sent him another look. He tried out a second smile and wondered just how he might weasel into her medicine cabinets. Cassandra's cats ran toward him, giving him the unrestrained welcome that he'd expected from her. He bent to stroke a hand over each—nothing else would get them to back off—then followed their owner even as the cats continued their meowing demands for his attention.

The kitchen was barely big enough for her and half his larger frame as she bustled about putting the groceries away. Another of her wary glances slid his way. Smiling hadn't been doing much for him, so he just looked back.

Coming to a sudden halt, she closed her eyes, as if in pain.

His chest constricted and he took a step forward. "Froot Loop—"

She halted him with a hand. "Please. Could you get me some ibuprofen?"

"What? You need me to go to Rite Aid?" He tried to think if he had any pain reliever at his place.

Cassandra's hand rubbed a spot between her arched brows. "No. I have what I need. It's in . . . I'm not sure. The guest bathroom? My bathroom? Check the medicine cabinets. There's a new bottle somewhere."

No. It couldn't be that damn easy. He had permission to do exactly what he wanted? Her request meant he could run down her hallway and use the excuse to check out all the likely spots.

Cassandra winced, her fingers pressing harder to her forehead. Without thinking, Gabe stepped closer to his nun/sister/friend and closed his hands over her shoulders so he could massage the muscles that led to her neck. "Headache, honey?"

At the endearment, she stiffened. Her gaze shot up. Gabe pretended that damn wide blue of her eyes wasn't dragging him down like a weighted anchor and slid his fingers upward so his thumbs could find that sweet spot where neck met shoulder. In a weird flash—memory?—he saw himself biting her there.

But the flesh was unmarked. Half-relieved, half-disappointed, he kneaded her tense muscles, aware that before today, he'd never intentionally touched her—in his memory, that is.

"Ah." Her head dropped back and she emitted a husky sound of relieved pleasure.

He went hard.

Gabe's arms dropped and he spun away. He cleared his throat. "Let me, uh, check those cabinets for you." That was what he needed to do, right? He needed to figure out whether there was a chance he'd made Cassandra pregnant.

Shit. Didn't that just freeze his feet. Cassandra pregnant. He could picture it. Her rippling hair reaching to her pregnant belly. She'd breast-feed the infant, of course, and every day, damn, so many times a day, she'd expose those incredible, full, beautiful breasts—

"Stop!" he said.

"Gabe?"

Gentleman Gabe. Jerk Gabe. Got-to-get-a-grip Gabe. "I'll be just a minute grabbing that ibuprofen," he said, and ordered his shoes to move.

It took more than a minute but less than five to find what she wanted and to find out the info he'd been after. Plastic bottle in hand, he returned to the kitchen with the certainty that Cassandra didn't stock condoms and with the likelihood that she wasn't on the pill. He'd discovered no evidence of either.

Which meant he was going to have to tell Cassandra he didn't remember bedding her. He had to know for sure that they hadn't risked a baby.

Her back was to him as she sautéed some cubes of tofu in a pan. His gaze trailed over that incredible fall of her rich brown hair, slowly taking in each ripple to where the ends brushed her hipline, right above her heart-shaped butt. He thought about those bruises he must have made upon her skin and damned himself again for not remembering what the cheeks of her ass felt like against his palms, what the globes of her breasts felt like in his mouth, what her wet heat felt like wrapped around his cock.

He groaned and Cassandra looked over. "What?" she said, eyes wide again. "Why are you looking at me like that?"

If the tails of his oxford shirt weren't untucked, she wouldn't have needed to ask the question. He shifted on his feet and pretended to peer at what she was cooking. A man couldn't just launch into the subject of forgotten sex when the scent of soybean curd was in the air, could he? "I'm just wondering how the hell you can eat that stuff."

And why the hell she hadn't invited him to share it with her. Yeah, this morning she'd asked for some "distance" from him, but distance just wasn't Cassandra's way. He hated thinking that being together in bed with him last night had somehow changed her.

Her head whipped back around as if she could read what he was thinking and she focused on the cubes she was stirring. "I've told you. I was brought up eating vegetarian on the organic farm."

That's right. "The place your mother worked and where both of you lived when you were a kid. From four until you were, what, eleven? Your mom did the books for the farm owned by the old MacDonalds."

"MacDougalls," she corrected. "She did the books and homeschooled the kids. The farm was pretty secluded and we all lived there together. Three generations of MacDougalls, my mom, and me."

"Three generations, huh? I don't remember that part." And he'd been certain he knew thousands of details of Cassandra's life, as from the beginning she'd filled every moment of quiet between them with any thought or emotion that crossed her mind. Since his black moods equated to many dark silences, Cassandra had given him hours of her bright and cheerful chatter.

For some crazy reason he couldn't explain, he'd found her impossible to walk away from or to shut off. She'd wrapped him around her finger that way, which meant he knew her favorite color—robin's egg; the name of her date to the senior prom—Carver Shields, now a drummer in some heavy metal band currently touring Eastern Europe; and the day she'd first picked up a pair of knitting needles—May 15, at her friend Claire's thirteenth birthday party. But he didn't recall three generations of MacDougalls living together on a secluded rural property, and something about the way she said it had the hair on the back of his neck rising.

"Froot Loop?" he prompted, cold trailing down his spine. "Did that MacDougall clan include a funny uncle?"

"No. The MacDougalls aren't a very funny lot." She added some soy sauce to her pan. "Especially the MacDougall kids."

Hmm. Gabe stepped closer to her turned back, twining his fingers in her hair. He pulled a swathe away from her face and tilted his head so he could better read her profiled expression. "Bullies?"

She slid him a quick glance, then shrugged a shoulder. "Cousins. Twelve of them, all first cousins, which made me . . . lucky number thirteen."

"Twelve little bullies," Gabe confirmed. And Cassandra the unlucky outsider. The only one not family . . . and without a family of her own except her mother who insisted she be called "Judith" instead of "Mom." A man didn't need to be named Freud to know what drove this generous, beautiful woman. From the beginning, from when he'd first met her and all the way through her making contact with her donor sibling sisters, she'd been clear about what she was looking for.

The bonds of family.

And now he thought he understood a little more about why.

"They didn't like me," Cassandra added, a new note in her voice. "And they made that very, very clear in very many ways." She sounded . . . bewildered? Hurt?

Because everybody always liked Cassandra. The woman had more close friends than most people had pairs of socks. But between her mother's choices and the MacDougalls' cruelties, she'd come to think they couldn't substitute for family. That friends couldn't provide the kind of support and comfort some people required.

She was right, in a sense. Who rubbed away Cassandra's headaches? Who stroked her hair like he was doing right now when she was blue?

Gabe had experienced that kind of intimacy once. Juliet had it with Noah now. Nikki with Jay. But Cassandra was still searching for that tight emotional and physical bond. He palmed his hand down her hair again and she sent him another glance. He could read those big blues of hers like a book. Sweet Cassandra, who had put up with his sour tempers and nasty disposition so many times, was having herself a bad day.

It unsettled him, more than a little, because Cassandra didn't have bad days. And shit, was he the one who had delivered hers?

Without thinking, he turned her and pulled her against him. His arms held her close, her soft breasts aligned with his chest, her hip bones pressed to his groin. "Froot Loop . . ."

"You know I hate that name." Looking up, her lower lip slid out in a pout.

And he kissed it, gently and slowly and nearly asexually, because she was so sweet and still his nun/sister/friend. She was still in his arms, too, and her blue eyes looked a little lost and Christ, he didn't know where to go from here.

No condoms. No birth control pills. So damn it, man, no putting tongue into this kiss!

No way could he let this embrace turn passionate. He sighed. Just as there was no way he could ever let her know that if he had fucked her last night he'd forgotten all about it.

Five

Marlys remained focused on her current customer when the
bells on the door of her boutique, Ms. M, rang out, though
satisfaction warmed her belly. A busy morning was the harbinger of a good day. Surely she was owed one of those.

Her gaze ran over the woman who had just stepped from
the dressing area. Fortyish, she was just the kind of customer
Marlys liked to see in her shop. Good taste, ready with
her credit cards, and willing to step out of the Nordstrom/
Neiman/Bloomie rut that her type too often traveled along.
Still, Marlys had to shake her head.

"Dark jeans are a good choice, but not *those* jeans."

The woman looked down, showing how artfully blond
and copper highlights were weaved into her blah-brown
hair. "What's wrong with them?"

"Nothing's wrong with the pants." Crossing her arms
over her chest, Marlys inspected the customer's midsection.
Other boutique owner's might soften the truth to make a
sale, but tact didn't come easily to her. At twelve, she'd

stopped nurturing that let's-make-nice female gene—which probably partially explained her lack of friends. Not that she missed them.

"Nothing's wrong with the pants. It's you," Marlys said, gesturing toward the small roll of flesh hanging over the waistband of the woman's jeans. "It's your muffin top."

A choked-off cough caused her head to jerk around. Oh, damn. Harbinger shmarbinger. This was going to be a very bad day, after all.

Dean Long was in her shop. All too many feet and too many hard muscles of him were pretending to inspect a tray of costume jewelry sitting on a small table near the narrow rack of shoes. But he wasn't looking for an accessory; she could guarantee that. He was looking for answers.

The other day, when she'd encountered him at Juliet and Noah's guesthouse, she hadn't told him she was Ms. M. Between the shock of seeing him and then learning he didn't remember any of his time in Malibu, it had been impossible for her to do more than make an excuse and hurry away.

Her customer had turned to look at herself in the full-length mirror and was pinching the skin at her hips. "I substituted Pilates for lattés. I walk up those damn treadmill steps four times a week, forty minutes each time. It must be the wine."

Marlys returned her attention to the woman and shook her head. "It's the rise. You need to choose a pair of pants that has a longer distance from the waist to the crotch—that's the rise."

"You're telling me I'm too old for hip-huggers," the customer said, an expression of dismay on her face.

"Yes." What was the point of prettying it up? In the mirror, she saw Dean glance over at her. He had questioned her plain-speaking before and didn't like it now either, apparently. So what? It was part of the secret to her success in the fashion business.

But watching the customer grab her waistline with evident self-loathing gave Marlys a little pinch, too. "Hip-huggers with a two-and-a-half inch zipper, that is," she clarified. "Leave those to the women who never get to taste ice cream. Let them at least have something."

The woman paused, then laughed. Her fingers eased on her flesh and she smiled at Marlys in the mirror. "Too-thin women have saggy breasts."

"And sallow skin," Marlys added. "Not to mention the bad moods that are brought on by chocolate and fat deprivation. Very scary. Very sad."

She saw the customer's shoulders relax as she crossed to a stack of denim on a nearby shelf. "Try these," she said, handing over the jeans. "There are more inches to the rise and the back pockets will accentuate your, um, natural assets."

The woman took them with a grin. "The natural assets that my best buds Ben & Jerry get the credit for."

"All hail Phish Food and Chubby Hubby," Marlys murmured.

The customer laughed. "I've always liked this shop, but now I think I like *you*, too."

As the dressing room drapes closed behind the woman, Marlys took a quick breath and steeled herself to face the man browsing through the Ms. M merchandise. Stalling wasn't an option. Running had only sparked his curiosity about her. What she needed to do now was deal with him head-on and without hesitation.

Then lie through her teeth if it became necessary.

Dean never needed to know what they'd once had . . . and the manner in which she'd thrown it away.

She tacked a smile carefully in place and marched right over to him, where he was standing by a selection of scarves and belts. "We meet again."

He dropped the gossamer-weight chiffon he was fingering to pull the battered business card from his front pocket. "You didn't tell me the other day that you worked at Ms. M."

"I *own* Ms. M."

"You didn't tell me the other day that you own the shop that the card I carry advertises."

She kept her smile in place. "An oversight."

"Or an underestimation. You must underestimate *me*. Didn't you figure I would venture into Santa Monica?" He wiggled the little piece of cardboard in front of her face. "The address is right here."

"I . . . I guess I didn't think about it." More like, she'd been praying he wouldn't.

He slid the card back into his pocket and crossed his arms over his chest. It was a wide chest, and she could see the outline of his pectoral muscles under the cotton knit of his shirt. She remembered sitting on his lap. She remembered leaning her head against that strong shoulder.

She remembered how he'd made her weak and womanly, both things she couldn't afford to feel.

Given that she had those man issues. Especially those man-leaving issues.

"You didn't think I'd be curious as to why I'd be carrying this business card around Afghanistan?"

"I don't like to think about you in Afghanistan," she confessed. Giving herself a mental jab, she hurried to the nearby counter to put a barrier between herself and the man who followed, his expression giving nothing away.

"I'm trying to reconstruct the missing pieces of my life," he said.

She wouldn't let him. At least not the pieces that involved her.

"Marlys—"

"You know my name." Her head jerked up. "I didn't introduce myself the other day."

His brows rose. "It's right there." His finger pointed to one of the two sets of business cards sitting on the counter. One small stack was the generic advertisement for the business—like the card in Dean's pocket. The other was new. Last month she'd had different cards printed that included her name, which was convenient for handing out to vendors and special customers.

"Oh. Yeah." She blew out a breath between her lips. For a moment there, she'd thought his memory might have returned. Having Dean recall what she'd done was too damn close to reliving the event. She rubbed her upper arms with her palms as if she could wipe away the memory.

"Cold?" His fingers reached toward her face.

Marlys scuttled back. No way could she let him touch her again. Her elbow still remembered the grip of his hand from two days ago. Though it was months past, her mouth remembered every searing kiss they'd ever shared.

Dean stared at her face. "There was something between us before," he said, his voice certain.

She made a face at him. "Why would you think that?"

"Marlys . . ."

The fact was, Marlys Weston was pretty. Maybe even beautiful. She knew that. And she was also short, which meant that she'd had more than her fair share of attention.

Once she'd wandered through a Tall Singles Club barbecue at a nearby park and been accosted by an Amazon who demanded she stick with the height-challenged. But she couldn't control who hit on her, and at twenty-five, she'd been hit on by dozens of men—the five-foot-one guys, the seven-foot-two types, the geeks, the gods, and every kind in between. She had the freeze down pat and she turned it on now, icing her gaze and her words and her attitude.

"If there was something between us before," Marlys stated, "*I* certainly don't recall it."

His eyes narrowed. "You—"

"I love them," interrupted the customer as she hurried from the dressing room to the cash register. "They fit just right."

Marlys took the jeans to ring up the sale, smiling because she saw that Dean was backing away. "I'm sure they're fine."

She was, too—fine, and safe, now that the man was in retreat.

Her customer took a glance over her shoulder and then turned back to Marlys. Her voice lowered. "Cute."

Marlys checked out the woman's ring finger. A platinum and diamond honker clinched her marital status. "Taken," she said anyway.

Too soon, the other woman was gone and Marlys was left alone again with Dean, who had resumed prowling the shop. "Look," she said, calling to him from the other side of the room. "I don't mean to be rude, but I have boxes to unpack in the back and—"

The bells on the door rang out again.

"—customers," Marlys finished, blessing whoever was coming over the threshold. She headed for the front of the store, mentally promising the newcomer an instant 10 percent discount.

Then she noticed it was another man. Weird. She hadn't had this many male customers since last December 24, twenty minutes before closing time. As she got closer, she realized which man it was.

Her ex-boyfriend. Pharmaceutical rep Phil. AKA her one-time fuck buddy.

She closed her eyes. Karma. Damn. That vindictive bitch was really pissed off. "What do *you* want?"

Phil gave her that smile he'd been offering up ever since he'd walked into her boutique one November day and she'd begged for a no-strings boff later that afternoon. It was a grateful smile. Hopeful.

"Just poking my head in to say hi," he said.

In case she was in the market for another kind of poke altogether. Last fall, he'd hummed to himself while he'd rocked on her body in her bed. She'd closed her eyes and pretended she was in the kitchen making toast.

"I'm busy, Phil," she said, her tone clipped. And if she ever felt sorry about how she treated men, she might feel sorry about that, because Phil had been doing her a favor that afternoon. As Dean had pointed out when he'd arrived for the date she'd set up with him to find the pharmaceutical rep leaving and Marlys dressed in her robe and smelling of the other man's cologne, Phil hadn't deserved to be used.

"You sure?" he asked, hopeful again.

Really, though, she didn't think Phil had felt used. "I'm sure."

"Okay." He gave a little wave and half-turned. Then he stopped, his gaze going over her head. "Hey, don't I know you?"

Marlys swallowed her groan. No. *No.*

Dean's arm reached around her. "Dean Long."

A quizzical light sparked in Phil's eyes. "Where do I know you from?"

Shit! She didn't want Dean knowing they'd had a relationship before, let alone one that she'd ended in such an ugly way. Phil wouldn't spill the beans, would he? He wouldn't say, "Oh, yeah, you're the guy on Marlys's porch that miraculous day when she offered up some afternoon delight." Would he?

Phil rubbed his chin, and he appeared to be thinking back. "We know each other somehow."

Dean shrugged. "I couldn't say—"

"Because he's busy, too, Phil."

"Busy with what . . . ?" Phil murmured, as he seemed to be thinking harder.

Oh crap. Did she say bad day? Let's call it a disaster and get it over with. Pharmaceutical Phil might be slow, but he didn't suffer memory loss like Dean. Any moment now—but she couldn't let that happen.

In a move of total desperation, to get rid of Phil and to derail this dangerous conversation, she turned and launched herself toward Dean.

"Busy with me," she declared, then latched her mouth to the tall man's, as behind her back she made urgent "get lost" gestures with one hand. The other had creeped around Dean's neck.

By the time his palms pressed the small of her back to hoist her closer, worries about Phil and doom had burned away in the heat of the mouth-on-mouth. She thought she heard the bells of the boutique's door ring out again, but that might just be the disturbance caused by the bats in her belfry that had led her to commit such a crazy act.

Because he tasted so crazy good.

Dean snatched his mouth from hers. He was panting, his chest moving hard against hers. "We've done this before."

Instead of answering, she kissed him again. She couldn't help herself. She heard more bells, not the goofy, girly, he's-kissing-me kind this time, but the ones on her shop door that told her she had another customer. So this was going to have to end soon, and end forever, but for this moment, was it wrong of her to indulge?

Ah, well. She'd always been a bad girl.

Cassandra pulled slowly into her carport, aware during every inch of pavement she crossed of the man waiting on her porch. Gabe. Again.

Gabe, who over the last few days had become a ubiquitous presence, just when she'd determined to cross him out of her life. She eyed him as she climbed the steps to her front door, for a silly minute wishing she was wearing something sexier than a pair of boyfriend-cut khaki pants and a white cotton-knit Henley shirt that had a dozen tiny buttons marching down the front.

As if Gabe ever noticed what she was wearing. But maybe he'd surprise her, because he was breaking all sorts of character molds, she realized, as his mouth turned up in another of those startling, unpracticed smiles. Just when she'd hardened her heart to him, he was melting it with things like that smile.

He stepped forward, his mouth brushing her cheek.

And with things like these casual kisses.

He lifted a bag and waved it in front of her face. "I brought dinner."

Not to mention the edible gifts. The night before he'd shown up with frozen yogurt for dessert.

Why would he feel the need to give her smiles, kisses, food? She'd better figure it out, and figure it out fast, before she fell into the old bad habit of caring too much for him. She was over that.

With a sigh, she let him into her house, and both of them were occupied for a few minutes greeting the critters who delighted in the fact that Gabe was visiting again. Then they made it to her small dining table and he began setting out the meal. "Grilled portobello sandwich for you," he said.

It smelled delicious. One of the best things about Malibu living was Malibu takeout. While Gabe continued unpacking the bag, she opened the bottle of merlot he'd handed over and poured it into two glasses. She set them on the table.

He frowned at the ruby-colored wine. "Maybe I shouldn't have brought that."

"You don't like red with your red meat?" she asked. "Don't even try to tell me you chose something healthier than roast beef or a burger."

Still frowning, Gabe pulled out her chair. "After the other night . . ."

"We don't have to talk about that," she said quickly as she took her seat. Before, they'd never spoken openly about his drunken bouts, let alone her Florence Nightingale activities, and she was afraid if they did he'd read too much into her two A.M. rescues.

He sat in his chair. "But—"

"It ended differently than other nights, I'll grant you that," she said, "but it doesn't change a thing between us."

They ate a few minutes in silence, she sipping at her wine and focusing on her plate, even as she was aware he was studying her from across the table. Her pulse jumped, but she ignored the feeling as she chewed. *Remember. Remember he's hung up on his dead wife and child. Remember you're no longer hung up on him.*

His hand slid across the small table and covered hers. Heat warmed her skin, but she held tough, keeping her palm flat to the table when the only thing she wanted to do was curl her fingers around his. "Cassandra," he said, the command in his voice making her look up. A lock of his too-long hair fell across his temple and curved toward his stubby black eyelashes. Her gaze snagged on a single silver hair mixed in with the mussed black bangs. She stared at it, aware of what had put it there, aware that the ghosts that haunted his life were every reason she had to keep her hand still beneath his and her heartbeat steady and even.

"You're hurting again," he said, his fingers leaving hers so he could stroke his thumb across her temple. "I can see it in your eyes. Another headache?"

She jerked her face from his touch. "I have things on my mind."

"Me."

"What? No." She couldn't let him think he had a place in her head when he certainly wasn't in her heart. "It's not about you. Nikki and I had words today."

It was true. She'd again brought up the idea of contacting their father with her sister, and Nikki's refusal had been Cassandra's prime concern—until she'd spied Gabe standing on her porch.

"Tell me about it."

She frowned at him. What was this? Smiles, kisses, food, and now *conversation*? While she talked to Gabe all the time, it had always been more of a talking *at* Gabe. Not once had he prodded her to divulge a single thing.

"Maybe I can help," he said now.

Oh. *Kay.* His behavior was still oddly out of character, but she could use an objective viewpoint and, face it, who could be more objective than he? When it came to her—except when he was drunk—Gabe had always seemed downright disinterested.

She scooted back her chair and he followed her into the small living area, carrying their wineglasses. From a bookcase, she pulled a manila folder and laid it on the coffee table. "It's about this," she said, dropping to the couch so she could open the file of newspaper clippings. "It's about him."

Gabe sank into the cushions beside her and set the merlot on the table. His long fingers brushed the stack of tabloid articles to spread them out. The headlines screamed.

SECRET SIBLINGS SHOCK DADDY SCISSORHANDS!

SPERM-EGG ON FAMOUS DOC'S FACE?

CELEBRITY PLASTIC SURGEON FATHERS THREE MALIBU BABES!

The last piece came complete with candid photos of the three donor sibling sisters, as well as a professional head shot of a handsome, mature man wearing a white medical coat and a reassuring smile.

She didn't know how much of the story Gabe had absorbed when it had come out last November. "Do you remember? Marlys learned that the man who fathered Juliet, Nikki, and me—our sperm donor—was none other than Hollywood's favorite go-to guy for new noses and tighter tummies, Dr. Frank Tucker."

"And she tipped off the gossip rags."

Cassandra nodded. "Just to cause more trouble for Juliet. So what was supposed to be anonymous became public."

"But I remember that you were going to make yourselves known to him anyway. He'd registered at a website for donors who want to make contact with their progeny." Moosewood jumped onto the couch and Gabe shifted to make room for the cat, his thigh pressing Cassandra's.

She was up against the upholstered arm, so there was no way to put more space between them. Ignoring the heat and hardness of his muscled leg, she grabbed up her glass to take a healthy sip of wine. "We were still in the early stages of how exactly to manage that. We put it into Juliet's hands, but then we got sidetracked by the holidays and Juliet and Noah's wedding. Not to mention that Noah was never exactly keen on the idea."

"He's very protective of Juliet."

"Yes." Cassandra smiled a little. Her older sister didn't always appreciate Noah's need to watch out for her, and like any married couple they were learning to compromise, but Cassandra thought the way he cared for his now-wife was . . . She didn't have words for it. She only knew that she envied the security of that kind of love.

"He wanted me to talk you out of the plan."

Surprised, Cassandra glanced up. "What? Why?"

"He tried to persuade Jay, too. He suggested a united stand among the three of us—the three men in the lives of you and your sisters."

The temperature of the blush crawling up Cassandra's face was hotter than the press of Gabe's thigh to hers. Noah was married to Juliet. Jay and Nikki would be wed in a few months. But Gabe was nothing like that to her. "I'm sorry he involved you. I hope you told him that you're merely my landlord."

"Is that all I am?"

She stole a look at him as she slid her wineglass back to the table. His dark eyes compelled her to tell the truth, but she shifted her gaze away to stare at that ghostly strand of silver in his hair. "Of course."

"Even after—"

"You're a . . . a friend, too," she put in hastily, again worrying that he wanted to delve into a discussion of her past rescues. She was done with them. Done with him in that way. "No doubt a friend, but Noah shouldn't have put you in that position."

"I didn't agree with him, anyway."

"What?" Her head jerked toward him and she put her hand on his knee. "You think we should contact Dr. Tucker?"

He ran his fingers over the backs of hers. "I think what's right for you, Cassandra, might not be the same thing that's right for your sisters. I think you should do what you need to do."

The light touch on her skin was mesmerizing her, the same as that hypnotic darkness of his eyes. She leaned toward him, astonished that he had an opinion about her life, touched that he seemed to be interested in what was best for *her*. With his free hand, he tucked a piece of hair behind her ear and goose bumps skittered across the surface of her skin.

It took her a moment to bring her mind back to the subject at hand. "But I made a promise to Nikki today that I wouldn't introduce myself to him," she said, frowning. "At least not until Juliet gets back from her honeymoon and we have another talk about it."

His fingertips brushed the top of her hand again. "But you don't want to wait that long."

"I need to do something," she agreed, her voice low. "It's . . . time." Her sisters had their loves, and she'd given up on Gabe, so she had to have something else to focus on now. "If I could just see him in person . . ."

"Why don't you go for that? That's how you worked things with Nikki and Juliet, right? You enticed them into Malibu & Ewe so you could get a look at them before you made contact."

He surprised her again. Blinking, she drew back, sliding her hand from beneath his. "You remember that?"

"Cassandra, you are aware that pretty much anything you think and feel goes right through your head and then comes straight out your mouth, right?"

But she'd never realized he'd been listening. "You probably thought that was all weird and New Age-y of me, that I wanted to get a feel for them first."

"I always think you're all weird and New Age-y. I blame it on the overabundance of beta-carotene in your diet."

That sounded like the old Gabe. The pre-smiles, -kisses, -food, and -personal-interest-in-her Gabe. Comfortable with him like she hadn't been in days, she leaned back and grinned at the man. "So you wouldn't be surprised if I told you I wanted to meet my sisters and my father before talking to them because I'm able to read auras?"

"I wouldn't be surprised, but I wouldn't believe you either. Froot Loop, everyone, New Age, old school, and anywhere in between wants a chance to size up a person before they make their move."

Her smile widened. "Your aura is very peanut brittle brown right now. Did you eat that junk for breakfast again?"

Gabe grimaced. "Froot Loop . . ."

"Okay, okay." She left off teasing him to consider her

options. "So you think I could do that. Just get a . . . get a glimpse of him to satisfy me until Juliet returns? I don't think an invitation to Knitters' Night at Malibu & Ewe would work, but I suppose I could drop by his offices or something."

His shoulder brushed hers when he shrugged. "Or something. If you want, I'll help you with that."

She pinched her bottom lip between her thumb and forefinger and continued thinking, her gaze on the bookshelf across the room. "I suppose I could make an appointment . . . not with him, but with one of the other doctors in his practice, and then hope I see him in the hallway. What could I say I wanted a consult about? What do women my age typically see a plastic surgeon for?"

Her gaze shifted to Gabe's. "Breast augmentation, right? I could say I wanted breast augmentation."

His eyes didn't move from her face. "No."

Cassandra glanced down at her D-cups and made a face. "Right. How about breast reduction? I've often thought about—"

"*No!*"

His vehemence startled her. There was a little flush across his cheekbones though his gaze was still trained on hers. She narrowed her eyes. "Gabe?"

"Don't change those at all, okay? They're perfect just as they are. Trust me on this."

Wow, she thought. "I didn't realize you'd ever really noticed me, um, like that. I mean, particularly, um, there."

Though she'd deny it to her dying breath, she'd tried using "there" only about a zillion times to get his attention when he was sober. He'd never seemed to notice. When he was drunk, he always talked about his proportions, not hers. "And frankly, with the exception of you, men usually can't seem to help themselves when faced with . . ." She made a vague gesture toward her chest.

Gabe swallowed. The flush on his cheeks deepened and his hand came to her face, his thumb brushing back and forth against her bottom lip. "If I didn't pay proper homage to your incredible body when we were in bed the other night, I was not only drunk I was a fool."

She didn't hear a word he said. Her mouth stung where he was touching it and she could only stare at his face as his gaze finally, finally, shifted from her eyes and moved to a spot south of her collarbone.

In that moment, everything changed between them.

Her breasts swelled and their centers tightened as the heat of his leg still pressing against hers shot up her torso. Flames erupted around them, swallowing the oxygen in the room. Her head spun with the sudden onslaught of a combustible, sexual burn.

She couldn't catch her breath. Where had the fire been all this time? How had Gabe managed to keep it smothered? He wasn't managing now though, because there was definitely sex in the air, rising off their skin to mingle in the atmosphere. His hand dropped from her mouth to her thigh. More heat. She started to tremble.

"Cassandra," he said, his voice hoarse. His gaze returned to her eyes, then dropped to her mouth where it lingered for a moment. Finally, it shifted lower again. "Cassandra, I didn't do right by you, did I?"

She shook her head, unsure what he was referring to. He wasn't doing right by her right *now*. Because if he didn't move that hand from her leg and touch her someplace better, preferably one of those tight, aching someplaces he was staring at, she was going to burn up with want. She didn't know why things had changed between them or what the change meant exactly; but if she could really read auras, theirs were mingling in an explosive combination of simmering yellow and passionate red.

She licked her lips, trembling as he continued to look at her. It was like there was a beast under her skin, a hot, sexy, demanding beast that didn't remember Gabe had been kicked out of her life. *Touch me, damn you,* it wanted to shout at him. *Touch me.* But when Cassandra opened her mouth, a sultry voice—her voice—said something else altogether.

"Is this what you meant when you said everyone wants a chance to size up a person before they make their move?"

Six

The great gift of family life is to be intimately acquainted with people you might never even introduce yourself to, had life not done it for you.

—KENDALL HAILEY

The half-laugh, half-groan sound that Gabe made in response to Cassandra's question rubbed against her skin like she was desperate for him to do. Maybe he heard her silent plea, because finally his hand slid upward from her leg, slowly smoothing the soft khaki covering her thigh, passing the front pocket, skimming the waistband to the cotton knit of her Henley T-shirt. The flesh over her ribs twitched as his palm tickled her there and then it was cupping her left breast, still not touching, damn him, but transferring his body's heat to the already sizzling temperature of hers.

She didn't move.

She had to move.

Then they both moved at once, and she fit her swelling, aching flesh to his hand just as he moved to cover her.

He groaned again.

Her belly—no, lower—clenched. But she held still, not wanting to spook him, not wanting to rush the delicious sensation of his hand over the soft fullness beneath her bra.

"Look at me," Gabe ordered.

She was afraid to. She was afraid of what he'd see in her eyes, so she lifted her head but let her lashes drift half-closed. His mouth came against hers.

She jolted into the kiss, her nipples tightening unbearably with just that first touch of hard mouth to willing lips. This wasn't one of those casual, howdy-neighbor busses he'd been doling out lately. This was a man's demand, a demand that she open immediately for the swift surge of his tongue. Fire flashed over her body as he thrust inside her.

Cassandra widened her mouth—he gave her no choice—and Gabe, usually detached and often so distant except in her fantasies, went greedy on her, feeding her long kisses, commanding kisses, drugging kisses. She leaned into him as she took each one, leaned into that maddening hand that just held her breast, caging it but not caressing it. Her fingers speared into the long hair at the nape of his neck.

He tore his lips from hers and raced more kisses over her cheek, against her ear, across her jaw and then down her neck. His mouth was hot there, open, and when he sucked at her skin, a stab of pleasure speared between her thighs. Swallowing a moan, she squeezed them together to sustain the bright flash of sweetness. Gabe pulled back to stare down at her, his breath coming fast, his nostrils flared.

"Jesus, Cassandra," he murmured. "Jesus, you make me dizzy." His gaze dropped from her mouth to focus on his hand, the one over her breast. With a deliberate movement, his fingers flexed.

She gasped, even though the touch was muted by the thin layer of molded foam that was the bra's cup. Her breasts had always been sensitive, but who could have thought just this whisper of feeling would make her blood burn in her

veins? His thumb swiped over the center and she closed
her eyes, trying to absorb as much of the sensation as she
could through that damnably thick material. She'd bought
into the bra maker's hype—*Perfect Under T-shirts!*—but
she could kill the advertisers or the intimate apparel de-
signers or someone, anyone, because this ridiculous thing
was surely invented to dull a man's touch.

Gabe's touch.

He slid his thumb over her again and she hoped he
didn't hear her frustrated little whimper.

"Baby," he said, and she knew from the tone of his
voice that he had. "Obviously I didn't do this right before.
I suppose I didn't do right by you at all, selfish ass that I
am. But I can make it better now."

Better was a million buttons away. She could feel him
begin to unfasten them and she flushed hot again, wondering why he didn't just lift the damn shirt and then dispel
with the ugly, confining, can't-feel-anything-with-it-on bra.
This was taking so long . . .

And the anticipation was making her feel so good, she
realized, as pleasure pulsed in little bursts between her legs.
She was aching there, too, feeling swollen and open and
needy. She whimpered again, and Gabe flicked her a glance,
a tight smile curving his mouth.

"Shh, baby," he said, leaning down to deliver another
kiss. This one was gentle, sweet, but his tongue was in it,
too, and she rubbed hers along the velvety surface of his.
"This time I'll take care of you, I promise."

She quivered. Men had never made her promises. She'd
searched all her life for one who might, but maybe her
longings and her lonely soul sent them running in the wrong
direction. Or maybe it was because she had looked at the
wrong men. Wrong men like Gabe, who was so preoccu-

pied with his ghosts that he couldn't see the rest of life going on around him.

But he seemed to see her now. His fingers had unfastened buttons as far as a point just below the lower edge of her bra. "There," he whispered, again in that soothing voice. "There now."

In one sure movement, he pushed the sleeves of her Henley off her shoulders, taking the bra straps with them. He slid all the material down, until her arms were trapped at her elbows and the cups of that infernal *Perfect Under T-shirts!* dropped, releasing her breasts.

She trembled harder. He gazed at her bare flesh, his breath coming fast again. Cassandra glanced down, noting the stiff jut of her dark pink nipples and the way her swollen flesh quivered along with the rest of her body.

Gabe's thumb brushed across the tip of her nipple. She looked for sparks, the pleasure flared and flamed just that much. "My imagination wasn't this good," he said.

"You . . . you've been thinking about my breasts?" She wiggled a little, trying to move her arms out of their trap.

"Hold still," he said, and he caged her breasts again with his fingers, touching, but not really touching. "If you don't hold still I'll stop."

He couldn't stop! She closed her eyes and surrendered, willing her muscles to relax even as every cell and every nerve was on alert for his next move.

"Nice," he said, and he rewarded her by rubbing his thumbs around each areola, tracing a light circle. Reward, punishment, it was all the same because in seconds it wasn't enough.

"Gabe, don't tease."

He laughed, a low, sexy sound that had her thighs clenching again. "Silly darlin', this is all about the tease."

"Gabe."

Then his mouth was on hers again, his tongue thrusting deep, just as his thumbs rasped across her nipples.

Her back arched, her mouth took in more of his tongue as she gasped, her fingers curled into fists at her sides. Who would have thought this would feel so good? He chafed her tightened flesh again and she felt another burst of wet pleasure between her thighs. She moved into him, still constricted by her clothes, but so turned on she needed to get closer, to press nearer, to put all her soft parts against his hard ones.

Gabe controlled that urge, too. Instead of letting her rub against him like she wanted to, he gripped her at the shoulders and held her away from his body. "No," she protested, breaking the kiss.

"Shh," he said again, and kissed the corner of her lips, her chin, the notch of her collarbone. Then he dipped his head deeper and she held her breath until she felt the touch of his tongue on her nipple.

Gasping, her back bowed. He slid an arm around her so that she had support against her shoulder blades. With his other hand, he plumped up one breast and latched his lips around its throbbing center.

And sucked.

Her mind spun, her nipple throbbed, her center melted. She moaned, and kept on moaning as he kept up the heated pressure. His tongue was working, too, flicking the stiff nub, lashing it with sensation that she never wanted to end.

But end it he did, and she cried out until he'd transferred his mouth to her other breast and tweaked the now-abandoned wet nipple with his fingers, pinching just enough to add a little bite to the delirious, drugging sweetness.

Her knees slammed together, and she couldn't help but rock her hips against the cushions. She knew what she wanted, but Gabe wasn't hurrying, Gabe refused to be hurried, as he shifted from one breast to the other, tasting her and teasing her.

"Please. Please, Gabe," she heard herself whisper to him in a hoarse voice. She struggled to free herself from her shirt again, though she was really struggling to free herself of the tightening, maddening coil of pleasure. For that, she knew, she needed more nakedness, and Gabe naked, and a bed, and more of him—her darkest, deepest fantasy—against her.

"*Please*, Gabe."

His mouth still busy at her breast, he lifted his gaze to meet hers. Her lungs ceased to function. Time stopped. It was exciting, erotic beyond any of her late-night imaginings, to look into Gabe's dark eyes, the expression in them burning, as his mouth continued to suck at her breast, his cheeks hollowing.

Her womb clenched, releasing more slick heat. "Gabe," she mouthed, her voice robbed of sound as her body throbbed with want. "Please."

She saw the satisfaction in his eyes. Without taking his gaze from her face, he slid his palm away from her free nipple and slid it down her body. He found the juncture of her thighs, still tightly pressed together. The heel of his hand ground firmly against the soft pad of flesh at her mound.

Moaning, she felt her thighs part. It was what he wanted because he made a hum of approval and then slid his hard fingers into the narrow gap. He had to feel her heat, the dampness, but she couldn't do anything but tilt her hips to meet his firm, knowing touch.

Through the thin cotton of her pants and the light fabric of her panties, he found the exact right place to rock and roll. He did both, taking her closer . . . and closer . . . And when his teeth bit down on her nipple, she reacted like a band groupie to her favorite singer's signature song . . .

She screamed.

He rode with her through the waves of orgasm. His mouth and his hand easing up as the ripples receded. When the last shudder died away, he lifted his head and took a breath. Then he placed a quick kiss on the tip of each nipple, her chin, her nose, then back to her mouth.

No tongue.

No heat.

No intent to move on to the next act.

"Gabe, what? . . ." she said, even as he was pulling up her bra and her top in the same efficient move he'd used to take them down. Her face felt hot with embarrassment. She wasn't practiced at this after-the-scream thing, but she couldn't just *take* from him, could she? "What about you?"

"That was yours, honey. Just for you."

Her face burned hotter. Had she been too loud? Had she done something else to turn him off?

"Gabe . . ." she said, agonized. "Did I do something wrong?"

He buttoned her up almost to her chin. "No. It was me that did wrong the other night. To you."

"What?"

"I was evening the score, Froot Loop. Us together in bed like we were—bad idea. But it happened, and I feel like a heel that I left you high and dry then."

Us together in bed like we were . . .

The words sank in. He'd said something similar earlier, and now she finally understood what he was talking about. He thought they'd had sex the other night after she'd brought him home from the Beach Shack! He'd woken in her bed and assumed . . .

Which meant he didn't remember a thing.

Which explained why he'd been Mr. Nice Neighbor the last couple of days, handing out kisses and concern and now . . . climaxes. He'd felt guilty for sleeping with her.

The warmth on her face and kindling in her belly had nothing to do with sex or shame now. She was pissed. He thought she thought so little of herself that she'd let some drunken barfly talk her between the sheets.

And he hadn't questioned his assumption—or questioned her. Apparently he figured that them naked-to-naked could be just that forgettable.

Oh, she was going to make it very clear that—

But wait. His mistake had gotten him out of his bat cave. It had got him eating and talking and taking an interest in something other than his ghosts and his grief.

That was good. And despite her anger there was still enough Nightingale left in her when it came to Gabe that she wasn't ready to see that end.

So she wouldn't correct his wrong impression that they'd slept together. Her gaze slid over to him as he straightened on the couch. His grimace made her eyes narrow, and then she noticed the bulge in his jeans. Hah. That little session they just had might not have been shared, but it had certainly gotten to him a little. Well, good.

It only strengthened her decision. She definitely wouldn't correct his wrong impression that they'd slept together. But she *was* going to make him pay for it. And now that she knew he wasn't as immune to her as he'd always pretended, she thought she had an idea of just what it was going to cost him.

Don't look at her, Gabe told himself, staring out the passenger-side window of Cassandra's veggie car and pretending a fascination with the light rain. Don't breathe, because then you'll take in her perfume. Don't think about the sight of her incredible breasts . . . The pale globes, their nipples red and sweet and wet after he'd loved them with his mouth.

Find your detachment, buddy. Remember, she's like a nun. Okay, not with the image of those breasts branded into his brain. Sister, then—uh, can't go there now either. Then friend. Yeah, Cassandra was a friend, though one he needed to keep a decided distance from—and hadn't she asked for it herself just days ago? He couldn't take the chance on letting his lust take over for his common sense.

She pulled into the parking lot of the medical building in Beverly Hills, and found a spot in the first row of patient spaces. "It looks like the staff will have to walk right past us to get inside," she said, turning off the ignition. "Now we just have to sit back and wait. I was told Dr. Tucker would be in this morning."

"Are you sure it *is* morning?" Gabe grumbled, peering out at the dim light. "Morning is when birds sing and sun shines and I've had at least three cups of coffee."

Cassandra unhooked her seatbelt and kneeled on her seat to reach behind it. From the corner of his eye, he gave himself two seconds to check out her curvy behind in blue jeans. Her waist was tiny, flaring to hips and ass that were in proportion to that pair of spectacular . . .

He was not thinking of those spectaculars.

She flipped around, and settled back behind the steering wheel, a cardboard carrier in her lap. She had a colorful knitted hat perched on her head with tassels on its two upstanding corners, making her look like a jaunty, sexy milkmaid. "Here," she said, handing over a cardboard cup. "Thirty-two ounces of mood enhancement."

Hesitating, he eyed the beverage with a frown. "Froot Loop, that's not the sick seaweed stuff you usually drink, is it?"

"It's one hundred percent caffeinated, he-man java, Gabe," she replied. "Black and ugly, just like you seem to be feeling today."

Though he maintained his scowl, inside he perked up. This was the way things usually were between them. He baited, she poked, they both used the activity to maintain a safe space between them. He took the coffee from her and raised it to his lips.

"Thank you for coming with me, by the way," she said, her voice low. "Thank you very much." Her slender hand landed high on his thigh and squeezed.

He jumped, and his fingers curved around the cup matched the movement of hers. Hot coffee burped out of the small drinking hole, scalding his fingers. "Damn!"

"Ouch," she said, commiserating. She grabbed up a napkin from the cardboard carrier, and when he transferred the coffee to his other hand, she tended to the burned one herself. She dried it with the paper square, then inspected his skin.

He tried pulling away. "I'm fine."

She held on. "Let me make sure."

Gritting his teeth, he kept still for her ministrations, though the feel of her warm breath against his wrist might as well have been her tongue. The sensation tickled up the smooth inside flesh of his arm.

Then she brought his hand to her mouth and kissed his fingers.

"What?" He yanked his hand from her grasp. "What do you think you're doing?" With a panicked shift, he slammed his back against the passenger door to gain some extra inches from her body, her breath, her soft mouth. "What the hell do you think you're doing?"

"Kissing it to make it better," she said, pulling her own paper cup from the container as if she didn't notice his alarmed posture. "Didn't anyone ever do that for you? Didn't you ever kiss Maddie's little hurts?"

Maddie.

Inside him, everything went quiet.

When was the last time someone had said her name aloud? Who would speak it to him? Her mother was dead, too. And he supposed Lynn's parents would find it too painful to call him up and talk about her. Maddie's other grandparents—his own mother and father—had given up on him before he'd left San Francisco for Malibu. Perhaps they'd not given up on him, precisely, but they'd stopped trying to get him to answer his doorbell or his telephone or their e-mails.

"Maddie . . ." He tried the name out. When was the last time he'd said it aloud himself? Probably when he'd had to make those horrible, terrible, can't-think-about-them-without-wanting-to-get-drunk calls to Maddie's two sets of grandparents.

"Your daughter," Cassandra confirmed, as if he could have forgotten. "I thought I saw a picture of her in your wallet the other night. Would you show it to me?"

The other night . . . His spine pressed painfully into the door's handle. He still had an infuriating hole in his memory bank about that other night . . . and he remembered much too much about another night, that night on her couch, when Cassandra had almost bewitched him into losing his cool. He'd wanted so much to sink inside that heat he'd felt between her thighs.

"Gabe?" She was looking over her cup at him with those bluer-than-blue eyes, the ones that could send out a spell with just a flutter of her lashes. "The photo?"

Like always, her magic worked, and he found himself slipping his coffee into a plastic holder hanging from the dash and then reaching into his right front pocket. His wallet fell open to the picture of Lynn and Maddie. He quickly flipped the clear sleeve, unwilling to meet the eyes of his dead wife, which he always avoided in case the smiling gaze had turned accusing. From behind it, he pulled another photo free. This one was of him and Maddie. She'd been . . . three? He carried her piggyback and she had her chin propped on his shoulder as she mugged for the camera.

Offering it to Cassandra, he had the sudden urge to hide it away, but she already had her mitts on it, and he found himself letting go.

As she studied it, he felt the weight of his daughter pressing onto his back, much heavier than it had been that day, her legs digging into his ribs, her hands in a stranglehold around his neck. He couldn't swallow. He couldn't breathe.

"You both look happy." Cassandra looked up. "Very happy."

Happy. *Very happy*, said his neighbor who had never had

a father to carry her like that, Gabe realized. Cassandra had never grinned for the camera from behind her daddy's back. At the thought, he could breathe again, the strangling weight he'd felt vanishing, leaving only a lingering ache in his throat. He glanced at the photo and felt his lips curve. "Yeah. That day we were very happy."

Cassandra continued to study it. "Maddie. Madelyn . . . what?"

"Madelyn Rosemary."

His neighbor snickered. "Gabe. You named your daughter after something green. Who would have thunk it?"

He was obliged to frown at her. "We named her after my *mother*."

"Still green."

"What's your middle name?" he asked. "No, wait. Let me guess. Thyme. Tofu. Bamboo Shoots. Wheat Grass."

She laughed and tossed her hair over her shoulder. The fragrance of her shampoo infused the air, but it was too late for him to shut down his lungs. It invaded his chest, his nose, his head. He grabbed up his coffee.

"No middle name," she said, with a little shrug. "Maybe because there's no paternal grandmother, either."

He swallowed down the renewed ache in his throat with a slug from his cup of coffee. "Cassandra's a mouthful," he mumbled, staring out the window again.

"You should know," she murmured.

His head jerked toward her. Had she just said what he thought she'd said? Did she mean to make the three words a sexy little innuendo? He couldn't tell, because she was looking out the window, too, and it might just be the brighter morning light putting that pink cast on her cheeks.

And shit, it didn't matter what she'd said, because it was

in his head: her fragrant, hot skin, the taste of her kisses, her berried nipples, the way she moaned when he rubbed the sweet spot between her thighs. His cock stiffened as his blood chugged hot and steadily southward.

Damn woman. She took away his ability to think.

And she didn't even seem to realize it. "I wonder," she mused, her gaze still on the view outside the windshield. "If we shouldn't have done this differently."

"Huh?" he grunted. "Differently how?"

"I don't know." She gave a tiny shrug. "Surely we could have put our heads together and come up with something about me a plastic surgeon would want to get his hands on."

Get his hands on? Gabe's cock jumped, thinking of his hands on her, of their heads together, of those wet, hot kisses they'd shared and how easy it had been to get her off with his mouth and with his touch. Christ, he probably could have given her an orgasm just by sucking on her nipples.

And didn't he just want to try.

His hand reached out, tangling in the ends of her hair. He made a fist, about to yank her close for just such a test.

Only to realize they were in a public place.

And this was Cassandra, who didn't deserve to be his experiment . . . or his anything else.

In an abrupt move, he shoved open the passenger door. "I need some air," he said, and slid out of the car. Air, space, distance, common sense. He forced himself to think of Lynn's face instead of Cassandra's. Lynn, the very reason Cassandra was not for him.

The light rain was more mist now and it felt good against his too-hot skin. He loitered on the sidewalk leading into the building, taking in deep breaths and thinking of innocuous stuff like the sticker on the front bumper of the car:

CHICKS WITH STICKS
♥ MALIBU & EWE

He considered what it would be like to spend time taking bumps out of noses and removing ill-conceived tattoos as cars pulled into the lot and people—obviously staff—juggled briefcases and purses and Starbucks cups as they headed for the front doors. Some were in business attire, some wore scrubs, a few white-coated doctors, their names embroidered in dark blue against the cotton, all strode past him. Preoccupied with their prework thoughts, no one gave him a second glance.

Then around a corner came two young men. He wouldn't have given *them* a second glance except that they were such a contrast in appearance. There was a lean guy with dreadlocks wearing Levi's, flip-flops, and a long-sleeved T-shirt emblazoned with "Responsible Recycling, Inc.," talking in vehement tones to his opposite. The slightly older man had a business haircut, silk tie, expensive loafers, and a doctor's coat.

A doctor's coat that read DR. PATRICK TUCKER.

Through the rain-splattered windshield, he shot a look at Cassandra. She was sitting straight in her seat, clutching her cup as if it was a teddy bear and she was here for a tetanus shot. No way could this thirtyish dude be her dad, but she was on edge all the same. And the last name . . . had Cassandra called the wrong clinic?

Because this wasn't, of course . . . "Dr. Frank Tucker?" Gabe said the name out loud, just to see what would happen.

The two men immediately bristled. "Who wants to

know?" the doctor said. The younger one seemed to be scanning the lot for a threat.

Gabe lifted his hands in casual surrender. "I'm here with my"—he glanced over his shoulder at Cassandra, still sitting in her car—"wife." Like Maddie's name, he hadn't said that word in a long while and it stopped on his tongue.

Hell, he should have said he was here with his nun, sister, neighbor, friend, anything but *wife*. He wouldn't have one of those again. But the word seemed to calm the men. The guy with dreadlocks ran his gaze over the Mercedes and then Cassandra.

"We're his sons," the doctor said. "I'm Patrick Tucker, this is Reed."

The one with all the hair nodded. "And you're not a reporter, right? We're not real fond of the press."

"Hell, no. No reporter here." Gabe gave them an easy grin. "It's just that my wife"—there was that word again—"she wants a little work done."

"Oh?"

With a subtle tap of his forefinger, Gabe indicated his chin, mouth, then finally his nose. "And we've heard good things about your dad, and thought we might, uh, book a consult." Of course, normal people would make a phone call, but neither of these two seemed to notice.

Maybe people who came here to have their beaks tweaked and their lips enlarged were a bubble off normal anyway.

Dr. Patrick stuck his hands in his coat's patch pockets. "Sorry to say you're out of luck. My father's been in Switzerland working at the university in Geneva for the last five months. He won't be back for another couple of weeks, and I know for a fact his appointment book's full until late summer."

Tacking on a professional smile, he leaned around Gabe to beam it Cassandra's way through the wet windshield. There were dollar signs in his eyes. "Maybe I could . . ."

"We'll let you know," Gabe interjected, making a hasty turn toward the car. Christ, if they saw the perfection that was Cassandra's face, the jig was up. "Thanks for the information."

He hopped into his seat. "Move it, Froot Loop."

As the car started, the two men continued on into the medical building. Cassandra flipped on the wipers to clear the misty droplets off the windshield. "Am I wrong, or did you tell them I wanted a nose job?" she asked, an edge of accusation in her voice.

Whoops, she'd noticed that. "I hope you have nothing against collagen injections and a chin implant, too."

"Gabe." She yanked the steering wheel to pull off the road and onto a side street. There, she put the car into park.

Uh-oh. Oh, well, mad would work if it would guarantee a healthy gulf between them. "C'mon, Froot Loop. Should I have said all your vegetarian vittles had given you a bad case of cauliflower ear?"

Instead of giving him a piece of her mind, her hands tightened on the steering wheel. As he watched, a tear tracked down her cheek.

Hell. He froze, digging his fingers into his thighs to keep himself from doing something stupid. Determined to keep that wedge between them, he tried again. "Tofu tongue? Jicama hips? Mushroom mouth?"

Another tear chased the first. He swallowed his groan.

"Switzerland for the last five months?" she said, her voice husky.

"That's what was said," he confirmed.

Cassandra wiped at her face, but another tear rolled down. "That's before the tabloids took up the story."

"Yeah."

"He may not even know about that dumb gossip." She shot him a look from drenched blue eyes.

His short nails could delve through denim, he discovered. "He may not."

"So . . . so maybe it wasn't something about me that made him want to avoid us."

And damn, distance was something he couldn't take anymore. As more wetness flowed down Cassandra's face, he hauled her over the console between the two front seats. In his lap, his arms went around her, her nose found a niche in the crook of his neck and shoulder, and her tears were soaked up by his shirt. "Froot Loop," he murmured against her scented hair. "No sane man would willingly stay away from you."

Seven

Good family life is never an accident but always an achievement by those who share it.

—JAMES H. S. BOSSARD

Gabe told himself he'd been keeping an eye on the action at Malibu & Ewe because they'd had that incident with the kids playing with fire. It didn't have anything to do with the fact that he couldn't get Cassandra's tears off his mind or the memory of her curled in his arms out of his head.

Because she didn't need him, he thought, as he glanced through the rain-spattered windows across the parking lot to her shop. It was Tuesday night and the knitters who got together to share their yen for yarn and companionship were straggling out the door and into their cars. For sure she didn't need him, not only because she knew now that her concern about her father was misplaced, but because all evening she'd had a roomful of women at the ready to offer her advice. He'd heard them doing just that—whether it was about a project or about a personal problem—dozens of times when he'd been at the shop to make a repair or to deliver Cassandra another cup of contraband coffee.

The last of the visitors exited, two of them waving to

each other as they headed home to their families. Leaving Cassandra alone. He saw her figure moving about the shop, tidying the counter, and then putting some errant skeins back in their bins. She looked so . . . solitary.

But that was no different from what he was, he reminded himself. The clock read half-past nine P.M., and he was alone at the fish market fiddling with a recalcitrant kitchen fan. He was content enough, wasn't he?

For the moment. Until another one of his black moods tackled him and dragged him under.

A car circled the lot. He followed it with his gaze, wondering if one of the women had returned for something she'd left behind. The sedan made a couple of slow laps, and the hair on the back of Gabe's neck rose. He skirted the counter, heading for the front door, when he spied a dark figure approaching Malibu & Ewe on foot, its movements stealthy.

Gabe ran into the parking lot, part of him noting that the anonymous car accelerated toward the exit and shot onto the Pacific Coast Highway. The other part of him saw the stealthy figure burst into Cassandra's yarn shop.

Under the interior's bright lights, she whipped around, her hand going to her throat. Gabe picked up speed, and then Cassandra did the same. She rushed the unknown person—a man, he could tell now—and leaped into his arms.

Gabe yanked open the shop's door just as her long legs wrapped around the stranger's waist.

Lonely, my ass, he thought, as she laid a lavish kiss on a guy Gabe had never seen before in his life.

He considered backing out, but planted his feet and crossed his arms over his chest instead. "Another long-lost relative?" he inquired, as the shop's door shut behind him.

Grinning, Cassandra slid down the man's body so that the soles of her shoes once more touched ground. Then she tugged the other man toward Gabe. "This is Carver!" she said, face flushed, eyes bright. "Carver Shields. I've told you about him."

She didn't bother waiting for Gabe to answer. Instead, she turned to the other man. He appeared about thirty and Gabe supposed Cassandra thought him good-looking, given the way she wouldn't let go of his hand. He wore his light brown hair to his shoulders and a tattoo of a naked woman with long flowing tresses was sprawled on the skin of his arm like she was waiting for a lover. Her face was hidden by the short sleeve of his shirt. "I thought you were touring in Europe until summer," Cassandra said.

Ah, yes, Gabe remembered now. Carver Shields. Cassandra's prom date and the drummer for the mega-successful heavy metal band Mercy.

Carver grimaced. "We had to cut it short. Lou—" He glanced at Gabe. "Lou's our bass guitarist—developed a little substance abuse problem while we were in Berlin. I dragged him back here and checked him into rehab."

Though there was a treatment facility for each and every mile of Malibu coastline, Gabe couldn't figure out why the drummer had to bring his buddy here of all places. Was it so he could then drop in on Cassandra, his beautiful, obviously enthusiastic former prom date?

"Stop looking like that, Gabe," Cassandra said, frowning at him. "You're not one to judge."

A trickle of shame slithered down his spine. Shit. He didn't deserve the feeling, damn it. Neither Froot Loop nor her dedicated drummer boy knew the demons he faced or if they would do any better against them.

Carver's eyes narrowed. "So, this is your curmudgeonly landlord?" His voice was easy; his gaze wasn't.

Gabe gritted his teeth. "I take her rent money every month."

"Yeah, and what else?" Carter asked. He crossed his arms over his own chest, his pose matching Gabe's. Except Gabe didn't have a voluptuous babe inked on his skin, one with truly awesome tits and red-painted toenails that seemed to balance on the band of his platinum-and-steel watch. "What else do you take from her?"

Cassandra stepped between the two of them. "Healthy meals, whenever I can wean him off saturated fats and high-fructose corn syrup. Now, Carver, stop bristling and tell me you're coming back to my place for tea and cookies."

Looking into her pretty face, the other man relaxed. The backs of his fingers trailed down her cheek. "That's the plan, doll. Knowing the cell reception's shit out here, I told my people I'd be heading to your place. Gave them the number because I'm expecting a call from the president of my fan club. You've still got that landline, right?"

"Yep." She gave a little bounce of pleasure. "If you'll wait just a minute, I have a few things to do in the back and then we can go."

"Take your time, doll," Carver called to her retreating form. "I'm sure Gabe and I can find something to talk about."

When she disappeared around a corner, the younger man pivoted toward him, his face set. "I just have one thing to say. Screw with her and I'll kill you."

Gabe shook his head, trying not to let his annoyance show. "What do you think you know about me or about the two of us?"

"I've got e-mail, all right? And this is Cassandra, dude. She can type almost as fast as she can knit. You know her. She's pretty much set on 'Spill All' all the time."

Christ. Was she telling the world he'd bedded her that night after the Beach Shack? "Look—"

"No. You look. She's special and I can't figure out why she'd think you're worth scraping off bar floors, but—"

"I've heard this lecture before," Gabe ground out, impatient with the second round of shame snaking through him. "And I'm not inclined to listen to it another time." Especially coming from some too-pretty, globe-trotting musician who'd bought Gabe's nun neighbor sister friend a wrist corsage once upon a time.

"Cassandra—"

"What is she to you, anyway? So one time you two slow-danced across the gym floor to a Celine Dion tune."

Carver took a quick step forward. "We're close. We—"

"Close? This from the man who's been on tour for the last couple of years." Christ, did no man do right by this woman? And yeah, Gabe was fully aware he could include himself in that group.

"We have an . . . an understanding, okay?" Carver shoved a hand through his long, rock-boy hair, his frustration palpable. "This is Cassandra. Her heart's so big and she gives so damn much—"

Bells rang out as the door of Malibu & Ewe opened. A long-legged blonde walked in. Her stride hitched and her eyes went wide as she took in the man confronting Gabe. Carver glanced her way, then froze. After a moment, he slouched and a charming smile crossed his face.

He put his hands in his pockets. "Oomfaa. Darling."

One of the Most Famous Actresses in America didn't move. She was a Malibu & Ewe regular, another of Cassandra's friends, and apparently shocked to run into Carver Shields.

Then she seemed to get over her surprise. She walked

farther into the shop, using an exaggerated runway model heel-to-toe that made her slender hips sway. Her worldwide-recognized smile spread across her face, but she had eyes only for Gabe now. She flicked a careless finger along Carver's jaw as she passed him. "Where's our girl?" she asked.

"In the back," Gabe answered. "She'll be out soon."

"I can't wait even that long. I've got to get going," Oomfaa said. As an actress, she was good. Nothing about her body language gave away a thing, but she couldn't control her body's response. She was radiating sexual heat and none of it was radiating Gabe's way.

Carver was staring at the back of her head, that smile still on his face. "Don't let me scare you away, sweet thing."

She snorted, but didn't turn to face him. "As if you've ever frightened me, Carver. Why are you here? Running from another of your amorous groupies? I grant you that they're pretty scary."

"Ah, you're just mad that I didn't invite you to star in our latest music video. I saw you in Timberlake's and you know I don't do seconds."

Her spine snapped straight. She held out a pair of knitting needles to Gabe. "Take these before I shove them somewhere the drummer would find very painful."

Carver's smile widened. "You already broke my heart once, Oomfaa. I'm made of stronger stuff now."

Their repartee had a decidedly familiar ring to it, Gabe realized. He and Cassandra used to regularly spar like this . . . and hell, he couldn't close his eyes any longer to the fact that it was a tool to dilute a supercharged sexual chemistry. What was going on between Carver and Oomfaa could be sold back to the energy grid at premium prices.

"So you two know each other . . ." he ventured.

"We met at a Coldplay concert," Oomfaa said, still not looking at the man behind her. "Gwyneth introduced us."

"And then there was Paris," Carver added.

Oomfaa whipped her hair around to shoot a dagger-sharp look at him. "Oh, yeah. We'll always have Paris. Me, you, and . . . Guinevere?"

"Genevieve."

She repeated the name just as Carver had said it, except with a heavy dose of venom. "Ah. *Oui.* Jen-vee-ev."

"I don't know how she got into the hotel room."

"But you didn't kick her out of the shower, either."

"I had soap in my eyes. I thought she was you."

Without responding, Oomfaa spun, and made for the door again. "Later."

"Really?" Carver called after her. "Promise?"

Again, Oomfaa's stride hitched.

Carver slid a glance Gabe's way, and his hand shoved through his hair again. *What are my chances?* was clearly written on his face. He forked his fingers once more across his scalp.

As his arm came down, Gabe stared at the detailed tattoo inked there. He noted the voluptuous body. Took in the long, rippling hair. The face was still obscured by the other man's sleeve, but shit, Gabe thought he knew who was the inspiration for the other man's tat. "Hey . . ."

Carver noticed Gabe's regard and dropped his gaze to the artist's rendering on his arm. Then, grinning, he hurried after Oomfaa. "A minute of your time, sweet thing."

They exited the shop.

Cassandra appeared a few moments later. Her brows drew together. "Where's Carver?" she asked.

"Oomfaa showed up," he said. "I guess he's walking her to her car." He handed over the knitting needles.

"Oh," Cassandra replied.

He had no idea what she was thinking. "I'm sure he'll be right back in."

"Sure."

Clear thought was difficult with that tattoo branded on his brain. Rippling hair. Incredible breasts. "What's with you two anyway? Carver's your . . . what, exactly?"

"Close friend."

"Exactly how close?" he asked, though it was none of his business. "He comes back from tour and you two . . ."

She frowned, his insinuation seeming to sink in. "No! You know I . . . that I don't . . . I made a promise to myself . . ."

He rocked back on his heels. "Are you babbling about your celibacy? I used to consider it amusing, a kind of hippy-dippy affectation like your car that runs on used vegetable oil and your devotion to organic eating, but now . . ." He thought of that familiar naked figure on Carver's arm. "Now I'm sort of wondering if you've been bullshitting me."

Anger gave a sharp edge to his voice. It certainly wasn't jealousy. But she claimed to be going without sex, when for all he knew she'd been bedding guys right and left while he was being best buds with barroom floors and bottles of booze.

"Why wouldn't I be telling the truth?" A flush rose on her neck.

He shrugged. "It's just hard to understand."

She rolled her eyes. "The answer is simple. You know about my mother, right? Artificially inseminated. She's never had anything against men or sex, she just doesn't consider either of particular consequence. So maybe it's classic rebellion on my part, but a while back I decided not to be so . . . offhand about either. I'm not casual about how I regard other people and I'm not casual with my body."

He couldn't say whether her explanation satisfied his curiosity or just pissed him off even more. And as for bringing up what had happened on her couch the other night and in her bed before that . . . no way. "Doesn't it strike you as, I don't know, sublimation, that you've so devoted yourself to work that keeps your hands busy and your fantasies firmly in G-rated territory?"

She slammed her arms across her chest. There'd been a lot of that going around lately. "You don't know everything about me, Gabe. Certainly not where my hands and my fantasies have been."

Now his face felt hot. "Cassandra, it's just that—"

In the parking lot, an engine turned over and headlights flashed on. They both glanced out the shop's front windows. Oomfaa's car. As they watched, the passenger door opened, then slammed shut on Carver. The car reversed, then Oomfaa and the drummer drove off.

"Oh," Cassandra said. A moment of silence passed. "He's not coming back, is he?"

Was that a forlorn note in her voice? Gabe couldn't tell, and he didn't dare look at her. Yeah, it appeared her close friend the rocker boy wasn't coming back, yet Gabe hated having to be the one to confirm that yet another man had failed her.

Which just went to prove that Gabe didn't feel offhand about her.

At all.

Cassandra smiled to herself as she drove home from Malibu & Ewe, Gabe's headlights in her rearview mirror. Carver and Oomfaa. Months earlier, they'd each told her their half of the story of meeting in London and then their rendezvous in Paris. Both halves created a very entertaining whole.

Though she was disappointed she wouldn't be spending time with her old friend tonight, she was delighted for the two former lovers, who just might be returning to that state. She wouldn't be surprised by it, since so many around her were pairing off.

Which made her sigh a little, too. With Juliet on her honeymoon and the plans for Nikki and Jay's wedding in full swing, she had romance on the brain. It wasn't good to be thinking in terms of twosomes, though. There was her thirtieth birthday coming up. She should think about that.

She should think about the fact that her father wasn't avoiding her. She'd been surprised by how relieved she'd been to know he was out of the country. And then there was his sons—her research had informed her that Dr. Frank Tucker and his wife had adopted them when they were small. Not really her kin, but it was interesting to get a look at them. There was the white-coated one, all Dr. Serious, and then the younger, more laidback guy wearing the Responsible Recycling, Inc., T-shirt. She'd done some googling and determined that Reed Tucker was the vice president of operations for a small start-up that recycled computer equipment from schools and colleges, diverting what was useful to needy organizations before selling as scrap what wasn't. He sounded like her kind of guy.

Rain pounded on the roof of her car and she eased her foot onto the accelerator. Malibu had remembered it was winter and the temperatures had been lowering and the rainfall amounts rising for the last several days. She inched her window down to let in some fresh air and the smell of wet greenery mingled pleasantly with the fumes of the fuel that powered her car. The fragrance was reminiscent of a nighttime KFC-bucket picnic on damp grass.

Levering up the speed of her windshield wipers, she took another glance at the rearview mirror. Gabe had slowed, too. This was one of the less-traveled canyon passes that traversed east from the beach, and the windy, narrow stretch of road was empty of any but them tonight. Their private lane that led to Gabe's property was a half-mile or so ahead, but here there was nothing on either side but muddy hillside planted with straggly foliage. A brushfire had gone through last year and the natural growth had yet to return.

She steered around another turn, losing sight of Gabe's car. Her heart stuttered in her chest at the new darkness behind her, and she slowed more. Then, feeling foolish, she forced herself to bring up her speed. Gabe would be along, or he wouldn't. He wasn't following her home. He just happened to be going in the same direction.

Her life was full with friends and work and future plans. Invitations had already gone out for her party. She needed no man at her back, or otherwise. Her foot pressed harder on the accelerator.

The next curve came, this one pinched even tighter by yet another steep slope. Cassandra glanced back, still no Gabe. Despite herself, the sole of her shoe left the gas pedal and the car decelerated. She looked forward again. Her heart jumped.

Up ahead. Something tumbling. A big boulder, rolling down the hill. Onto the road. Her foot, already jerking to the brake, slammed down.

Slammed harder.

Her tires skated on the wet asphalt. The heavyweight Mercedes continued forward, headlights bright on the vehicle-sized chunk of earth settling onto the road straight ahead.

Her hands gripping the wheel, her eyes squeezing shut, she stood on the brake pedal. The Mercedes slowed, but still slid . . . slid . . . slid . . .

As it did, her mind kicked into high gear, ticking off regrets. No birthday party. No meeting with her father. She would never know if her mother met the Dalai Lama after all.

Worries followed. Juliet and Nikki. Would they be all right? They had each other. They had Noah and Jay. The only one alone like her was Gabe, and Gabe—

Car met boulder in a crunching crash.

At impact, her rear teeth snapped together. Her torso jolted forward, then was caught by the harsh straps of the seatbelt. Her left knee jerked up and banged the dashboard, while her right foot stayed jammed on the brake, muscles locked like rigor mortis.

As the noise of the crash died away, she could hear her own harsh breaths. They soughed from her lungs, loud in the suddenly quiet night. Apparently she was alive.

She opened her eyes. One headlight was out, but in the light of the other she could see the boulder. It appeared to be weeping—no, that was only the rain, rolling down her windshield. The still-moving wipers couldn't keep up with the deluge.

She continued breathing, continued clutching the steering wheel with panic-cramped fingers.

A shout came from somewhere—inside her head? Then big hands were banging on the driver's-side window. Wide and wet, they looked like the starfish in the aquarium at the Santa Monica Pier. It was said there were even larger ones at the bottom of the Pacific, but Cassandra had only seen those in the aquarium's touch tanks and then others that were baby-sized in the local tide pools where they snuggled next to tiny sea anemones and were tickled by the spiderlike legs of traveling hermit crabs. Though she'd lived beside the ocean all her life, she'd never done any scuba diving or even taken a snorkel mask below the water's surface. She was terrified of sinking into deep depths and that no one would care enough to come looking for her.

The pounding and shouting was getting louder—man, did she have a headache—but even if she could find some pain reliever in her purse, it had toppled during the crash, its contents spilled all over the floor of the passenger side. She'd likely never find her favorite pen, she thought absently. Her Mercedes was to writing implements what a dryer was to single socks.

Suddenly, a ghostly face pressed itself to the glass of the windshield. She shrieked, rearing back in her seat. Had she died after all? Was this creepy, ghoulish . . . Gabe come to take her away?

Gabe?

He slid his palm over the rain-dotted glass to clear a patch. She read his lips and heard his words at the same time. "Unlock your door, Froot Loop!"

It was Gabe all right.

"Unlock your door!"

Blinking at his vehemence, she did as instructed. Then wished she hadn't. The instant she reached over and popped the lock, Gabe wrenched open her door, letting in the cold and the rain and the heart-in-the-throat knowledge that she might have died.

An instant later, Gabe had turned off the ignition and was pulling her from the car. Already she was shaking in delayed reaction. She knew her knees wouldn't hold her, but she didn't need them to, because Gabe kept her steady, one arm wrapping her against his chest. His other hand cupped her face. "Are you okay? Are you hurt?"

"F-f-fine." Her teeth started to chatter and her heartbeat raced. For a few minutes shock had held the adrenaline at bay, but now it was speeding through her system, making her hyperaware of what was going on both inside and outside her body. "Just c-c-cold."

"Damn it!" Tucking her close to him, Gabe drew her toward his SUV. "You need to get warm."

Both of their clothes were soaked. He helped her into the passenger side of his SUV, giving her bottom a boost with his hand and then shutting the door with a thunk. The vehicle's engine was running and the heater was on, but the warmth didn't register. Her limbs were quaking and she looked over at Gabe as he slid behind the wheel, a little scared by her own physical reaction.

He cursed again. "Here," he said, long-legging it over the console between the seats. Somehow he managed to get into her place, with her on his lap. His arms came around her. "See if this helps."

She clung to him. "I-I-I w-want to g-go home," she said.

"In a minute. We'll have to take an alternate route. I can't make it past your car and that rock."

"I-it j-just came down," she stuttered. "I couldn't stop in time."

His body stiffened. "I know, baby. I know. Maybe it's all this rain."

"C-course it's the r-rain."

"Yeah."

"D-didn't you s-see what h-happened?"

"I saw what happened," he said, his voice gruff. His

arms tightened around her. "You did a good job slowing the car. It's not as bad as I thought it was going to be."

Cassandra realized how it must have been for him. Gabe behind her, watching her heading for that boulder, watching her crash, a vivid reminder of what had happened to his wife and daughter a few years before. "Gabe." She looked up into his face. "Gabe, I'm so sorry."

He closed his eyes a moment. "Froot Loop. Cassandra. You are so . . . so—" Breaking off, he gazed into her face. "I'm so damn glad you're alive."

His mouth met hers.

The kiss was hot, demanding, frantic even. She met his tongue with her own, rubbing it, sucking on it, taking as much of him inside of her as she could. He groaned, his hands roaming over her body as if to assure himself she was in one piece.

She moaned, loving his touch, the warmth of him, the absolute yearning she felt inside her that let her know that yes, yes, yes! she was alive. Alive and in Gabe's arms and it was his mouth that was sliding down her neck, it was his voice murmuring words she couldn't understand, his face that he suddenly pressed to her throat as if to inhale her scent into his lungs. She held him to her, cradling his dark wet hair in her hands, both of them shivering with chill or leftover fear or panic or a potent cocktail of all three.

He made a frustrated, hoarse sound, then lifted his head. "This is not the place and time," he said, but continued to kiss her cheeks, her nose, her forehead. With a deep breath, he reached a hand over the seat and pulled something from behind him.

An old beach towel, soft and worn. He wrapped it around her shoulders like a shawl, then maneuvered himself back into the driver's seat with a grunt. "No cell reception as usual," he said. "I'll get you home and then call in this mess from a landline."

She leaned her head against the seat and clutched the towel as he turned the car around. She was shivering again, but whether it was from the temperature, the accident, or the desire that he'd ignited with his kisses, she didn't know.

Closing her eyes, she felt his fingers brushing her face. "You okay, Froot Loop?"

She pressed a palm against her stomach. Too many different emotions in too short a time. "I feel a little queasy," she admitted.

His hand dropped. A different kind of tension filled the air.

Her eyes popped open. She turned her head, looking at him in the light of the dashboard. "Gabe?"

"Right beside you."

For now. But from the tight expression he was wearing, she was reminded once again that she couldn't count on that forever.

Eight

He that hath a wife and children hath given hostages to fortune.

—FRANCIS BACON

It was after five P.M. when Marlys locked the door to her boutique, then turned into the wall of a man's chest. Leaping back, her shoulder blades rattled the door's glass and her heart rattled, too. "Dean," she said. "You scared me."

The streetlights glinted off his black hair. His teeth glowed white in the gathering dusk. "I know."

The smile he wore made her regret her choice of words. "I'm not afraid of anyone or anything," she muttered with a scowl as she pushed past him. His pectorals were solid slabs of muscle and if she took a quick breath of his clean scent he wasn't the wiser.

"I brought you a gift," he said from behind her back.

Her footsteps halted. She didn't want to turn to face him, yet still she did. "I don't want presents—" she started, then her gaze fell on what he had in his hand.

Flowers.

Marlys had been given flowers before, of course. Exotic orchids. Spiky birds of paradise. Once, a man who wanted her in his bed sent her two dozen, long-stemmed, blood-red roses. She'd pricked herself on a thorn when she'd thrown them in the trash.

Dean was bearing roses as well, maybe again two dozen of them, but each was a delicate baby rose, the petals a fragile, kittenish pink. They were encircled in a matching wrap of tulle and bound by organza ribbons of gold and silver.

It was all Marlys was not—girlish and sugary and everything nice.

She despised the flowers because he thought they would appeal to her. So she snatched them out of his hand, determined to dump them in the nearest garbage can like she'd done with that homicide-red bouquet.

What was in his other hand stopped her. A rawhide bone the size of a tyrannosaurus femur.

He noticed her staring at it. "Not for you. You just get the roses."

Her fingers tightened on the stems. No thorns. "Why?"

"As a thank-you for the kiss. I haven't had one quite like that in . . . well, I don't remember when."

"And the bone's for Blackie? Gratitude for how he's slobbered over you?"

He grinned. "Nope. It's a bribe. Something to keep him occupied tonight while I visit with his beautiful owner."

She narrowed her eyes. They'd shared that kiss in her boutique, but a burst of business that day had managed to get rid of him. She needed a way to make that happen again. "Maybe I have plans."

"Date with Phil?"

"No!" The vehement note in her voice embarrassed her, so she cleared her throat to cover the moment. With her free hand she found herself rubbing her arm and then her thigh, as if washing them clean. A memory flashed in her mind: She was facing Dean just like this, wearing her bathrobe and nothing else, while Phil jogged down the stairs from her bedroom, whistling.

"So what are they then?"

She'd lost the thread of the conversation. "What are what?"

"Your plans. Because I'm trying to nudge my memory by revisiting every place in Malibu I went to before."

"How do you know you were ever at my house?"

With his free hand he tucked a piece of hair behind her ear. Her skin burned, heat zigzagging down her neck like a lightning bolt. "We kiss like I've been at your house before."

"You've never been in my bed," she retorted. But then a guilty flush made a liar out of her. "Well, once you stayed the night, but nothing happened."

His eyebrows rose. "Nothing?"

She wouldn't confess that the note he'd left her the next morning after sleeping beside her that night—just a brief couple of lines saying he'd be back in a few days—was folded origami-style into a size that fit in the second tray of her jewelry box. "Nothing."

He shrugged. "I'm not limited to a mattress and sheets, Marlys. So tell me, where *did* we, uh . . . kiss? In a bathtub? Under a tree? On the stairs?"

The stairs. The recollection swamped her again. The surprise in Dean's eyes when she'd answered the door with mussed makeup and bed head. Just a few hours before she'd agreed to get intimate with him for the first time. They were supposed to go to dinner and then they both knew that the sexual chemistry that had been bubbling between them would finally have its chance to explode.

Instead, he'd come over to the house to find out that he'd just missed dessert—and that she'd shared it with some other man.

Her stomach roiled remembering how the expectant good humor in Dean's eyes had died as Phil's jaunty whistle drifted down the stairs. The nonexpression on his face had made it clear he'd added two and two together. She'd counted on him being good at math.

"Hey," he said now. "What's wrong? I'm teasing, you know. If you really have plans, or if you don't want me to come over, then—"

"No!" she said again, again vehemently. "I do want you to come over." Because clearly he wasn't going to give up on her so easily. If a visit to her place could assuage his curiosity about her . . . then fine. Perhaps after that he'd go away for good.

Twenty minutes later she pulled into her driveway in Pacific Palisades, Dean behind her on his motorcycle. Be strong, she told herself, even as the thrum of the engine seemed to echo in her very foundation. But she wouldn't be shaken from her goal: Do what was necessary to satisfy his interest in her. No secrets need be divulged, she assured herself. Just enough detail to send him on his way.

It should work out. No male had ever stuck by her before.

"Except Blackie," she said aloud, as she opened the front door, the bouquet of roses in the crook of her arm. Her dog bounded out, hopping knee-high in greeting. But then he looked past her, and with an ecstatic bark, left her in the dust.

Marlys sighed, and walked into the house without a backward glance. "Abandoned again." But she liked her solitary lifestyle, she told herself. She'd been virtually on her own since she was twelve.

Apparently Blackie was bought off with the faux dinosaur bone because Dean was alone when he found her in the kitchen. She poured beer into a glass for him, then debated on what could quiet her jangling nerves.

When she turned to him with the frosted glass, he was looking at the scattering of family souvenirs spread on the kitchen table. She hadn't put them all away after displaying them at a launch party for her father's book months ago. "I remember," Dean said.

She started. "What?"

"I remember who this is," he said, pointing to the framed photo of her father. "General Wayne Weston. I've read about him and I recall that Noah worked for him until he died."

"And Noah just married Juliet, the general's widow."

"And Marlys Weston, the general was your father," Dean added.

There was no reason to deny that fact. Her hand pressed the silver tear she wore on a chain under her thin sweater. "Daddy dearest," she confirmed, while her gaze focused on her handsome father's face. He'd died of cancer over a year ago now, and it had left her feeling . . . feeling . . . but that was one of her secrets. That she didn't like feeling anything and that she did her best to smother inconvenient emotions when necessary.

"I'm sorry for your loss," Dean said, and he looked at her, his eyes like mirrors.

She refused to peer at her reflection. "Thank you," she said, "though we weren't close. My parents divorced when I was twelve. That military life you told me you rebelled against until you were eighteen or so—" He'd confessed last fall that he'd grown up with an army father as well. "I swam in it like a fish until my mother turned us civilian."

"And unhappy," Dean said, as if he read her thoughts.

She shrugged. "Waah, waah, waah. Now I'm done whining about my past."

Dean tucked that hair behind her ear again. More lightning. More heat. She swayed toward him and quickly considered the consequences of having sex with him. Right now. Tonight. Surely he wouldn't turn her down and she could hate him so much easier if he took her to bed knowing nothing more than the few facts she'd doled out. The act would mean less than nothing, and she'd get this yearning for him out of her system.

Yeah, right. But still, if it made him move on, it would be worth the risk.

"So how did it end with us before?" he asked. "Did we, what, just fade away?"

She couldn't stifle her smirk. "I get that. It's from that General MacArthur quote: 'Old soldiers never die; they just fade away.'"

He smiled.

She melted. Marlys Marie Weston never melted, which was why he was absolutely wrong for her. Absolutely dangerous.

"How did it end?" he asked again.

Her throat felt tight and she turned away from him. The bouquet was on the counter and she busied herself finding a vase and filling it with water. "You were going to Afghanistan. We decided that, well, you know."

"That's the problem. I don't." The easy humor was gone from his voice. He sounded serious. "I don't understand what happened between us."

"With the future so uncertain . . . It seemed best . . ." He'd told her that before meeting her he'd had a reputation for being impetuous. Reckless and rash. And then he'd told her he was going to carry her picture in his head as he went into battle.

It had been like a punch in the chest. She couldn't imagine being that woman, the one in his head, waiting for him to return from war. As a child she'd waited for her father to rescue her from her bitter mother and her lonely civilian childhood. That had never happened, and she knew waiting for a lover who might never return would be so much worse. But because she couldn't trust herself to break it off with him, she'd arranged the Phil episode so Dean would do the job.

"That uncertain future," he prompted now. "It seemed best . . ."

She cleared her throat. "You were leaving."

"I'm back now."

What she'd done with Phil would make anything between them impossible, however. But that was one of the secrets she didn't need to share. She found her kitchen shears and cut the ends off the roses' stems, wishing she could cut out as easily that ugly piece of her past. Blinking against the sudden sting in her eyes, she settled the flowers into the water.

Dean's heat was at her back and she wanted nothing more than to take the half-step that would press him to her, that would allow her to lean against his strength. He reached around her to touch one of the delicate rosebuds. "I saw these in the flower shop and they said, 'Take me to Marlys.' They're like you."

"Girlish and sugary and everything nice," she scoffed, trying for her old sarcasm.

"Small and fragrant and probably a pain in the ass to keep happy."

She laughed, when she should have been crying, because maybe he *did* know her.

"I'm still scaring you," he said.

She was too tired to deny it.

"Pull out a few pints of Ben & Jerry's," he suggested. "Then gather some girlfriends and spend a whole night talking about me. Bet they say we should give this another try."

"I don't need girlfriends," she was quick to say. "I don't need anyone."

His big hand swiped the hair off the nape of her neck. He laid a gentle kiss on that vulnerable skin. "When you realize you do," he said, and he was already halfway across the kitchen and heading for the exit, "look me up."

And the scariest thing anyone could find out about Marlys Marie Weston was just how tempting that offer sounded.

Gabe's worst days started like this: He'd wake in the morning with shards of dark dreams rattling inside his skull. Lynn's smile. The arc of her bouquet on their wedding day. That same arc mirrored in the curve of her belly when she was eight months' pregnant and they were calling the baby WhatsIt because they couldn't agree on a name. The sound of Maddie's first cry. The sound of her last one, the one that he could only imagine. "Daddy! Daddy! Save me!"

On his worst days, he drank oily coffee with his daughter's pleas in his head. He thought about the photograph in his wallet and his wife's smiling eyes turning to a glare of accusation.

That's when he knew he couldn't save anyone. That's when he knew that he could save himself least of all, and he'd pick up a beer or a bottle of something stronger and start that slide into the abyss always yawning at his feet. "Come to me." The tempting words drifted from that inky void, in a whisper made hoarse by the smoke of hell. "Come to me and you'll forget the pain."

For three years, whether it had been a month since the last episode or merely a few days, he'd always fallen for the seductive promise. This morning, it was whispering to Gabe again as he stared at the obsidian surface of his first cup of coffee and saw instead the ruined car his wife and daughter had been riding in when a drunk driver hit them at four in the afternoon on the way home from Maddie's dance class.

The irony that he drank to forget the actions of a drunk was not lost on him . . . it just didn't stop him from hearing that voice, from sensing that hole at his feet, from succumbing to the longing to slide into the welcome amnesia of too much alcohol.

Setting the coffee aside, he walked from the house to his second, smaller garage. There it was, the 1963 Thunderbird, the same make and model that Lynn had been driving on the day she and Maddie had died. He'd bought it a few months back, with some notion that he could restore it and somehow restore—what? Not his past, he'd known that was lost to him forever.

His sanity. He'd thought, in his tequila-influenced state, that it might save him from crazy.

But today, when he looked at the gleaming new paint job and then noted the garden hose hanging from the exhaust pipe, he saw crazy.

Yet he didn't immediately make tracks for the nearest bottle of booze and that first, easy step into oblivion. There was something else stirring in his head, another bad dream, but this one kept his feet on the floor and kept him moving through his ordinary-day schedule. By mid-morning, he was at his business across the parking lot from Malibu & Ewe.

He made the motions. Checked in with the manager, bullshitted with the cook, pretending he gave a crap that the order of cabbage they used in making their most popular menu item—Baja tacos—was short. Earlier that morning, he'd also played the I-give-a-rat's-ass game with the assistant who helped him manage the other various properties he owned about Malibu.

The residences rented for exorbitant prices, and he found an odd pleasure in going on maintenance calls himself—the owner of the multimillion-dollar property showing up to unplug a toilet. Today, there was no shit to deal with. Too bad, because he was in just that kind of mood.

He didn't take a morning latté to Cassandra. He was self-aware enough to know that witnessing her accident had stirred up all the black ash inside his chest. He'd nearly choked on it as he'd seen the boulder tumble, heard the crash, felt her bones rattling in her skin as he pulled her from the damaged car. The recollection hammered at him.

And honed his need to see her—even as he knew he shouldn't.

Until three P.M. he managed to stay away. Then, arguing with himself the whole while, he strolled across the asphalt to Malibu & Ewe. He carried the coffee that she would just happen to drink if he just happened to set it on the countertop by the cash register.

Inside, he found her sitting on one of the couches beside a customer. Her long hair rippled down her back and her attention was riveted on the piece of knitting in her hands. She didn't notice he was in her shop.

"Oh, how sweet," she said, her voice soft. She held up a tiny garment. Peachy-pink.

A baby's sweater.

The blackness ever present at Gabe's feet shot up, rising as dots in his vision. He would have admitted it to no one, but he had the distinct concern he was going to drop to his knees. Cassandra with an infant's clothing in her hands. Fear couldn't come close to describing how he felt at the sight. Petrified was better. Claustrophobia was in the equation.

This was the other nightmare he'd been living with since waking up in her bed. Cassandra pregnant. She'd been queasy after her accident with the boulder. He'd tried telling himself that was normal, not natal, but now, like then, a wave of heat washed over him, followed by a dousing of icy cold.

Cassandra. Pregnant. If it was true, he couldn't allow himself the indulgence of alcoholic amnesia. If it was true, he'd have to resist with all he had because it wouldn't be right to check out on her like that.

Why couldn't that night after the Beach Shack be clear in his head? Why couldn't he recall that they'd had great sex without the fear of the consequences? But he couldn't remember and she'd never brought up the issue.

Her friend Carver claimed Cassandra was set on "Spill All." If that was so, why couldn't she have said something simple about that night? Something like, "Hey, we had a phenomenal time in the sack, and there's no worry that I'm knocked up."

But of course it had already been made clear that he hadn't provided her with a phenomenal experience that night. Though that still didn't solve the mystery of whether or not he was less than nine months from disaster.

He could ask . . . but no, he couldn't. He was just that terrified of the truth.

His knees were going soft again. He had to get away. He had to get air.

Outside the shop, he dumped the latté in a can and pulled in deep breaths of salt-laden oxygen. He scanned the cars coming in and out of the lot, and like the other night, noticed a vehicle cruise the area a couple of times before settling into a space. He kept his eye on the little car, surprised to realize that the driver was none other than Marlys Weston.

He didn't think she'd been the one circling the lot that other time, but he waylaid her anyway as she approached Malibu & Ewe.

"What are you doing here?" he asked.

She scowled at him. "I thought maybe I'd get into knitting."

"There's a lot of other yarn shops in the Los Angeles area."

"Excuse me, but I didn't consult my yellow pages. I thought about knitting and then I thought about here."

Gabe wanted to leave it alone, but Christ, this was the woman who'd caused Cassandra and her sisters grief by dishing to the tabloids about their father. "Your mischief won't be welcome here."

"You mean *I* won't be welcome here." For a moment, her cool mask slipped and he caught a glimpse of vulnerability in her eyes. "The mean one isn't in there, is she?"

He could almost laugh. It was easy to guess who she was thinking of. "Nikki?"

Marlys nodded. "Definitely the mean one. Juliet's too well-bred to make a scene if I walk inside the shop. And as for Cassandra, she's . . ."

Now it was Gabe's turn to scowl. "Cassandra's no push-over."

"No. She's incredibly talented, though. I saw some of her designs the night of my father's book launch party."

"Incredible covers it," he murmured. He glanced over his shoulder at the shop, thinking of the woman inside. Her clever fingers, her generous spirit, her honest heart. No way would she keep something so important from him, he thought, relief making him unsteady again. Of course Cassandra would have told him if pregnancy was a real concern.

"What's with you two, anyway?" Marlys asked. "Nikki's got Jay, Juliet's married to Noah. Does that make you Cassandra's . . . ?"

Man. The word popped into his head and, damn, it startled him, coming three seconds after the realization they hadn't made a baby. Why did he find it so easy to claim Cassandra? Maybe because he'd already done it once, when he'd spoken to her father's sons outside the medical building. The word *wife* had slid from his mouth.

"I'm her friend," he said now instead, as if he'd ever actually been one to her. The truth was, their relationship had all been one-sided. It had been like that with Lynn, too, in the last years of their marriage, and God, wasn't it easy for old patterns to reestablish themselves.

"Friend?" Marlys repeated, then her attention shifted away from Gabe. Gazing over his shoulder, her eyes narrowed. "There are those kids," she said. "From the other day. They have matches again. And cigarettes."

He whipped around to catch a glimpse of a posse of scruffy preteens descending the path that led to the beach below the bluff. He took off after them, just as one glanced over his shoulder. Shouting something to his buddies, the kid sped up, herding the other boys along with him. At least three of them had lit cigarettes in the forks of their skinny fingers.

Half-sliding, half-running along the narrow, sandy path behind the boys, Gabe stopped the chase when they hit the firm sand of the beach and took off like bullets. Two of the little shits ran backward, their middle fingers up in the air, we-got-you grins on their faces.

Shaking his head, Gabe turned back up the path. Maddie would have been closing in on that age, he thought. If she'd lived, would his sweet little girl have turned into a smoking, swearing hellion?

He'd never know.

At the thought, the despair he'd been holding back all day engulfed him. Stilling, he closed his eyes and suffered through the first crippling pangs of grief and remorse. Lynn's annoyed voice in his head: "Couldn't you at least once take her to dance practice?" Maddie's plea: "Daddy, Daddy, don't you want to watch me pirouette?"

He tasted ash in his mouth and he knew it was from his heart incinerating all over again, just as it had done with such regularity over the last three years. It was a wonder he was still alive.

It was no wonder he so regularly wished he wasn't.

His feet started to move, knowing that he wouldn't find what he needed to cope out here. Breaching the top of the beach path, he glanced over at Malibu & Ewe. He could go in there. He could pretend he had a repair to do or that he wanted a mug of her disgusting dandelion tea and then he could hope that her presence or her chatter might stifle the voice drifting from the beckoning blackness. Already it was loud in his ears. *Come to me. Come to me.*

But squaring his shoulders, he turned the other way.

There was no reason to resist the call and avoid oblivion, and his friend deserved better than to be subject to his despondency. Instead, he'd join other old acquaintances. Good ol' Bud. That wily Jack Daniel's. Jose Cuervo was always up for a night on the town. He'd just meet his companions some place where the bartender wouldn't call Cassandra.

As he walked through the parking lot, he noticed Marlys's car had gone. Apparently they'd both decided there were other places they'd rather be.

Nine

The only rock I know that stays steady, the only institution I know that works is the family.

—LEE IACOCCA

"Come to me," Cassandra said into her phone.

"What?" On the other end of the call, Gabe coughed out the question.

"Come to me over here at Malibu & Ewe. Better yet, just meet me on the beach down below the shop."

"Why?"

She looked out her window and across the parking lot, dimly lit by the security lights that switched on at dark. His SUV was angled in one of the painted stalls, so she was certain he was still inside the business, though it had closed fifteen minutes before. "Stop asking questions and just do as I say. I have chocolate."

The suspicion in his voice turned to disbelief. "You do not."

"I do." And she hoped the surprise of that would render him curious enough to do as she asked.

"I'll bet it's carob," he said, with mild disgust. "You

know how I hate carob. It tastes like stale malted milk balls. So I think I'll pass on your offer."

She'd been afraid he'd say that. From what she'd been told, he was heading for a more destructive diversion altogether. "It's real chocolate, Gabe."

"Froot Loop—"

"You owe me. Didn't you tell me that the other night?"

"What other night?" His suspicion was back. "Exactly when?"

She hardened her voice. "I think it was right after the bartender informed me that the stink on you was, indeed, exactly what it smelled like."

There was a weighty pause.

"Please, Gabe." *Please don't go for the booze over the beach with me.*

His sigh was heavy, too. "Give me a few minutes."

A few minutes were enough for her to build a tidy little bonfire in the concrete fire ring at the bottom of their bluff. She always stored some wooden pallets in her small side storeroom for just such a whim—though it was usually a summer impulse. Yet tonight was perfect for what she had in mind, with clear skies, little wind, and temperatures that had swung once more from winter to spring.

Spread on the sand near the flames was a beach blanket she'd bought on a trip to Tijuana. Unpacked on it were the contents of the basket that she'd used to lure Gabe to the beach. She heard his voice before she saw him, the sound of his footsteps absorbed by the soft sand.

"That actually looks like real chocolate," he said. "What is all this stuff?"

"It's s'mores makings." She'd already punctured a marshmallow with one of the expandable forks she'd found inside the basket. "What kind of roaster are you? I prefer the slow toast, going for golden brown."

"Wait a minute." She heard the raised eyebrows in his voice and congratulated herself. Curiosity was proving to be a successful means of distraction after all. "Not just chocolate, but marshmallows, too? Aren't they made of that Evil White Stuff, namely . . . sugar?"

Could he see her shrug in the light from the fire? "The gift is from Edward Malcolm the Fourth. Graham crackers, chocolate, and marshmallows. I was going to dump it all, but why should I when that's exactly what he did to me two years ago? Worse, months later he decides he wants me back and he still can't believe I won't fall into his arms. Ergo, the persuasive present. It isn't going to work, but I've decided we shouldn't waste the goodies."

Instead of sitting on the blanket as she was, Gabe continued standing. His voice was sharp. "He came to the shop today?"

"If he did, I didn't see him," she answered, remembering she'd told Gabe about Edward's ongoing and annoying insistence that they retry their relationship. Apparently her landlord had been listening then, too. "I looked up at one point and the basket was on the counter accompanied by a note with his name on it."

Gabe stepped onto the blanket and she gave herself another metaphorical pat on the back. "I don't like it," he said.

"I don't like Edward." Cassandra held up the second fork that she'd already threaded with an uncooked marshmallow. Her hands were covered with fingerless gloves that matched the thick sweater she'd handknit herself. "But I haven't had a s'more since I was sixteen."

Hunkering down beside her, Gabe took the fork, though still obviously reluctant. He wasn't wearing anything warmer than a pair of jeans and a denim workshirt.

"You're not cold?" she asked.

He shoved the unmarshmallowed end of his fork in the sand and then reached into his back pocket. "I brought a hat," he said, and pulled the beanie over his hair. She'd made it for him months ago, in the blue-and-gold colors of his alma mater. As far as she'd known, he'd thrown the thing out. There was a matching extra-long woolen scarf, but she'd never seen it again either.

She shot another glance at him. It gave her a silly little thrill to see him wearing something she'd made with her hands. He picked up his fork and shoved the tines into the hottest part of the fire.

"Why am I not surprised you go straight for flame?" she asked, as the white confection lit and started to burn.

He brought it to his mouth and blew on the marshmallow to put out the little fire. It looked more like a lump of coal than a treat.

"Who gets to eat something gooey and sweet first?" he asked, and to prove his point, he created a graham cracker and chocolate sandwich, biting into it just as she was turning her fork yet again.

"You'll burn your tongue," she warned, worrying he'd selected the speedy method in order to hurry back to his original plans for the evening.

His next words were somewhat muffled by the sticky treat. "I survived your kiss, didn't I?"

That shut her up for an uncharacteristic ten minutes. But maybe her silence was as effective as his curiosity, because Gabe stuck by her side on the blanket. Of course, knowing him, it was probably the sugar that kept him from running off. They made s'mores to the sound of the surf, Gabe's cooking style enabling him to out-eat her three-to-one.

She was licking chocolate from her thumb when he groaned and fell back onto the blanket. "I'm warning you, getting sick is another possibility."

"But you won't have a headache later, which makes it so much better than the vice you were heading for tonight."

He didn't move. "What makes you think that?" he asked slowly.

"Jay called me. He said he stopped in to get swordfish steaks for his and Nikki's dinner and that you were . . . in a mood that told him there was trouble brewing."

"I was in a mood because my manager, Charlie, told me at four this afternoon that he'd forgotten an appointment, which meant I'd have to stay and close." A long moment passed. "Ah. I smell a second conspiracy."

"I'm not the only person who sees what's going on with you, Gabe. Charlie worries, too. And Jay was concerned enough to call me."

"I'm surprised he did," Gabe admitted.

"Why?" Though she'd known her almost-brother-in-law was reluctant and had heard Nikki in the background objecting and cautioning throughout the phone call. *Tell her I can keep him off a barstool*, Cassandra had told Jay, *while keeping myself out of trouble*. While keeping her emotions unengaged. "Why would Jay be reluctant to call me?"

"In a few weeks you'll be related by marriage, Froot Loop. A good man does the right thing for family."

With a sigh, Cassandra lay back on the blanket, mimicking Gabe's pose. Overhead, the swathe of the Milky Way lay like a thin film over the twinkling stars, just as she'd heard Jay's concern for her coating his words during their conversation. He did care. Nikki and Juliet and Noah as well. It was exactly what she'd been seeking after her mother went off on her global adventure. Family ties to take away her loneliness. Her feeling of rootlessness.

What a success! Her sisters were everything she'd dreamed of since childhood . . . and yet she hadn't updated that dream once coming to understand about husbands and marriage. Both of those changed the relationships she could have with her siblings.

Not that she didn't want Nikki and Juliet to find their men and matrimonial happiness. And if she wanted the same for herself, well, Edward popped the question on a biweekly, if increasingly peevish, basis. He didn't take her "no" for an answer, nor did he seem to believe her when she said she liked running her own business and was not interested in closing it or selling it so she could devote herself to becoming his devoted wife.

"Where did you meet Edward anyway?" Gabe asked.

Had she said his name out loud? Cassandra frowned. "It was before you owned the fish market . . . I met him there. He was with his mother and his two sisters. They'd gone for a Sunday drive and stopped in for lunch."

"Ah," Gabe said.

" 'Ah'?" She glanced over at him. The firelight and the starlight illuminated his chiseled features but didn't make clear his expression.

"Sisters? A mother who goes on Sunday drives with her children? All you've ever wanted, Cassandra. Can't-Take-No-for-an-Answer Edward was just a bonus. Or, as we know now, just an ass."

She scowled at Gabe, resenting his flip, beachside analysis. "So, if we're into swapping facts and then making something more out of them, where did *you* meet your wife?"

"What?"

Yeah, that shoe didn't feel so comfortable on the other foot, did it? But she refused to back off. Gabe's daughter and wife—particularly his wife—were taboo subjects she'd been tiptoeing around as long as she'd known him. She wasn't any good at it, not really, no better at it than she was at keeping her emotions unengaged when it came to Gabe.

Because here she was, despite her promises to Nikki, lying next to him, her body aware of every inch of his body next to hers. And worse, her heart was pounding and her lungs were tight as she brought up the woman whose ghost had always hovered between them.

Her failure to keep her emotions unengaged made her voice sharp. "Where did you meet her? Lynn. We can say her name, right?"

Lynn. We can say her name, right?

Yet it was another of those unspoken words in Gabe's vocabulary. *Lynn. Maddie. Daughter. Wife.*

The s'mores sugar buzz had done something to dilute the day's earlier grim mood. With the darkness still hovering all around him, he'd been forced to put off his next bender because of staffing problems. But now, lying beside Cassandra and with the taste of chocolate and marshmallow on his tongue, the voice in his head was muffled and those verboten names slid into his consciousness without the usual wrenching pain. God, it felt good. It felt like he could breathe, and maybe even live a little.

He stared up at the sky. The stars overhead looked like the surface of the play table after his little girl had been into her craft box. The mess of sequins and glitter would cling to her small fingertips and be sprinkled like fairy freckles across her short nose. *Look, Daddy, I made you a card. Mommy's mad that you're late, but I'm not.*

"Lynn was mad the first time I met her, too," he murmured.

"What?" Cassandra said. She scooted closer to him on the blanket and he could feel the warmth of her shoulder brushing his. The black mood moved even further away.

"Lynn was mad the first time I met her," he repeated.

"I can sympathize," the woman beside him said, with a teasing nudge to his side. Now her whole arm was against his. "What did you do to tick her off?"

It startled him to realize that he could smile, thinking about it. "I was riding my bike near campus and mistook her for someone I knew. I came up behind her, and as a joke, when I passed by I swatted her on the butt."

"But it was the wrong butt."

Cute all the same, he remembered, but yes, the wrong butt. "When I looked back to laugh at my friend, I was looking into the fuming face of my future wife."

"So what did you do?" Cassandra asked. "Leap off your bike, drop to one knee, and propose right on the spot?"

"Not even close," he said, recalling his embarrassment. "I put on the afterburners and pedaled away as fast as my legs would carry me."

"And?" She nudged him again, and then the back of her hand brushed the back of his. Hers was encased in some sort of half-mitten thing that left her fingers bare. Their pinkies twined. "What happened then?"

Gabe glanced over and saw the moonlight washing Cassandra's beautiful face with a silver light. Like the sugary s'mores, the sight of it zapped a jolt of energy through his system. But she was his friend, his platonic, assuredly unpregnant friend, and it would be wise to remember that. "She caught up with me at the next stoplight."

"Then gave you a piece of her mind," Cassandra finished for him.

"Not to mention her phone number, before all was said and done," he added, and realized he was smiling again. "Believe it or not, I used to have a surfeit of charm."

"You've proved that a time or two," she said, her voice light.

Looking back up at the sky, he threaded the rest of his fingers through Cassandra's. She was such a pretty liar, because he'd never tried to charm her. He'd never tried with Cassandra at all.

It made him feel regretful and protective—the former on his own behalf and the latter on hers. He wished he could give her more at the same time that he wanted more for her. Yet here he was, already hand in hand and unable to move away from her slender fingers and warm body.

"So was it wonderful?" she asked softly. "The marriage? Making a family with Lynn and Maddie?"

He stiffened, the wistful note in Cassandra's voice piercing that chink in his armor she'd been able to find so easily of late. The stab hurt like shit and only served to piss him off as his lungs tightened again. "I don't want to talk about it."

"Oh, Gabe." Her fingers squeezed his. "I . . . I shouldn't have brought it up."

"Damn right," he ground out. Damn right, because that way lay danger.

"But don't you think—"

"No," he said. Implacable. Completely certain that he didn't want to talk about his marriage, that he didn't want to share a second of it.

She looked over. He could feel her sympathetic gaze, but he kept his own away from hers, determined not to fall victim to the concern he was certain he'd find in her big blues. Next thing you'd know he'd be reassuring her, rewriting history and telling his own lies, anything not to extinguish the stars reflected in her eyes.

Or worse, he'd tell the truth, and shatter her illusions forever.

Since when had it become so important to him that Cassandra keep her confidence in love and forever afters? Or was it her image of him as the perfect husband that he didn't want to damage?

Her gaze was still resting on him, he knew it, and he couldn't resist the lure any longer. Turning his head, he found himself nose to nose with her, their mouths inches apart, his cheek resting on a cool length of her rippling, perfumed hair.

He wanted her. Yes, she was his friend, but he still wanted to fist his hands in that hair and roll onto her body. Cassandra would cradle his cock between her thighs and he could rock them both away, far away from the truths and the danger that being this close to each other wrought. Funny, but it suddenly seemed like sex was the weapon that he knew would keep emotions between them at bay.

With his body, he could put off honesty.

"Gabe . . ." she whispered.

And he could almost admit to himself that those words were just his own lie to give himself permission to taste her again, to touch her again, to feel her warmth. Using his free hand, he brushed her hair away from her face. A strand was caught in the corner of her mouth, and he worked it free, seeing how her breath hitched at his gentle touch.

He was such an asshole, he thought to himself, as he gave up the struggle and leaned in to take her mouth.

She turned into his body and pressed closer as her lips opened to his invasion. He slid his tongue in her mouth and stroked it against hers, soft and sure, until he heard her moan. Then he couldn't leave it soft anymore. Thrusting hard into the heated cavern of her mouth, he slid his hand along the indentation of her waist to her hip and then her rounded ass. She moaned again and he tucked her hips against his, grinding his cock against the cushioned mound of her sex.

At their feet, the fire crackled, and he could smell the smoke, but both were almost drowned by the sound of the blood rushing through his veins and the delicious fragrance of Cassandra, her lemony skin and her flowery hair.

He wanted to wrap himself in her and take them both away. Driven by the image, he inched up her sweater to bare the warm skin of her belly and then her breasts, her bra covering their abundance. His hand cupped one and squeezed with a gentle pressure and Cassandra bowed into his body and his touch, her mouth widening to take the deeper thrust of his tongue.

Then he left her lips to run his along her soft cheek, her slender neck, the pulse point that thrummed with excitement. They were both excited, aroused, and he couldn't deny that it was only harder to resist her every time they got this close.

But he couldn't worry about it, not when her skin was so hot and her little whimpers such a turn-on, not when she was chanting his name with such sweet desperation.

"Gabe." Her breath hitched. "Please, Gabe."

He caught her earlobe between his teeth and felt the bite of her fingernails in his scalp as he tugged. "Please, Gabe. Aren't you listening to me?"

Aren't you listening to me?

The question repeated in his head, jolting his conscience

out of its sexual stupor. Lynn had always said those words. *Aren't you listening to me?*

Anger at himself poured through him, overriding the lust that he'd let drive his actions. He released Cassandra's tender flesh and then yanked her tight against him, pushing her head into his neck. "Easy, baby," he said, using his other hand to jerk down her sweater. "Easy. We're taking this too far."

"Gabe?" He heard the uncertainty and the thread of embarrassment in her voice and cursed himself again.

"It's all my fault, Froot Loop. This has nothing to do with you."

She shoved him away in a sudden flurry, scooting back on the blanket so there was a good eighteen inches between them. Her mouth was swollen and her eyes accusing as she sat up and stared at him. "What the hell are you talking about, Gabe?"

"I just can't do this, Froot Loop. You need someone better in your arms."

"Better? I still don't know what you mean."

"My wife. Lynn . . ."

"The one who had no trouble giving you a piece of her mind? Because that sounds like a good example for me to follow."

"Cassandra." He reached out to touch her, but let his hand drop with a sigh. "You're right. She had no problem telling me what she wanted. But I had trouble hearing her."

In the moonlight, he saw Cassandra's eyes narrow. "Meaning what?"

"Meaning you have this wrong idea about my marriage, about me." Damn it. He cursed Charlie and Jay and everything that had gotten between him and the booze that promised blessed forgetfulness. Except Cassandra. He couldn't curse her, he could only save her from himself by telling her the truth.

"Lynn wanted another child," he confessed. "I kept saying no. I kept saying maybe later, when I meant maybe never. I told her we'd talk when I stopped working so hard when I meant that I found my job more interesting than I found our marriage. Then, the last year she didn't ask for another baby anymore. She didn't ask me for anything."

Except that he drive his daughter to her dance lesson that afternoon. And if he had . . . how might that have changed the outcome of that day?

"Gabe . . ." There was sympathy in her voice. She touched his arm.

He didn't deserve it, but Cassandra was so damn tempting that he wanted to forget all the reasons why he couldn't have her. Why not just let her skin and her scent and her sex take him away from his past and keep him out of the darkness?

His fingers curled into fists. Over the shushing surf and the dying fire, came the sound of a siren. A vehicle, speeding its way down the Pacific Coast Highway. He almost laughed, it was such an apt soundtrack for this moment. They were at a dire crossroads. Their own personal emergency.

But the vehicle's wail didn't pass on. They both glanced up, and then jumped to their feet, as they realized that something was happening at their businesses on the bluff above. Jesus!

What could it be? He dashed toward the trail leading upward, certain only that his good intention to keep their relationship from going in the wrong direction wasn't the only thing at risk tonight.

Ten

The happiest moments of my life have been the few which I have passed at home in the bosom of my family.

—THOMAS JEFFERSON

Trying to keep her alarm at bay, Cassandra scrambled in Gabe's wake up the path that led from the beach to the bluff and both their places of business. She lengthened her stride to keep up with him, but her slick-soled shoes couldn't find purchase on the gritty sandstone path and she felt herself sliding back, her balance off.

Gabe's hand latched on to her wrist. How he knew she'd been about to tumble, she couldn't figure, but he yanked her upright and pulled her along, his pace slowing a little for her shorter legs.

"Don't fall," he ordered.

She glanced at the strong fingers clamped around her arm, then shifted her gaze to his face, turned toward her. In the moonlight, she could see his frown. She could remember his emotional confession on the blanket and then those hot kisses. "Working on that," she replied. *Working on that.*

The sirens had stopped wailing, but red lights were

pulsing against the face of the sky. As they breached the top of the path, her gaze honed in on them, flashing on top of the pair of red engines. Even in winter, fire was serious business in Malibu.

And the attention of the firefighters, she realized with a sick jolt, was trained on Malibu & Ewe. She froze, stomach shrinking and heart squeezing as she saw flames and smoke emitting from the side of her shop.

Throat choking on a plea, she surged forward. Gabe's grip, still circling her, hauled her back. "No, baby," he murmured, clasping her against his chest and wrapping his arms around her. "This isn't our fight."

He was right, but that didn't stop dread from shooting through her bloodstream. She and Gabe were just the audience, as water was trained on the side door of her shop and smoke billowed into the sky. "What happened? Why?" she cried out, as she tried to move forward once more, but Gabe only held her closer against him.

Tears stung her eyes, and her lungs seized in a sharp sob. Her business. Her *life*. Gabe palmed her cheek and pressed her face into his shoulder. "It's okay," he said. "It's going to be okay."

He repeated the mantra as the firefighters quickly extinguished the blaze, as she and Gabe waited around to give information to the sheriff's deputy who eventually showed up, as the building was secured and the mopping up was completed. It had been a small blaze, caught early.

Gabe said that, too, as he drove her back to their canyon. When he'd insisted on driving her home, even though both their cars were in the parking lot, she hadn't protested. Preoccupied by nightmarish thoughts of what might have been, she'd let him usher her into the passenger seat of his Jeep.

He glanced over now. "The damage is minimal, sweet-heart."

He never called her sweetheart. No one ever had.

"I heard what they said," she answered, her voice hoarse. With a cough, she tried smoothing it out. "Lucky for me the nine-one-one call came in from the crew who cleans the fish market at night."

"And lucky that you didn't have anything but more of those pallets and some empty boxes in that side storage area. The shop itself isn't even smoke damaged. Your other store-room, the back one, where all your inventory is, is fine."

"I still shouldn't have left that side door unlocked." It was something specific to fret over, though there was so much more bothering her. "I thought we might want more pallets later."

"It wasn't you who threw burning, wadded up newspaper in there. And the fireproof door between that area and the rest of your shop means the worst that happened is we have to phone the insurance company and for a few days you have to listen to some construction workers' hammers and their lousy taste in music."

"Right." Except that "worst" didn't include the vulner-ability she now sensed in her foundation. That couldn't be repaired by a guy with a hammer and some Toby Keith cowboy songs.

Gabe continued. "I told them about those delinquents that have been playing with matches around the shop. The sheriff's people will be looking for them."

"Heard that, too," she said, remembering the smoke, the fire, the way her imagination had leaped to total loss. Some other woman would be feeling relieved now. Celebratory. But instead she still felt sick inside. A breath away from falling apart.

When he pulled up to her house, he gave her a once-over as the car continued to idle. "Are you going to be okay?"

She took a breath. "Sure." Everybody knew that Cassandra Riley could keep it together. She was the epitome of calm, the kind of woman who made others feel that way, too—so certainly she could be okay. Was okay. "I'm totally fine."

"Liar."

Her body twitched. "No. Really." Admitting how shaky she was would only serve to make her feel more exposed. She needed to shore up her defenses, and she only had practice doing that one way—alone. "I'm good."

"You could fool just about anyone, Froot Loop, but you can't fool me."

Her arms creeped around her body, as they'd been wanting to the entire drive, trying to hold herself together. Ah, that was better. *You've always been your own best friend, Cassandra*, she reminded herself. *Everybody says you're so warm, so calming, so nurturing. Nurture yourself!*

Gabe twisted the key, killing the car's engine. "Let's go inside."

She fumbled for the door handle. "No need for that." Her voice came out sharp. "I said I'll be fine."

Instead of settling back in his seat, Gabe followed her out of the car. She sent him an exasperated look over her shoulder but he just gazed back at her, and she was forced to unlock her door and push it open. With his warmth at her back, she stepped inside.

He followed.

Moosewood, Breathe, and Ed rushed forward. She left them twining Gabe's ankles and moved into the tiny kitchen where she automatically hit the PLAY button on the answering machine. A hang-up. A reminder of an upcoming

Chamber of Commerce meeting. Then the aggrieved tones of Edward Malcolm IV. "Cassandra," he said. "Now can you admit I was right about closing the yarn shop? You could have been killed in that fire tonight."

She stilled. Killed? But she'd been on the beach, not at the building on the bluff.

Though with her car in her usual parking space, someone else might not have known that. There'd been a few lights left on in the shop, consistent with the owner working late on paperwork as she so often did.

But the damage had been minimal!

Thanks to the prompt call from Gabe's cleaning crew. With different timing, the fire could have gained a stronger foothold—and could have trapped her inside.

No. If anything, it had been her livelihood at stake, not her life.

"Cassandra?" She whipped around to face Gabe.

His eyes narrowed. "What now?"

"Nothing." She jerked her finger away from the answering machine and tucked both hands in the crooks of her folded arms. "Nothing at all."

Eyebrows rising, he reached around her to punch a button on the machine.

"Hey—" she started to protest, but he just put his palm over her mouth, muffling what she had to say. Rolling her eyes, she tapped her foot while the messages replayed, including the last one from Edward.

Gabe glared at her as that call clicked off. "Why were you covering that up? How the hell could Edward already know about the fire?"

She pushed his hand away from her mouth. "I don't know how he knows," she said, sidestepping him and heading for the refrigerator. Turning her back on Gabe, she tried to pretend an interest in hummus, olives, and a plastic-wrapped plate of rice pilaf. The s'mores had ruined her appetite.

Gabe's hand on her shoulder spun her around, his other slammed shut the refrigerator door. "Cassandra—"

"He surfs the Net all the time," she said. "Malibu? Fire? I'll bet it's already out on the Web. Think how long we were kicking our heels waiting for the sheriff."

He stomped over to her laptop, which sat on the countertop a few feet away. His body visibly tense, he pulled up the Internet browser, punched a few keys, then grunted as text poured onto the screen. Then he checked his watch. "All right. It's out and the time on the first posts jive with the time stamp on the message left on the machine."

"Told you."

"But hell, Cassandra, could you stop involving yourself with these freaks? First it's that druggie drummer—"

"Carver's no druggie!"

"—and now it's this creepy, can't-let-go Edward."

Why didn't Gabe go away? "So I should start spending time with someone normal you're saying?"

He'd taken his beanie off on the ride home and when he forked a hand through his hair, it stuck up like a little boy's. "Yeah."

Glaring, she stepped up to him, her breasts brushing his chest wall. "Someone normal, say, like you?"

He jerked back his head. "No. Not like me. Not like . . ." Then his eyes closed and he groaned. "Not like me," he said, yet his arms moved, clamping around her to bring their hips flush, too. "Never like me," he said against her mouth.

The fear she'd felt at seeing the fire rushed over her again, making her bones watery. She clung to Gabe, her insides shaking. Her imagination had decimated her shop, and it was then she'd realized that her business was the only thing she could count on. The only steady feature in her life.

There were friends. There were even sisters. But everyone had someone else as their number one, and Cassandra only had Malibu & Ewe at the top of her list.

Without it, she'd be lost.

A cold, unsettling, lonely notion. Her business was all she really had. The only thing she took to bed with her each evening. Tonight, she couldn't let it be the same.

She tore her mouth away from Gabe's kiss and looked at him through eyes stinging with tears. "Help," she said, her earlier alarm closing in on full-blown panic. Tonight, she needed something to think about beyond her empty life and her lonely heart, and she couldn't do it all by herself. "Rescue me."

It had been leading to this for months, days, two years. Two years' worth of stifled and subjugated lust that took only two words to set free, Gabe realized. *Rescue me.*

Face it. There wasn't a chance in hell he'd be finding his scruples and stop this time.

"Cassandra . . ." He said her name not to refuse or warn her, but because he could say it now with all the pent-up desire he'd been trying to deny. With a smile, he pressed his forehead to hers.

"For tonight," she whispered. "Please give me something else to think about."

As he'd wanted her to do on the beach a few hours ago. And didn't he owe her sweet payback for the many times she'd taken him away from his dark moods? For the many occasions she'd rescued him from barrooms and booze and the self-destruction that he couldn't say still didn't sound damn tempting so often.

But not now. Not tonight. Cassandra was the temptation now.

His neighbor needed him. The only friend in his fucked-up little world was quivering in his arms and he could smell the faint hint of smoke in her hair. He felt something inside him tremble, too. What if she'd been in the shop tonight?

He leaned back to put a breath of space between them and cupped her face in his hands. Before he could get a word out, her gaze turned fierce. "If you tell me no after the day I've had, I'm never going to feed you tofu fritters again."

He laughed. "Um, sweetheart, listen to yourself. Tofu fritters, not an incentive."

Her hands came up to tighten on his wrists. "Gabe, please just take me away for a little while."

He knew what it was to want that so very badly.

He bent down and kissed the pillowed bottom of Cassandra's lower lip. "Sweetheart . . ."

"Just keep calling me that," she said, her voice infused with a sexy huskiness. "Just keep kissing me and touching me . . ."

He pressed a tender, prolonged kiss against her mouth, and something tight inside him eased. God knows he'd been a failure before, but Cassandra knew about that now, knew him better than any living person, and with the truth between them, he could focus on something else. Focus on her.

With her, with this, he'd be damned if he provided anything less than success.

"I'll do my best, Froot Loop," he promised.

"You know how much I hate when you call me that." She frowned.

He kissed it off her mouth, then took her hands to draw her toward the bedroom as he walked backward. "C'mon. Sweet and juicy? What's not to like?"

Her lips curved and he could tell she was trying not to laugh. "Sure. But that means that though it provides an intense sugar rush, you'll be hungry again soon after."

They were crossing the threshold to her bedroom, lit by a small lamp at her bedside. He raised his eyebrows and gave her a wicked look. "Exactly."

She laughed.

He used it as a distraction to release her hands and reach for the hem of her sweater. Its softness caught at her hair and when he tossed the garment to the small chair beside the bed her cheeks were pink.

The tops of her breasts over her bra matched their color. Did any woman ever look more like a dream? He reveled in the freedom he had to take in that wealth of flesh with his gaze. To stroke the back of his fingers over that hot skin. "You've been making me crazy with these for way too long."

She looked at him through the veil of her lashes. "Your resistance—"

"Until recent times has been mighty." He brushed the shoulder straps of her bra off her shoulders and then tucked his forefingers into the top of the cups to edge them below her nipples. His breath caught. "Obviously."

She was trembling again, which made her breasts quiver as he looked at them. Her nipples were already hard, their color darkened, and he thumbed them, watching closely as they stiffened further. Lust shot through his body, bouncing around like a pinball, only to settle in the hard spear of his erection. He let out a long breath.

His hands were shaking—shaking!—as he moved them around to her sleek back and found the clasp of her bra. Someone was looking out for him, because he didn't fumble. The clasp released without any reluctance. The garment itself fell to the floor, landing on top of Gabe's shoes.

There was no glance to spare for it; his attention was wholly engrossed by her truly incredible breasts. He cupped each in a canoe made by his thumb and forefinger. Weighing them, lifting them, appreciating them. A quiver ran through her body and her flush deepened. He smiled again. "So . . . am I in trouble for thinking I am really, really lucky right now?"

She swayed into his touch. "Only if you're going to just talk about it all night."

"As the lady wishes," he said, releasing her flesh and then taking a moment to throw off his shirt. Bared above the waist, he grasped her ribs and jerked her close. They both gasped as their skin met. Her hard nipples burned brands into the skin beneath his pecs. Without his will, his hips ground forward, and his hands slid down to her ass to press her mound against his erection.

He groaned at the goodness of it, his head dropping back. It was inconceivable to him that he could have forgotten the incredible feel of this, no matter how drunk he'd been. Swear to God, there was no way he wouldn't remember the sleek burn of his flesh against hers, the soft give of her sex.

"I never dreamed . . ." Cassandra murmured.

The whisper pierced his arousal-fogged brain. Eyes narrowing, he inched back, despite the protest of every cell in his body, to get a clear shot at her face. Her eyes—big, blue, dazed by the same kind of wonder he felt shooting through his body—met his.

"We've never done this before," he said. A declaration of fact.

She hesitated, then capitulated. "We've never done this before."

He wasn't sure whether he was relieved or grateful or pissed off that he'd been such a fool. But then he realized he was only glad that he hadn't forgotten even an instant of such potential pleasure. "Hey, wait a minute," he said. "The other night you didn't object when I thought I owed you that org—"

She put her fingers over his lips. "You did owe me that, for being such an idiot to think I'd hop in the sack with a guy who—"

His palm clapped over her mouth this time. "Never mind. But I also wondered . . . Never mind that either." She didn't need to know he'd worried—feared—she carried his child. There were places he didn't need to go to make this a success. "However, *you* are in trouble."

She kissed his palm, ran her tongue along its center, sensitive skin, so that he had to drop it in order to touch her lips with his own. "You're in big trouble," he said, lifting his mouth from their latest kiss.

Her hands slid up his chest, and the edge of her thumbs brushed over the hard points of his nipples. He sucked in a sharp breath. She smiled. "Trouble? What does that mean, exactly?"

He cupped her breasts. "It means I'm going to make you crazy. Make you wait."

She huffed out a breath as he pinched the tight crests of her nipples. "I've waited long enough," she murmured.

That's right. There was that whole celibacy kick of hers.

He took her nipples between his thumbs and forefingers again. Squeezed with light pressure. Her spine went rigid.

He squeezed a skosh harder, curiosity compelling him to discover the details. "About that. Exactly how long have you gone without?"

Her breaths came fast and light. Her pupils were black discs trained on his face. "Wha—?"

God, she was beautiful. He tightened his fingers again. "I'm interested. Exactly how long have you been celibate?"

She licked her lips, her mouth going slack as he continued playing with her sensitive crests. "Uh, well. A long time."

"Yeah?" He bent to run his tongue along her neck. "How long is a long time?"

Her pulse rioted. "A really long time," she answered, her voice faint.

He froze. *A really long time*? Shit. Shit! Was she . . . ? Could she actually be . . . ? He couldn't form the words, because he'd never even considered the idea. Straightening, he gazed into her face again. "Cassandra?"

She was looking back at him, but he could tell it wasn't her brain that was running the show at the moment. Good. Leaning down, he took her mouth, thrusting deep to put her even more off balance. When he lifted his head, he swiped his tongue across her bottom lip, then framed her face with his hands. "How long have you been celibate?" he asked.

She didn't blink, her gaze now fixed on his mouth. Then she answered, and what she said confounded the success of his goal.

"Uh, almost thirty years?"

Eleven

Other things may change us, but we start and end with family.

—ANTHONY BRANDT

Gabe groaned out loud. Cassandra wasn't celibate, she was a virgin, for damn sake, and for all his talk of success, wasn't that just a recipe for failure?

"What's the matter?" she asked, her hips still pressed against his, her naked torso still warm against his bare flesh. Her tight jeans rode low on her hips and cupped the curve of her ass like he wanted to.

He glanced down, taking in the lush fullness of her breasts, the jut of her hard nipples, the curve of her waist and the sweet hollow of her navel. A shudder ran through him as he thought of laying a ring of kisses there, of tonguing that intriguing well, of letting the head of his cock take a shallow dip into that narrow pool before heading down to hotter, wetter territory.

He groaned again. "The matter is you're a virgin."

"Gabe . . ."

"I'm too old for this, Froot Loop." A virgin! It kept hitting him like a slap to the forehead.

"Me, too," Cassandra said. She slid her hands up his chest and linked her fingers behind his neck. "So let's do something about that."

"But don't you want—"

"Tonight I want you," she said. "I want you, and you want me, too, right?"

As if he could lie about it when the evidence was poking her in the belly. "Maybe we should talk . . ."

She sighed. "Don't tell me you're going to be sentimental and schmaltzy about this, are you?"

He frowned. "That sounds like an insult."

"It's insulting to me that you think I don't know my own mind, Gabe." She tugged his head down to insist on the next kiss. "I haven't had sex before. I want to now. What will it take to get you to cooperate? An exchange of mushy notes in math class? Do I have to write your name in pink gel pen in my school binder first?"

Her teasing annoyed him, which only added to the heat bubbling between them. "No, damn it."

"Just be a pal, then, okay?" Twining her arms tighter, she pressed another kiss on him.

Be a pal and take her to bed? Take her virginity that she'd been saving for twenty-nine years? Take, take, take. What else was new when it came to him and the best friend he had in the world? He couldn't take more from her. But he couldn't back away, either, not when she was needy and bare and breathless and . . . Cassandra.

"Pink gel pens, my ass," he muttered against her mouth, tucking an arm around her hips to draw her even closer against his throbbing cock.

"Gabe, please," she said, squirming against him.

"I'm going to give to you, baby," he promised. "All for you."

Her skin burned hotter as he pushed her mouth wider with his tongue, starting a rhythm that was heavy thrust and keen demand. Soon she was chasing his tongue back into his mouth with her own, and he bit lightly down and sucked on its firm, velvet wetness. She moaned, crowding closer to his body, and he kept her tongue trapped in his mouth as he worked one hand at the button and zipper of her jeans.

She moaned again, not helping at all as she rocked her hips, trying to ride her mons against the pressure of his knuckles. Her obvious need sharpened his lust and he felt his balls yank tight to his body. Christ! She could make him come just by the sound of her deep-throated moans and the roll of her pelvis.

Gritting his teeth against his own urgency, he slid his hand into the vee of open denim and over silky panties. She pressed against his palm and he broke their carnal kiss to catch his breath and slow the speed of his pulse. Cassandra pressed her mouth to his neck and he thought about his beard stubble—and then about the ever-groomed almost-brother-in-law of hers and of that pretty boy drummer she'd dated in high school.

Her tongue flattened against the side of his throat and he tossed away any thoughts that didn't have to do with Cassandra and her mouth and her incredible breasts and that melting heat between her thighs. He walked her backward to her bed and then pushed her down, not even letting her bounce before he was on her body, her thighs opening around his hips.

"Oh," she said. "Yes."

Oh, *yeah*. Rolling to the side, he hooked his fingers in her jeans and caught her panties, taking them both along for the ride. They pooled at her ankles, prevented from going anywhere by the short boots she wore on her feet. She jackknifed, reaching toward them, but he pressed her back down on the mattress. "You don't have to do anything," he said. "Just lie back—"

"And think of England?" She thrust out her bottom lip to blow a lock of hair from her face.

"Think of how good I'm going to make you feel," he corrected, leaning down to catch her little pout between his teeth.

He suckled the soft skin, savoring Cassandra's flavor as she squirmed against the length of his body. His head felt light, and he figured that was due to all the blood pooling in his southern hemisphere, so he moved south himself, trailing his lips over her chin, down her neck, across her collarbone. She was arching upward, asking for other touches, other kisses, and he smiled against her bare flesh, knowing that while she might have had years of anticipation, she didn't really *get* anticipation.

She made a frustrated sound and he glanced up to grin at her. "Is my earth goddess a little impatient?"

And maybe this was the benefit of sex with someone who knew your worst moods. Because she didn't hesitate to show him hers. With a little flounce, she tried turning to give him the cold shoulder, and he let her, distracted by the incredible sight of her naked, peachy ass.

His cock twitched as he palmed the sleek skin of her haunch and when he nipped a tempting spot high on her rump, she jerked. Her squeak was the absolute funnest, girliest, cheeriest sound he'd heard in half a lifetime. He pushed her all the way onto her belly, and pulled back so he could stroke his hands up her thighs to the taut thrust of her butt. She wriggled under his touch, but he didn't relent as he continued his caresses, exploring every creamy inch from the nape of her neck to the backs of her knees.

She buried her face in the pillow, but he grabbed a fist of waving hair to turn her head so he could lean down and take a kiss. Her cheek was hot as he tickled the corner of her lips with his tongue.

"Gabe." She was panting a little. "I asked for sex."

"This *is* sex, Froot Loop."

She flounced again, but her tongue reached out to greet his. "This is torture."

He chuckled. "You want fast and without finesse, you do it in backseats with bare-assed adolescents. You wait this long, you get the edge that experience brings."

She wriggled again and he relented this time, letting her face him again so that they could share another long, wet kiss. Then he abandoned her mouth for another exploratory foray, but he didn't get farther than her breasts. He'd meant to give them a grazing caress, to tease her even longer, but his sophistication—his so-called edge—began and ended when his cheek brushed one hard nipple.

Instead of moving on, he moved his head, covering the hard center with his mouth. Her body tensed, not arching, not squirming. He didn't even think she was breathing, and when he started to suck he felt an answering quiver shoot through her muscles. He lifted his gaze to take in the flush on her cheekbones and the rosy color of her parted lips.

Cassandra . . . Wholesome, irksome Cassandra. He was doing this to her. He was putting that expression of pleasured passion on her face.

His mouth took in more of her flesh, sucked harder, as a new lust drove away the last of his concerns. His hand plumped the other full breast and then he toyed with the nipple there, pinching lightly and pulling it away from her body as her gasps and whimpers told him she was running down the path he'd set her on.

He switched his mouth to her other breast, sucking and biting with delicate care. She bowed, her shoulders pressing low, her chest lifting for more of his hungry mouth. His head spun and his lust spiked, but he clamped down on his surging desire. This was for Cassandra. This wasn't about him.

He let his free hand slide down the center of her body to flirt with her belly button. Then he moved through the soft curls at the apex of her thighs and heard her moan as he skirted the top of her cleft. She was already flowering for him there, her labia unfurled and open for his touch. He eased the pressure on her breast as he took in the incredible feel of her silky inner flesh.

She whimpered, and he soothed her by sucking softly at her nipple. With a slow finger, he wandered around the layered heat of her sex, shuddering as silky wetness flowed into his hand. She was aroused—God, beyond aroused to enflamed—and the evidence of her desire electrified him.

Urgency clamored in his head and in his cock and he jerked his hand to his pants, shuddering as her wetness transferred itself from his fingertips to the skin of his belly. He toed off his shoes and shucked off the rest of his clothes, taking a moment to rescue the condom he'd put in his wallet as a precautionary measure the day following the Beach Shack debacle. Then he lay against her body again, treating himself to a decadent kiss as his cock slid along the slick flesh of her pussy.

He rubbed himself against her, ignoring the clamoring in his blood for action, for penetration, for completion. Her past abstinence at the forefront of his mind, he was able to take his clues from her hitched breathing, her hot skin, the way her thighs opened in sexual, needy abandon.

Rolling to his side, he propped his head on one hand

and put his other into play again. Using her expression as the measure of her readiness, he watched her face as he drew the back of his fingers down her quivering belly. At the juncture of her thighs, he found the hard kernel there and circled it with his forefinger, spreading the cream of her own excitement as the small organ throbbed beneath his touch. Her eyes squeezed shut, so tight that lines fanned to her temples.

"Look at me, sweetheart," he said. "I need to see you."

Her lashes lifted as if they were heavy and the unfocused pools of blue were darkened by the blackness of her wide pupils. His breath caught hard in his chest, and he couldn't stop his hips from pushing forward so he could slide his cock along the side of her thigh. She gasped, too, and he gritted his teeth, reminding himself that her pleasure was the focus. This was her first time.

His fingers slid down the wet slide of her cleft to circle the entrance to her body. Shit, he thought, his finger tracing the soft skin there. Was he going to have to hurt her? The thought stilled him—hand, lust, heart.

"It might not even be an issue," Cassandra said quickly.

It didn't surprise him that she could read his mind.

"Activity can make it a moot point. Horseback riding. Gymnastics."

He slanted her a suspicious look. "How much of either have you done, Froot Loop?"

"There's a guy who rents horses at Paradise Cove every summer," she said.

Though she didn't say she'd ever rented one of those horses.

"And I could probably still do a headstand."

His Froot Loop. He could barely restrain shaking his head at her, would surely have done so if she hadn't been looking so turned on and so anxious at the same time. "I'm sure yoga counts, too," he said, just for the hell of it.

"Yes!"

Good God. But he made it a prayer as he took his touch to another level. Blowing out a silent breath, he let his fingertip breach that tight entry. Her hot, wet flesh closed around him, robbing him of breath. On a moan, her lashes drifted down.

"No," he said, his voice gruff. "Look at me." To make sure he wasn't hurting her, he needed to see her eyes.

She obeyed, slowly, her eyelashes lifting again as he inched his finger into the snug passage of her body. She moaned; he swallowed his. His muscles trembling, his gaze trained on her face, he pumped his finger in and out of her in an unhurried, gentle rhythm that his heart took up. Then that organ's beat double-timed as a sudden blast of lust rocketed through him—urging once again for action, penetration, completion.

Cassandra, he reminded himself. Give to Cassandra.

"Gabe." Her flush deepened and her inner muscles started tightening on him each time he withdrew. It made his next gentle invasion more difficult.

"Sweetheart. Relax. Let me in."

She frowned, her breath panting in and out of her chest. "Can't . . . relax."

He tried pushing inside her again, but she was so snug he was afraid that pressing harder would cause her pain. A sneak attack was in order, he decided. Swooping down, he took her mouth for a kiss and moved up his hand for another round of play with the wet bead at the top of her sex. This touch electrified her; he could feel the energy pulsing through her body. He put all his attention into the touch and into the kiss, his heart thudding as he felt the tension in her tighten.

She clutched at his forearm as if to still his pleasuring fingers, but he ignored her tight grasp to circle her sex, to kiss her mouth, to take her higher and higher until she—

Broke.

Her body arched, her lips went slack under his, then she shook, as a blissful sound poured into his mouth. He eased his touch as she quaked and shivered through her orgasm. When her movements quieted, he lifted his mouth.

"Gabe?" she said, her voice languorous. "We're not done, are we?"

It was like the soft stroke of a brush against his thighs, his balls, his cock. "Shh, shh," he said, quickly donning the condom he'd left on the bedside table. With shaking hands, he took off her boots and stripped her of the rest of her clothes.

Then he rolled between her thighs and smiled into her pleasure-filled face. "We don't have to do this, you know."

Cassandra lifted a hand to his cheek. "I'd never let you off so easy."

But he'd make it easy for her, he promised himself. *Think how long she's waited. Make it worth it.*

The head of his cock slid into the softened entry of her sex. Her muscles were lax from her orgasm, and he pushed onward. "Don't tense up," he said. "Just let me in."

And Cassandra being Cassandra, she widened her thighs and tilted her hips and gave him the generous offer of her lush sexiness. And Gabe . . . he hung on to his control, pushing without hurry into her, parting her muscles, pressing against her inner flesh, giving her all the finesse he had even as he saw pain break across her face when he surged the final inches.

"God." Breathing hard, he laid a kiss on her mouth. "Okay?"

Her heart pumped against his. "Okay." She didn't sound sure.

He wasn't sure himself. But his body remembered the moves and swung into them without his permission. On his elbows so he didn't smother her with his weight, he pumped his hips and watched her own breathing quicken.

"Beautiful Cassandra," he said. *This is for you. This is because you asked me to take you away from your today.*

But then Gabe's day fell away. As he moved within the soft, tight clasp of Cassandra's body, he let go of her past abstinence, his past dramas. Her self-proclaimed loneliness and his self-imposed reclusiveness.

Gabe found himself living for the sensation of his body against Cassandra's. He lived in the moment, this moment, of intimacy and passion.

Someone had told him he needed to rediscover this, that he needed to learn to fully feel the now again, but in three years he'd never been able to let go of the deep despair that his personal tragedy infused in every moment. In the past three years, he'd felt loneliness, lust, despondence, desire, but this was delight, in Cassandra's skin, in the hitch of her breath, in her response as he slid deep and stroked her clitoris until he felt her second climax. It triggered his, and then the pleasure spun out, pulling from some infinite well of exquisite sensation and endless time.

If he'd had a pink gel pen, he would have written her name and how this moment was making him feel, with bows and flourishes and fat, cheerful clouds.

The success of the event was a success for him. Because his personal storm was, for this infinite moment, at bay.

Later he could laugh at how sentimental that sounded. Later he would have to acknowledge that he'd turned as schmaltzy and saccharine as she'd warned him against. But now, for once free of the rusty chains of grief and regret, he just felt happy.

"So," Cassandra forced herself to say in a teasing, yet dismissive tone. She had to keep this light, after all. "I waited twenty-nine years for *that*?"

She held her breath as Gabe lifted the forearm he'd thrown over his eyes after lifting from her still-tingling body. His head rolled on the adjoining pillow to meet her gaze. "Don't even try that with me, Froot Loop," he said, his voice hoarse. "That was some of my best work and all for your benefit."

"So I owe *you* now?" she asked, still trying for a little attitude.

"Nah." He moved again, this time off the bed to pad toward the bathroom. "We can call it even."

Even? He wanted to call it even? She didn't know if she could. She didn't know *what* to call it, except maybe more intimate than she'd expected, and it prompted her to yank the sheet over her nude body.

The intimacy was Gabe's fault, she decided. Some other guy—most particularly the bare-assed adolescent that she might have found herself in a backseat with ten or twelve years ago—would have touched her body but left her head alone.

But Gabe knew her so well that even before the physical act was accomplished, he'd figured out her celibacy was just another name for her virginity. His focus had changed with her admission. He'd focused completely on *her*, taking her up and then over before giving her what she'd asked for.

Him inside her body.

Because that's what she'd wanted, more than the mere end of her virginal state. She'd wanted that intimate connection with Gabe as a distraction from the fire and the feelings it had brought out in her.

Her breath caught as he strolled back into the bedroom, apparently unconcerned about his nakedness. Through her lashes she checked out his lean body, and she flushed, remembering all the hard sinew and strong muscle pressed against her. He hesitated beside the bed, and she saw him scoop up an opened foil square lying on the bedside table.

He'd used a condom. She lifted onto her elbows. "You remembered protection. Thank you." Her flush deepened. She should have thought of that.

Gabe scrunched the foil in his fist. "Yeah. I bought them after that morning when I woke up in your bed." He ducked into the bathroom to toss the packet away.

"Because you thought we'd . . . indulged that night," she said, curling her lip.

He turned, taking in the semi-scornful expression on her face. His lips twitched. "Apparently I flattered myself."

"You think? You were falling down drunk, Gabe."

Sighing, he sat on the edge of the bed, still naked, and reached out to trace the curve of her eyebrow with his finger. She told herself not to shiver at the touch, but it was hard to resist as the fine hairs lifted along her skin.

"Forgive me?" he asked.

She thought she might forgive him anything when he treated her to such gentleness and looked at her with those intent, dark eyes. "Maybe," she said, to show she wasn't so easy to win over.

His forefinger moved to trace her mouth. "What if I were to hold you now?"

Cassandra swallowed, unsure what to do. Was it right to

extend the intimacy? Would it be too much like the sappiness she'd professed she wasn't after to ask him for his arms around her?

A smile ghosted over his face. "Why don't *you* hold *me*?" he suggested, sliding in beside her.

He was reading her again, of course, but she didn't protest as he turned out the light and settled her against him. There was a little soreness between her thighs and she wasn't accustomed to sharing her bed, but she decided this decision was right.

Close against him, everything felt so right.

"In the interest of full disclosure," he said, twirling a lock of her hair around his finger, "I have to admit I jumped to another terrifying conclusion after finding myself between your sheets."

"Gee, thanks," she said, in a teasing tone again. "You found being in my bed 'terrifying?'"

"It was if we didn't use a condom. It was if I made you pregnant."

An icy burn swept across her skin. Pregnant. A baby.

His casual mention of it, his obvious relief that it was an unfounded concern shouldn't hurt. It shouldn't touch her at all. He didn't know it was the final piece of the dream of family she'd been carrying with her since childhood. Cassandra, with her own baby to love.

Gabe's great fear.

Her great hope.

She buried both thoughts as deeply as she could.

His chin was against the top of her head; her cheek was nestled on his chest. He smoothed her hair with his hand. "You okay now?"

"Mmm."

He smoothed her hair another time. "Sweet dreams, Froot Loop."

"You, too," she whispered, though she didn't think she'd be getting much sleep, let alone pleasant dreams. So as not to do anything silly like talk in her sleep and reveal how much his tenderness had meant to her, she'd have to be on guard until he left in the morning.

And she knew he would, as surely as she knew that there'd be gulls at the beach. He'd get up and go and their relationship—such as it had been—would return to its former state. He'd be her landlord, her occasional friend, her once-upon-a-time, one-time lover.

She'd asked for just that, after all.

Which meant it was a good thing that though she'd asked Gabe into her body and though he'd found his way into her head, that she hadn't been dumb enough to allow him into her heart.

Not that.

Never that.

Twelve

An ounce of blood is worth more than a pound of friendship.

—SPANISH PROVERB

Cassandra was assessing her reflection in one of Malibu & Ewe's full-length mirrors, when Nikki burst through the door of the shop, half an hour before the seven o'clock start of their regular Tuesday Knitters' Night. "Cute hat," she said, coming up behind her.

"Thanks." Cassandra reached up to pull off the hand-knit beanie covering her hair. A soft brown color, it fit close to her head and was embellished with antique ivory buttons and soft pink flowers that she'd knitted as well. Then, unable to help herself, she turned to her sister and grabbed her up in a hug much tighter than the casual moment warranted. "I'm so glad you're here."

"Whoa, whoa, whoa," Nikki said, pushing back with gentle hands. "I didn't just survive the *Titanic*."

"Right," Cassandra replied, taking a quick step away. Nikki had spent years defending her heart by keeping herself closed off from others, and she could still be prickly about physical contact.

"Oh, don't look like that," the other woman said, and yanked Cassandra against her for another brief, tight hug. "And don't try to tell me nothing's going on with you, either."

But Cassandra didn't want to divulge, not when she knew the event was over. Since then, she'd been finding ways to put it out of her mind. "Can't we leave it that I'm happy to see you?"

Nikki folded her arms over her chest and tilted her head. "Does this have something to do with the fire? It looks as if the damage is completely repaired."

"Mm-hmm." She turned her back on her sister and busied herself taking off the mittens that matched her hat. "It only took a few days." The few days that Nikki and Jay had been in San Francisco doing whatever engaged, in-love couples did in a beautiful city. Glancing at the mirror again, she tugged at the hem of her skirt.

"Great outfit, too," Nikki remarked.

Cassandra took a longer look at the reflection in the mirror. "Skirt's too short." She'd made it herself on the sewing machine set up in the back room, out of a remnant of thin-waled, camel-colored corduroy. The only thing that saved it from indecency was that she was wearing patterned tights beneath it. The cream color of her plain sweater matched the tights and she wore pale-pink suede boots on her feet. She plucked at the flat knit of the top. "Do you know how to make jewelry?"

"I can make omelettes. I'm good at decorating cakes. No jewelry."

"Maybe I'll bring someone into the shop to give lessons. Or do you think Juliet might want to learn—"

"Our sister will be more into her new husband than engaging in a new hobby, is what I think," Nikki said. Her bicolored eyes narrowed. "Wait a minute. How many FOs have you racked up since I left Malibu?"

FOs or "Finished Objects" usually afforded the knitter bragging rights. But her sister had suspicion, not admiration in her gaze. "You know I lose count of how many projects I have in progress," Cassandra said, hurrying away from the mirror and bustling to the back room where she could leave her hat and mittens and bring out the refreshments. Nikki didn't follow, probably because at that moment the bells on the front door rang out, signaling another knitter's arrival.

Not just any knitter, Cassandra noted as she returned to the main part of the shop. "Juliet!" Looking tan and rested, the oldest of the three sisters stood by the cash register, her husband, Noah, and Nikki's Jay nearby.

"Jay picked us up from the airport but I wanted to stop by the shop before we went home," Juliet said, pulling Cassandra close. A delicious mix of coconut oil and expensive perfume clung to her. "How have you been?"

"Never better!" Cassandra said, and turned to buss her brother-in-law, Noah, on the cheek and then give a second smack to Jay.

Nikki sent a pointed look at Juliet. "Ask her about the fire. Ask her about why she's completed an entirely new wardrobe, just in the past couple of days."

"Not an entirely new wardrobe—"

"What fire?" Noah cut in.

Cassandra tried ignoring the question. "—but I'm done with the matching bride and bridesmaids shrugs for your wedding, Nik."

"Oh, Froot Loop, I'm not that easy," Nikki said, then darted a look at her fiancé. "And no comment from the peanut gallery, please."

He grinned and looped an arm around her to drag her back against his chest. "Cookie. I'm nuts for you."

Rolling her eyes, she groaned. "Jay . . ."

"What fire?" Noah asked again, his voice sharper.

Cassandra sighed. "We think some kids were fooling around and started a small blaze in my side storeroom," she said. "The authorities haven't found the culprit or culprits, but the shop is as good as new."

Noah turned to Jay. "What do you know about this?"

The other man shook his head. "Not much. We left for San Francisco the day after it happened."

Cassandra recognized her brother-in-law's tension and guessed its source. "It was after-hours, Noah. Even if you hadn't been on your honeymoon, Juliet wouldn't have been working at the shop. She would have been safe at home—"

"I'm worried about you, too, Cassandra," he put in.

The steel in his voice warmed her heart, and she smiled at him. "I know. Thanks for that."

"So where's Gabe in all this?" Noah asked.

Nikki frowned. "If he's laid out on another barroom floor somewhere, so help me God, Cassandra, I'm going to—"

"Cookie," Jay admonished, tugging on the ends of her hair.

"No, no. He's not in a bar," Cassandra said quickly. "At least, not that I know of . . ." She went clammy, wondering if he just might not be on another of his benders, and that this time he'd made sure she wasn't called in as cleanup crew. Three days had passed since that morning when he'd brought over the contractor to do the necessary repair work on the shop.

She hadn't seen him since and she'd assumed he'd been avoiding her because, well, he went through periods when he avoided *everyone*. Rather than tracking him down, she'd let it be, because it made it easier on her not to think about him, not to think about him in her bed and in her body, when she didn't have to look at his unruly hair and his unsmiling face. Those only served to remind her that he'd smiled at her when they'd been together that night, that he'd laughed and spoken to her in a soft, deep, sexy voice. *You wait this long, you get the edge that experience brings.*

"Cassandra. Froot Loop." Nikki was snapping her fingers in front of her face. "Hello in there."

She started, aware that the other four were staring at her, their expressions puzzled. "Are you all right?" Juliet asked.

"Sure. I'm great." But it was a lie, Cassandra realized, as she busied herself getting ready for the knitters soon to arrive. Until now, until she was breathing in all the fragrant love-in-the-air that surrounded the two couples, she hadn't realized how third wheel she felt around them.

It was probably because Juliet and Noah were married now. It would only get worse once Nikki and Jay were wed.

She'd feel yet more alone.

It would be petty and mean-spirited and more than a little selfish of her if she didn't want her sisters to be happy—and happily coupled-up. But gaining siblings and then brothers-in-law hadn't rounded out her life as she'd hoped—it only seemed to push her further out of the circle.

With an inner sigh and a pasted-on smile, she waved Noah and Jay off and watched her sisters settle side by side on one of the couches, speaking all the while in a bridal shorthand that sounded like a foreign language she hadn't studied. To distract herself, she inspected the lists sitting beside the cash register counter.

She hadn't forgotten about that project she'd come up

with when talking to her mother. RSVPs were rolling in. A menu had been planned. It might not be a marriage, it might not be a man, but she could focus on her birthday party.

In a small side drawer, she found the one invitation she'd dithered about mailing. Sneaking a look at her sisters, she shoved the drawer shut, wondering if she really could make the event all that she'd promised herself.

Marlys couldn't say exactly what brought her back to Malibu & Ewe. She kept finding herself here lately. Once, on the evening of the posthumous launch of her famous father's autobiography, a second time when she'd found the cardboard burning, and then again when she'd encountered Gabe in the parking lot and then chickened out before walking through the door.

It was probably that chickening out that drew her back to the beachside shop. Marlys Weston didn't chicken out. Add to that the cavernous family house where she was living. The place was too large for one person and a dog. Blackie had a big personality, but even he couldn't fill all the corners and the gloomy quiet.

Within the echoing rooms, she'd had too much time to think about Dean Long. Tall, dark, her silver-eyed nemesis who had dared her to gather some ice cream and some girl friends and decide what she wanted to do about him. About them.

Of course, that had already been decided the November before, but she'd begun to think that including some women in her life wasn't a bad idea. Men had always failed her. If she could dress women, surely she could befriend women, too?

And maybe friendship could do something about those

holes caused by her father's death that had created in her this unprecedented need for a dark-haired, silver-eyed man who'd left her sleepless and yearning for too many nights running.

The bells on the door of the shop rang out as she pushed it open. Head down, she marched inside, not bothering to look around before making her way to the couches she could see in her direct line of sight. She took a seat on the first open cushion.

"Oh! It's you," a woman's voice said. "Marlys, right? And I'm Ellen."

Marlys turned, recognizing the woman beside her—Ellen—was none other than one of her boutique customers, the very woman with whom she'd discussed Ben & Jerry and low-rise jeans not long ago. She took it as a good omen, and tried on a smile, one she hoped was big enough to send amiable vibes as far as the other dozen or so knitters gathered in the center of the shop. "Hello. Small world, and all that."

"I've just taken up knitting and my mother-in-law suggested I come here," Ellen offered. "I don't dare say no to my mother-in-law. You?"

"Me?" Marlys said. "I—"

"Have absolutely no good reason to be in Malibu & Ewe," an angry voice finished for her.

Oh, shit. The mean one.

Marlys looked up, and sure enough, it was Nikki Carmichael, one of her evil stepmother's wicked half-sisters. Her arms folded over her chest, the other woman was glaring down at Marlys with fire in her bicolored eyes.

"Nik . . ." the woman at her elbow admonished. Long, wavy hair, big blue eyes, and big boobs, this one was Cassandra Riley, proving she wasn't so wicked after all as she tried pulling her sister away from the couches and the interested onlookers. "Simmer down."

"What do you want?" Nikki demanded of Marlys, shaking off her sister's hand.

"To . . ." *Find something to take my mind off Dean, my father's death, the fact that I still feel dirty for taking Pharmaceutical Phil to bed.* She cleared her throat. ". . . knit, of course."

"Juliet wouldn't—" Nikki started.

"Juliet doesn't have Marlys on her mind right now," Cassandra said, pushing her sister away. "You just missed her, as a matter of fact. She and Noah returned from their honeymoon today, so she cut out from Knitters' Night early."

Nikki was muttering under her breath, but her older sister ignored her to perch on the arm of the sofa next to Marlys. "She told me about the champagne and fruit basket you had delivered."

"I hope they had someone taste test the stuff first," Nikki murmured, loud enough for everyone to hear.

Marlys felt her lips twitch. Under other circumstances, she thought she and the mean one might have a good time together. "I hope they enjoyed themselves." She was almost sincere about it—well, she *was* sincere about it. Part of her didn't wish Juliet and Noah anything but happiness. Then there was the bitter, grieving daughter who still resented that her father had left her and ultimately loved someone else.

"She brought us pictures," Cassandra said, scooping a stack of glossy photographs from the low table between the couches. "Take a look."

It gave Marlys a few minutes to sit amongst the other women and get acclimated. After a short, stilted silence, their chatter rose around her. It was familiar. Shoppers came in pairs or trios to the boutique, so she was accustomed to the rhythm of women's conversation, the way it hopscotched from dinner plans, to a business dinner gone awry, to exactly what could Jennifer Aniston possibly eat for dinner to stay so skinny.

But around Malibu & Ewe more than one conversation bubbled, broke off, then restarted as knitters worked on their pieces, some without apparent concentration, others with their eyes glued to their needles. Marlys also learned about bad projects, bad parents, and bad romances in the short minutes it took her to sift through Juliet and Noah's pictures while pretending a tepid interest in them.

Beach. Sunset. Beautiful Juliet, in a hot pink bikini. Noah, tanned and laughing, as he ran for the surf, his bride in his arms. The blond woman wrapped in a green sarong and wearing a plumeria lei. The handsome man lying in bed, sheets puddled at his waist, desire stamped on his face as he beckoned the photographer to join him.

Damn! She was supposed to be appreciating the company of women, but now she was thinking of men and sex—oh, who was she kidding? She was thinking of one man, of Dean, who was a living, breathing beckoning finger, one that compelled her to forget that she'd never been able to depend upon the male species.

With a hurried movement, she shuffled the stack, hoping for a hula dancer or an innocuous tropical dawn. Instead, she found a snapshot of another tall, dark man. The one she was desperate to put from her mind.

Maybe she made some sound, because Ellen crowded closer, looking over her shoulder as her knitting fell to her lap. "It's that sexy guy who was in your shop the last time I was there, isn't it?"

It had to have been a picture taken before Juliet and Noah's honeymoon. It showed Dean, straddling his motorcycle, wearing that rash, reckless grin that had both tempted and terrified her. He'd looked exactly like that last November, strong and confident, and yet he'd gone off with all that bravado and still been wounded.

And yet . . .

"I'm in love with him," she whispered to Ellen. It felt good to say it out loud, not because she wanted to be in love, but if she no longer wasted energy trying to deny it, then she could start working on what it took to destroy the feeling. "I have been for a while."

"He seemed very interested in you," the other woman replied.

"That's what makes it worse," Marlys explained. "If only he didn't have any interest in me at all. But we can't be together. That possibility was lost months ago. I can't pretend that November didn't happen and I can't explain it to him either."

"November?" Ellen asked. "What happened in November?"

Marlys opened her mouth, then closed it on the sudden realization. The question was a trap. She saw it that way, anyhow, because the soft question and the concerned voice were like yawning metal jaws and the need to unburden herself was the piece of tasty cheese set squarely in the middle of the dangerous contraption.

Women really were the wilier sex.

And knowing that, and even knowing that the confession couldn't absolve her of guilt, she still opened her mouth again. "I . . ." She experienced the whole event in a flashback of sensory memory. The brush of Phil's lips as she turned her head and he missed her mouth to graze her jaw. The gentle touch of his hands as he undressed her, the deep groans he made as she undressed him. He'd once been her lover and at the onset it hadn't seemed like such a huge sin to take him to her bed again, but it *had* been a sin.

Not his sin, though. She'd never blamed Phil for accepting her offer of a casual roll in the sack.

But the act had defiled her in ways that had nothing to do with her body. It should have been nothing!

But it had been a dishonor of her heart.

A sin of the soul she'd been denying she owned.

"Here," Ellen said, pressing a tissue into her hand. Marlys stared at it, then lifted her other fingers to her face, only to realize she was crying. Waste of time, she thought, dashing at them with the tissue. They wouldn't wash her clean.

"Now," Ellen said, patting her thigh. "Why don't you tell us all about it."

Us? Marlys's stomach twisted, and she looked around the knitters' circle. Sure enough, the conversation had died down and though most were focusing their gazes on their yarn and needles, they were clearly really focused on her. "Where's the ice cream?" she murmured to herself in a wry voice.

Across the room, Cassandra jumped into the awkward silence. "Does anyone want to see the shrugs I made for Nikki's bridal party?" Quickly, several knitters piped up in emphatic agreement.

Grateful for the diversion, Marlys followed the shop owner with her gaze. As the woman headed toward the back and turned a corner, there came a muffled thump and then a smothered curse. Something that had been propped against the far wall—cardboard from a shipment maybe?—

toppled, then slid along the hardwood floor toward the center of the room.

Nikki came from behind the register to pick up the large piece. "You knocked over the general, Froot Loop," she called out.

Marlys rose from the couch as the other woman lifted the cardboard and she stared into the stern visage of her father, General Wayne Weston. Swallowing hard, she remembered that the nine-foot-tall cutout had been front and center at the book party held at Malibu & Ewe the previous fall.

As she walked toward it, she found herself pressing her hand against the silver tear she wore beneath her clothes. Suddenly, the shop walls felt too close, the ceiling too low, her chest too tight for the feelings brought on by seeing her father's figure.

It's just a piece of cardboard, she told herself.

Just like the pendant she was clutching at her throat was just an unshed tear.

Four feet from the cutout, she came to a stop. She was still standing there, staring, when Cassandra returned to the knitting circle, soft confections of ivory folded over her arm. She glanced at Nikki, who lifted a shoulder. Marlys couldn't explain her fascination either.

"I should go," she said, forcing her feet to back away. She'd accomplished enough for one night, with or without a pint or two of Ben & Jerry's.

Cassandra shot another look at Nikki. "Do you . . . do you want to take the general with you?"

She recoiled from the thought. Hadn't he always left her behind?

But a few minutes later she was on her way back to the house in Pacific Palisades, the convertible top of the Miata down so that the cardboard could be stuffed into the passenger seat beside her. Good God. Nothing ever did go her way, did it?

The woman who'd gone out looking for the comfort of female friendship was instead returning home with the embodiment of the man who had failed her.

Nikki stood next to Cassandra as they watched the Miata turn onto the Pacific Coast Highway. "That's one chilly chick," she said.

"Coming from Miss Warm and Fuzzy," Cassandra replied.

"But you know I'm a sap when it comes to romance these days." Nikki sighed. "You realize she got to me with that whole 'I'm in love with him,' thing."

Cassandra smiled at her sister. "You *are* warm and fuzzy."

"Don't tell anyone," Nikki replied, slinging an arm around her. "It'll be our secret."

Cassandra had another of her very own. Seeing Marlys drive away with the cardboard general had helped her make an important decision. She cast a look in the direction of that yet-unsent birthday party invitation and made a promise to herself. If Marlys could face her father, then so could Cassandra.

Thirteen

The family—that dear octopus from whose tentacles we never quite escape, nor, in our inmost hearts, ever quite wish to.

—DODIE SMITH

Gabe poured himself another cup of inky coffee and refused to look across the parking lot at what was happening at Malibu & Ewe. His fish market/eatery was shutting down for the night and the small, end-of-day staff didn't need him to oversee their efforts, but without groceries in his house and without any dinner invitations from Cassandra apparently forthcoming, he'd surrendered to his need for sustenance and dropped by for the last of the fish tacos and the dregs of the coffeepot.

The combination would probably keep him up to all hours, but what else was new? The last uninterrupted sleep he remembered was the night in his neighbor's bed. When morning arrived, he'd awoken to discover she'd already left the house. He couldn't exactly accuse her of avoiding him—by the time he'd roused himself it was past the hour that she opened the doors to her shop—but she'd left behind the air of someone who wanted to depersonalize their encounter.

In the bathroom, he'd found fresh towels—but no sign of the ones she'd used after her shower. The kitchen counter held the makings for a pot of coffee, but whatever breakfast she'd consumed had already been put away. She'd signed her name at the end of the brief note she'd left him—*See you!*— as if he wouldn't recognize her distinctive, arty handwriting. But the note had been devoid of any greeting, not even a simple "Gabe."

Do I have to write your name in pink gel pen?

Sue him, but it would have been a nice touch.

So, he'd followed her lead and been all business when he'd later brought over the contractor to repair the damage on her building. He'd dealt with the insurance company and followed up with the authorities from the distance of his home office.

She had thanked him while he was at her shop, but she hadn't followed it up with an offer to fix him a garbanzo salad and green tea. It surprised him, how accustomed he was to being disgusted by the food she tried to guilt him into ingesting.

He should be grateful for the respite.

He *was* grateful for the respite.

But he was annoyed, too, because now he was feeling a tad awkward about going over to her shop and collecting her for their usually joint attendance at this month's Malibu City Council meeting. She'd tricked him into the gig some time back. He'd missed another Chamber of Commerce shindig and she'd returned from it with the news that he had somehow, in absentia, "volunteered" to be the commerce's eyes and ears at the city government meeting. In that same manner she'd committed him to the parking committee a few months before. But he'd smartened up the second time around, and three days later informed her smugly that he'd volunteered her right back into the co-attendee position.

They were supposed to be at that meeting in twenty minutes.

This time he did sneak a peek across the parking lot. The lights were on in the shop, illuminating it in the surrounding darkness like a television set, which made it very easy to spy her eagerly embracing some other man.

They were going to be late if he didn't break that up, Gabe told himself, so it was purely a business decision that had him jogging across the asphalt toward Malibu & Ewe. It was their habit that he would drive and she'd ride shotgun, because he claimed to dislike the smell of her veggie car. Though it was still in the shop after its close encounter with that hillside boulder, and she was behind the wheel of a rental these days, he'd assumed that he'd be driving her tonight.

Of course, he'd also assumed that his once-virginal neighbor wouldn't just hop from her first experience into a second with some stranger. The man who she was hugging moved out of her arms and Gabe got a better look through the shop windows.

Christ, this was no stranger to Cassandra. This was her teen idol, the guy she e-mailed at will, that rock musician with an extremely familiar image of a tattooed woman pole dancing along his skinny arm.

Which reminded him, what the hell was Carver Shields doing with Gabe's naked, nearly virginal neighbor needled into his flesh?

Maybe he needed something else punched into his skin, Gabe thought, his hands fisting. Because Carver had to get the message that a globe-trotting, groupie-showering, Oomfaa-flirting rocker boy wasn't the right kind of man for the Froot Loop.

Friendly, generous, and beyond loyal, Cassandra needed in her life someone equally family-oriented, equally selfless, equally steadfast.

Someone who certainly wasn't like Gabe, he realized, his hand frozen on the front door.

And who wasn't Carver either, he reminded himself, and plunged into the shop.

Four heads whipped his way. He'd completely overlooked the two others in the shop. Two other men, who were, he realized as they rose off the couch, Cassandra's sperm donor's sons. Adopted sons, she'd told him. The last time he'd seen them he'd been lying in wait—and, uh, actually lying—outside the medical building in Beverly Hills. There was the doctor, Patrick Tucker, all buttoned up and intense looking, as well as the laid-back, younger man who sent Gabe an easy smile.

"What are you doing here?" Cassandra asked Gabe, her expression puzzled.

For a moment he couldn't talk. He hadn't been close to her in days and now here she was, looking like a soft, sweet dream in a pale blue blouse, a fuzzy scarf around her throat. Her black skirt was short enough to reveal fifteen miles of Cassandra's long legs covered in matching blue-patterned tights. A knitted band the color of her scarf held back her hair so he could see every inch of the smooth, flushed skin of her face.

In that getup she was a potent mix of girlish sexiness and womanly allure, which made his palms itch to explore every texture.

"What are you doing here?" she repeated.

He cleared his throat. "Uh," he murmured, sidling close to her, "because though I'm not your husband I once played him in a plastic surgeon's parking lot?"

She gave a little laugh. "I've already explained about that." Then she turned toward the Tucker brothers. "Patrick, Reed. This is my landlord and neighbor, Gabe Kincaid."

He stepped forward to shake hands. "Landlord and neighbor, among other things," he heard himself say.

"Yeah?" Carver asked, looking interested. "What other things?"

"What are you doing here?" Gabe shot back, instead of answering.

Cassandra patted her prom date's T-shirt sleeve, right over what Gabe suspected was her face and right above what he thought was a replication of her incredible breasts. Christ, he hated that tattoo.

"I asked Carver over to lend a little, um, support." She gave an apologetic smile to the two brothers. "I confess I was a bit nervous at the thought of meeting my sort-of brothers."

Carver? She asked *Carver* instead of Gabe when she needed manly backup? "You could have called me, Froot Loop," he said, trying to keep his tone mild.

She waved a hand. "You're always so busy."

With what? His black moods and his desire to drown them in alcohol? Ignoring the quick shot of shame, he scowled at her. "I seem to remember a recent request that I carried out to the extreme satisfaction of us both."

Carver's eyebrows rose another fraction, even as Cassandra ignored his comment and addressed herself to Patrick and Reed. "I appreciate you contacting me. I—we—it was never clear whether your family saw the press that came out a few months back."

"We did," Patrick acknowledged. "But with Dad out of the country we didn't feel it was our place to make any"—he seemed to search for the right word—"overtures."

"But the bumper sticker on your car," the other brother offered. "I noticed it that day at the medical building."

Gabe remembered.

CHICKS WITH STICKS
♥ MALIBU & EWE

"It kept niggling at me and then when I happened to come across your birthday party invitation on Dad's desk—his secretary opens all the mail that comes to the office—well, I put it all together. You were reaching out, so I thought I should phone you myself."

"Without consulting me first," the doctor added, with a frown.

"But you were eager enough to come along," his younger brother said. "And I, for one, am happy we did."

Cassandra smiled at him. "Did you know Reed runs a recycling venture, Carver? A project after my own heart."

"We're a family dedicated to good works," Reed added, nodding at the display behind Cassandra's cash register. "I see that you provide handknit blankets to homeless shelters and to the Red Cross."

She beamed again. Whether it was because the young man had noted her charity work or grouped them together as a "family" Gabe didn't know—but he didn't like it regardless.

Bristling, he stepped closer to Cassandra. "Another of your good works requires your attention now, Froot Loop," he said. "If we don't leave we'll be late to the council meeting."

She made a face. "Oh—"

"It's a commitment we made," he reminded her.

"Gabe . . ."

"We can't stay in any case, Cassandra," the doctor said. "I have late rounds and I made my brother promise that we wouldn't take up too much of your time."

"I understand." Though she was clearly a little disappointed.

"But we wanted to see you for ourselves and discover just how serious you are about meeting Dad," the younger man said.

"Oh, I'm serious," Cassandra said. She threw Gabe a guilty glance and he knew she was thinking about Nikki and Juliet and how they hadn't settled the issue between them. "And, um . . ."

He didn't think it wise for her to pledge further promises, so Gabe marched toward Malibu & Ewe's front door. "Get your purse and keys, Cassandra," he said. "I'll see your guests out."

The Tucker brothers took the hint. Patrick gave her hand a brief shake before departing. Reed kissed her on the cheek. Both Gabe and Carver stood at the door, watching the pair walk toward a dark Mercedes.

"So what's this I hear about a fire?" Carver asked, his gaze still locked on the sedan.

Gabe settled his arms over his chest and kept his own gaze off the X-rated tattoo the other man wore. "Some kids' prank, I guess."

"I guess." He folded his hands under his elbows to mimic Gabe's pose. "And then she says her car went nose first into a falling rock?"

Shutting down the instant replay in his head, Gabe nodded. "Yeah. They say they can fix it."

Carver groaned. "I was hoping she might start driving something better than that piece-of-shit veggie-mobile."

Gabe could smile, since he'd wished the same thing himself a number of times. "It isn't all that bad. It brings in a profit for me, as a matter of fact. Whoever she passes gets hungry and my place is an easy on-off from the highway."

The jingling of keys had them both turning back toward the shop. Cassandra bustled from the rear, her head down, her hand digging through her purse. She glanced up, her eyes meeting Gabe's. The connection between them snapped tight. It was all there in the shared look: that night in each other's arms, the trust it took for her to allow him into her body, the way he'd reveled in her mouth, her skin, her heat. But there was more, Gabe thought, rolling his shoulders to ease their sudden tension. There was the undeniable knowledge that they both wanted that intimacy again. That it was inevitable that they'd experience it once more. *Oh, yeah.*

Carver cursed. The look he shot Gabe felt like a punch to the solar plexus. "You'd better take damn good care of her."

"Count on it," he promised, walking toward the woman who was staring at him in a way that made his skin tighten over his bones. *I'll make it my business to do so.*

Cassandra shook the raindrops out of her hair as she reached the shelter of the City Hall building. It had started to rain as Gabe drove there from Malibu & Ewe and they'd dashed from the car to the door rather than bothering with unearthing an umbrella that Gabe said "might be somewhere around."

She'd welcomed the brief dousing to cool her flushed

flesh, a nervous leftover from the encounter with her father's sons.

Right. It had nothing to do with that searing look she'd shared with Gabe before they'd left the shop. She ran a finger under the short, knitted angora scarf she had tucked into the collar of her shirt, trying to give herself a little extra room to breathe. This wasn't supposed to happen again.

Gabe touched her elbow. She jolted with a gasp, flushing deeper as he raised his eyebrows at her overblown reaction. "The meeting's already started. We'd better get inside, unless you want to bag the idea and . . . ?"

It was the . . . *and?* that had her hurrying for the council chambers. With Gabe on her heels, she slipped into one of the seats in the last row and felt him settle beside her. She watched his long legs bend in the small space provided and then his knee casually brushed hers. Settled there.

Staring at the tiny point of contact, she tried slowing her overjoyed pulse that seemed in such a rush to deliver the news to every corner of her body: *He's touching me! He's touching me again!*

Her heartbeat sounded so loud in her ears that she took a surreptitious look around to determine if any of the other meeting attendees had noticed. But they were all grouped in the first few rows of seats, their attention focused on the council members and city department heads arranged in a horseshoe at the front of the room.

There was a call for the Pledge of Allegiance, and she obediently rose to her feet, obediently recited the words, obediently resumed her place in her seat. She gritted her teeth so she wouldn't jump out of her skin when Gabe resettled beside her and made contact again. This time his calf slid against hers and stayed there.

She wished she was wearing thick denim instead of the pale ribbed tights that matched her chiffon blouse. Going for nonchalance, she stared at the front of the room while edging her right leg away from his left one.

He bumped his shoulder against hers, leaning close to whisper in her ear. "Which one of us should take notes?" His warm breath sent chill bumps down her neck.

"Me." Happy to have something to focus on, she delved into her purse to bring out a small notebook and pen. Setting them in her lap, she gave her attention to the action up front.

Minutes passed, and all that she registered was the still-loud sound of her heart banging against her chest and the close proximity of Gabe's leg. She didn't dare look at his face, but she could feel the warmth of his shoulder just a breath away from hers.

He brushed it again. "You're not writing anything down."

She stared dumbly at her blank piece of paper.

"But I don't think the Chamber of Commerce cares that the Lin family has agreed to reduce their proposed roof-line height to below eighteen feet to preserve their neighbor's view," he added.

A few more minutes passed and his breath rushed across her ear again. "Aaah. They had to give up the tennis court they wanted, too."

She had no idea what he was talking about. The meeting's activity didn't penetrate the haze in her head. Every time she took a breath she took in Gabe's clean scent, warmed by his skin, and it made her stomach tighten and her palms tingle.

The mayor called for a brief recess and she was glad to move from her seat into the spacious foyer. There was cooler air there and she gulped it in, still so distracted that it took her a minute to realize Gabe had backed her into a shadowy corner. He braced his forearm on the wall over her head, caging her body.

Clutching her purse to her chest, she lifted her gaze to his. His dark eyes seemed to smolder. He used his free hand to push a stray lock of hair off her forehead, leaving sparks in its wake. She trembled, holding out against the urge to touch him back.

He gave her a little smile, as if he saw her struggle. "It doesn't have to be like this," he murmured. "We could do something about it."

Where would that get her, though? She frowned up at him, and he laughed a little, tapping on her bottom lip. "No pouting."

"I'm not pouting," she said, still wearing her frown—okay, pout. "I just don't understand why this 'it' exists. We did fine for two years without any 'it' getting in the way, didn't we? We traded insults, not kisses."

"It was one instead of the other, Cassandra, surely you know that now."

She sighed. "Juliet once said Noah threatened to rent us a hotel room."

Gabe smiled. "Would that have been so bad? Because when we finally got to a bed, it seemed to go okay."

"We wouldn't be here if it hadn't gone more than okay, and surely *you* know that," she grumbled.

"So . . . ?"

She wasn't finished complaining and she glared at him. "Still, I don't get it. I was doing just fine, Gabe, and now I can't sleep, I can't think, I can't breathe."

His mouth turned up in another small smile. "What's your favorite thing to eat, Froot Loop? And if you say something like frogurt or Tofutti, I'll have to spank you in front of all these nice people."

"Still with the insults," she said, her voice surly. "For your information, my favorite thing to eat is fettuccine Alfredo."

"So, having once tasted that, could you shrug off the chance to taste it again?"

Cassandra understood his point, but there was something else to consider. "What will happen afterward?"

"Whatever you want," he said promptly. "It's all whatever, however you want."

Such a lie. Because Gabe couldn't offer all she wanted—he had his limits. If she was willing to take what he now could give her, it would eventually end. Not well. She knew that, just like her mythical namesake had had the power to foresee the future yet suffered the curse of never being able to forestall it.

But here she was, almost thirty years old and she hadn't had a single love affair. She'd only had a single night in this man's arms and suddenly that wasn't enough, no matter what the future price to pay.

Biology, chemistry, whatever impulse was driving them together seemed impossible, at this moment, to duck, to distract, to deny.

Still holding her purse like a shield, she met his gaze.

"I want to taste you again, Cassandra," he whispered. "I want to touch you with my mouth and make you wet with my tongue and then take all that you have for me in great, greedy gulps."

Her skin flamed. Her head spun. In her dizziness, she clutched his shirtfront in her fist. His heart beat against her curled fingers. Strong but unsteady. The evidence that he was affected by her was almost as arousing as his words themselves.

"Cassandra . . ."

She stared at his mouth as he formed the syllables of her name. *I want to taste you again.*

"You're Satan," she whispered.

"Then let's go home, baby, so I can make you burn."

It was his wicked smile that melted any final vestiges of reluctance. No, that put blame on him, when it was her choice, not his fault, that had him leading the way outside into the misting rain. She slipped her hand into his and followed the gleam of his satisfied smile into the darkness.

The drive home seemed endless. Once inside the confines of his car, he flipped on the heat, though there wasn't any chill as far as she could tell. And when he shot a glance at her and then spoke in a low, husky voice, there was nothing cool about the insides of the car at all.

"That ladylike blue has been making me nuts all night, Cassandra. And you may think covering up your yards of leg with those tights is modest, but I spent that entire damn meeting watching the way your skirt inched up your thighs whenever you moved."

"Huh." It was a whimper, a half-choked expression of surprise. She hadn't noticed him staring at her legs.

"I got harder with each quarter inch."

"*Oh.*"

"Why don't you take the tights off?" he asked, his voice mild.

Her head jerked toward him. "W-what?"

"Take them off for me."

Whoa. She swallowed. "In the car?"

"No one can see." He paused. "But me. And I won't look. I just want to touch, Cassandra. I just want to touch your bare skin. I need to touch your bare skin."

Eeek. Her throat shut down. Her heart slammed hard

against her breastbone. Skin prickling, she wondered if she shouldn't have had a few more experiences before now, because then she'd have a better chance at dealing with Gabe's blatant sexuality.

What if she was too old or prudish or self-conscious to be what he wanted?

"C'mon, Cassandra," he said, one of his fingernails rasping against the ribbed texture covering her thigh. "Lift up and take the tights off."

Excitement and nervousness twined in her belly. Slowly, she rose a little on her seat, the belt across her hips placing an arousing pressure against her pelvis. She held her breath and tucked her hand underneath her straight skirt to curl her fingertips around the waistband of the tights. As she pulled them down, the fabric peeling away from her skin felt like a caress.

Gabe's caress.

Her breaths were coming fast and not one provided enough oxygen. She felt dizzy again as she toed off her shoes and stripped the hosiery away. Her newly naked skin felt vulnerable—

Gabe stroked her thigh, pushing her short skirt up toward her hips.

—and sexy.

It was better than fettuccine.

He drew gentle fingers up and down her leg, moving from her knee and up as far as her skirt's hem would allow, even then always pushing it up, so that he could tickle the insides of her thighs. Her hot blush didn't stop her from opening her legs and letting him explore as he wanted. He found the edge of her panties, then brushed across the satin that covered her most sensitive area. She gasped, but he didn't linger, moving on and down to touch her other thigh.

Cassandra turned her head to look out the window, because watching his hand on her flesh was making her too needy. Any second now and she'd beg him to pull over, when surely what he wanted was another slow session of lovemaking like they'd experienced that first night.

By the time they arrived at his house she was shaking. Her nipples throbbed, her breasts were swollen, and the place between her legs felt soft and achy. He touched the small of her back as he ushered her to the front door and the brief contact thrilled up her spine and down the backs of both bare legs.

In his bedroom, he didn't turn on the light, but instead flipped on the gas in the tiled fireplace that occupied the wall opposite the big bed. Then he sat on the edge of the mattress and drew her to stand in front of him. She'd already kicked off her shoes, her tights lay abandoned in his car, so all he had to do was unbutton here, unzip there, and soon she was standing in front of him, completely nude. She tried to hide her quivering as he pulled back the covers and urged her between the sheets.

Her breasts were heavy. She was so wet between her thighs that surely he could see the gleam of moisture in the firelight as he crawled, himself now naked, between her legs and gazed on her there. She swallowed, more aroused by the intent look in his eyes than she thought she could be if he touched her.

His gaze jumped to hers. "Your cats. Moosewood, Breathe, and Ed. Do they need to be fed tonight?"

Oh, God. Not only was the man sexy, he was thoughtful, too. "No," she answered, her voice husky. "I took a break in the late afternoon and took care of them."

Smiling, he bent his head. "Oh, good, then I can take care of *this* pussy."

She started. He hadn't just said that. He *had* just said that! Because he was laughing and pressing open her thighs with the palms of his big hands and then . . . and then . . . and then she was gone, reeling, rocketing, streaking skyward from the first lap of his silky tongue.

Coming back to herself, she was mortified to find him staring at her face, his expression bemused. "I . . . I messed that up," she said, embarrassed by how eager and easy she'd been. It was his fault—all that maddening foreplay in the car. "I'm sorry."

"Froot Loop," he admonished. "Shh. I'm thanking you, sweetheart." He leaned down to place a kiss on her still-throbbing center. "Because you're always giving me second chances."

He did so well with them, too, she thought, her head digging into the pillow as her neck arched. His second chance was her pleasure, the kind of pleasure that had her squirming, twisting, begging. He made her come again, and then he rose up and slid into her—no pain on entry this time— but just a delicious, satisfying fullness as he took her mouth and she tasted herself on Gabe's lips and tongue.

A taste worth the future she'd foreseen.

Afterward, they turned together and he drew up the covers. His body was curved around her back. He slid a hand down her hip, and then insinuated it between her thighs, petting her there in languid strokes. She wiggled a little and he smiled against her shoulder.

"Shh," he said. "Go to sleep."

She was drifting off, only half-aware when she felt one of his long fingers slide into the still-damp entrance of her body. It could have been sexual, but now it just felt like the connection they both needed.

"You won't leave my bed," he murmured.

She couldn't help responding with a whispered promise she knew she was going to regret someday. "I'm not going anywhere."

Fourteen

Where does family start? It starts with a young man falling in love with a girl—no superior alternative has yet been found.

—WINSTON CHURCHILL

Marlys had a good reason for calling Dean. "I require the transporting of a heavy object," she said, leaving off the traditional "hello" and "how are you."

When he tried that tack himself, she refused to respond. The first was a waste of time; the second was obvious. She would only dial his number if she was in desperate straits. "I require the transporting of a heavy object," she repeated.

"Will it fit on the back of my Harley?"

Oh, crap. She hadn't thought about that. She'd been so overwhelmed by that big-and-getting-bigger thing in her living room that she was ready to put a FOR SALE sign on the Palisades house and leave the two-ton object behind.

"I thought men always had access to utility vehicles." At one time, she'd considered it the only good thing about them.

"Maybe your friend Phil—"

"No!" Her free hand immediately rubbed at her arms

and legs. Poor Phil. He'd been relegated to spider status—in the way that once an arachnid was mentioned, a person would sense them crawling across their skin. And though it wasn't his fault, in her mind his name was now synonymous with "brown recluse" and "tarantula."

She scrubbed her skin again. "I'll . . . I'll find someone else to help me."

"I didn't say I couldn't help, Marlys." His voice was quiet. "Is that what you're asking me for?"

"Yes." She should have taken it back. She should have at least hesitated, but she was at risk of being flattened under the weight of what was growing in her living room. Even Blackie was affected. He had taken to slinking low as he moved about the house, always looking over his shoulder.

"I'll be right there," Dean said.

She and Blackie were waiting on the front porch steps. They both tried appearing nonchalant, lolling on the red bricks in the warm winter sunshine, but when Dean pulled up in a truck—she recognized it as Noah's—Marlys and her dog both shot to their feet.

Blackie rushed to the long-legged man and tried scaling his knees so he could plant a doggie kiss on the soldier's face. Marlys couldn't object, since she had approximately the same desire the moment his silver eyes met hers.

"Sit," he said.

As usual, like Blackie, she wanted to succumb to the command in his voice, but she kept her place as he strode over to her. "I've missed you," he said, and now her knees did bend, softened by the low note in his voice.

He kept her upright by cupping her face between his big hands and kissing her.

Heat flashed over her skin and her stomach turned inside

out. She clutched at him, sagging again, affected by the melting kiss and the way the weight of the object in her living room seemed to rest upon her shoulders. The weakness galvanized her, giving her the nerve-ridden ability to push off his chest and sway on her own two feet.

He was here so she could find a way to shore herself up, not strip herself down.

Dean rubbed his thumb over her lips. They burned, so she yanked her head away and looked over her shoulder at the front door. "It's in there."

With a puzzled glance at her, he headed up the front steps. "It's not a rat, is it? I charge extra for rodent extermination."

"It's dead," she whispered at his back. But it seemed alive enough to her as she moved about the house. It had taken on this living weight that she needed to be rid of in order to stop feeling so much about it. Stop feeling so much about the man it represented.

She plain wanted to stop all these damn feelings!

At the threshold of the open doorway, she lingered, her gaze on the wide vee of Dean's shoulders and the heavy muscles of his back. If only she were that strong. He was staring at the . . . the thing. The albatross that stood in the corner of the living room but also seemed permanently tied around her neck.

The cutout of her father had been sitting in that spot for days. She didn't give it ghost status—she didn't believe in those and she didn't think her father would choose to haunt her anyway. Instead she knew it to be the weighty embodiment of her disappointment, of her fears, of her grief.

She wanted freedom from them. From it.

Her hand crept up to grasp the silver tear that held a trace of her father's ashes. She'd started wearing it around her neck when Dean had left last fall, hoping it could contain all the emotions and weakness she didn't want to feel.

He turned to face her. "What are we going to do with the thing?"

"We're taking it to Malibu Creek State Park," she said.

She gave Dean directions. It was in the Santa Monica Mountains and a popular place for hiking and fishing and picnicking. Movies and television shows had been filmed there. She'd visited it with her father when she was twelve.

It was the first time she'd seen him after her mother had moved them off base. Her dad had been out of the country at the time and she'd counted on him reuniting them as a family when he returned. That day, he'd come early to the rental house where she was living. She'd been a typical preteen, nowhere near awake at seven A.M., but so happy to spend time with her father and so certain he was going to make everything right again that she'd agreed to go along on the hike he suggested.

She'd yawned through the first couple of miles, tramping on a trail that took them through oaks and sycamores and over chaparral-covered slopes. He'd been silent by her side.

They'd stopped at an isolated picnic spot. Sitting on the wooden table, he'd rummaged through the pack he'd had slung over one shoulder. She didn't take the orange juice he offered.

She'd been shocked when he dragged out a can of beer for himself and downed it without taking a breath. Her father never drank during the day. It was still morning!

Then he'd told her that he and her mother were getting a divorce.

She and Dean took a similar path to the one she'd hiked with her father that day. She didn't know if it was the same, and she didn't care. You could get to the site where they'd shot both the *M*A*S*H* movie and TV series. A replica of the iconic signpost was even planted in the dirt, but that wasn't the way Blackie chose. He was with them, and it was he that selected their path, his plume of a tail waving.

They didn't encounter anyone in the parking lot or along that trail, which she figured was Dean's good luck at work. He was the one carting the nine-foot figure of the general, after all.

Up ahead, Blackie came to a picnic site and plopped his butt on the powdery brown silt to wait for them. Marlys eyed the area, her gaze snagging on the fire ring. "This will do," she said.

Dean guessed what she had in mind. He held up the cardboard figure, glanced at the size of the fire ring, then without a word, proceeded to fold the cardboard into a manageable size. She looked the other way, not because she was freaked to see him accordion the image, but because it was so tempting to think that he could do the same with all that had been troubling her since last fall . . . since last year . . . since she was twelve. If she surrendered to Dean's confident hands, her sissy psyche wanted to think, she could be saved.

Hah.

If he knew what she'd done with Phil, Dean would be loathe to touch her at all.

Blackie whined—sometimes she thought he was as good at reading her as Dean—and she petted his head as she reached into the pocket of her jeans for the disposable lighter she'd brought along. When she turned back, the cardboard was stuffed into the fire ring.

Dean stepped back. He didn't offer to take the lighter from her.

She lit as many folded corners as she could reach. As the flames began eating through the layers of paper, she figured she owed Dean some kind of explanation. "He told me he and my mother were getting a divorce in this park." She watched a glowing piece of the board shrivel. "Just that brief statement, and then he said, 'You'll be fine.'"

Though she'd known she couldn't comply with what he'd put to her like an order, she hadn't contradicted her father. She was a soldier's daughter, after all. Instead she'd stood there in silence, less than five feet of stricken girl-going-on-woman and knew what it was to feel impotent and despairing and abandoned. Quite the preparation for the rest of her life.

She'd done okay, though. Sure, she'd always been a bit prickly with other people, but she hadn't felt the lack of any-thing until her father died. Until Dean entered into her life.

Then, emotions had risen from that deep place where she'd always stuffed them, growing bigger and heavier until she found she couldn't breathe. Those feelings were what she was hoping to burn away.

And as the fire consumed the cardboard, making it smaller and smaller and smaller, she began to feel lighter and lighter and lighter. She curled her fingers into the thick fur of Blackie's scruff and blinked away the sting the smoke put in her eyes. Her plan was working!

She looked from the fire to Dean's cool silver gaze, try-ing to put the past into perspective. "Surely he realized that it wasn't going to be easy for me."

He shrugged. "I suppose it was more convenient for him to believe the opposite."

"De Nile," she murmured, "not just a river in Egypt, huh?" Her attention returned to the firepit and the satisfyingly small pile of cinders that the nine feet of hurt and unpleasant memories had become.

Blackie pressed against her leg, and in the well of her belly, something released, a buoyant something that rose to hover in her chest. Her heart. Free?

"Marlys?"

Almost weightless herself, she turned to him, overjoyed to think that perhaps she'd left the past behind her. "Thank you," she said. "You once told me you'd take my tears away and I think that you just did."

"Have a little sympathy for your father if you can," Dean said softly, tucking a strand of hair behind her ear. "I'm sure it's hell to know you've hurt the one you love."

She froze, the general forgotten as her mind reversed, leaping to last November. *I'm sure it's hell to know you've hurt the one you love.* She saw Dean standing at the front door of her house, the anticipation on his face sliding away as Phil trotted down the stairs. Her palms scraped against her upper arms, her hips, her thighs.

Dean's eyes narrowed. "Marlys? What's wrong?"

Without a word, she hurried back on the trail the way they'd come, though certain this new feeling wasn't something she could leave behind at the park. The past just wasn't that easy to get rid of, she realized. Because though she might feel the weight had been lifted off her shoulders, she had the distinct sense that the rest of her would never feel clean.

Back at the house, she burst through the front door and headed for her bathroom. With every quarter mile they'd traveled away from the park, the shame of what she'd done in November tightened like a dirty, second skin. *I'm sure it's hell to know you've hurt the one you love.*

It was ugly, is what it was, and she needed to wash it away if she could.

Naked, she stepped under the scalding spray of her shower. She lifted her face, letting the needles of water bounce off her flesh, then picked up the bath sponge and doused it in gel soap. The scent bloomed in the steamy air, and she breathed gulps of it, hoping to dispel the olfactory memory of Phil's Armani cologne.

She scrubbed at her arms and legs, rubbed the sponge in harsh circles against her throat and over her breasts and between her thighs, her eyes squeezed tight as she tried to send the psychic stain on her skin down the shower's drain.

"Marlys." A hand clamped over hers.

Eyes flying open, she gasped, shocked to find a fully dressed Dean inside the tiled stall. His expression was grim as he used his free hand to adjust the temperature. "You'll be parboiled."

She'd never be clean.

"Get out," she said, yanking her fingers from his grip. Soap bubbles flew from the sponge. One landed on his chin. Stuck there. Marlys backed against the wall and told herself she wouldn't touch it. She wouldn't touch him.

He had no such compunctions. His hand slid behind her neck and she jerked away.

"No! I'm dirty."

He froze. Then his silver eyes narrowed. "Never," he said. "Never."

Without another hesitation, he pulled her into his arms, her naked body against his wet clothes. They scratched her overheated, overabraded skin, and she found herself crying at the tiny hurt. Crying, sobbing, falling apart like she'd never wanted to fall apart, had never allowed herself to fall apart, since she was twelve years old and her father had taken that emotional outlet away.

You'll be fine.

She hadn't been fine, she wasn't fine, she was a basket case who could no longer hold it together. But Dean was doing that for her now, holding her close, holding her so that she wouldn't shatter into a million pieces of emotional glass.

The catharsis lasted long enough for the water to cool. When she was crying *and* shivering, Dean lifted her legs and carried her like a child out of the shower. With one hand he reached for the towel and wrapped it around her. She watched her hair drip on the tile floor as he set her down on the closed toilet seat.

"Shut your eyes—or at least look away," he said, with a little smile. "I've got to get out of these wet clothes before they shrink while I'm inside them." She didn't have the energy to do either. Instead, she huddled under the terry cloth and watched more than six feet of sometimes lean and sometimes bulky muscle emerge from the chrysalis of his saturated clothing.

Another time she might have thought, Wow.

Now she could only reach over and hand him a second towel.

"Don't cry," he said, as he tucked it around his waist. "Don't cry."

Her trembling fingers confirmed that tears continued to run down her cheeks. He took her wet hand and used it to help her up, then led her into her bedroom. With a quick movement he threw the covers back and then inserted her between them, sliding the towel off her nudity at the same time. When she was covered back up, he rubbed the damp towel over her wet hair.

Drained, she drifted off to his touch.

She awoke to his touch, too. A finger traced the outline of her lips. Without thinking, she opened her mouth and touched the pad with her tongue, tasting him.

The hitch in his breath didn't pull her into complete wakefulness. Really, it all felt like a dream, the warm color behind her closed eyelids, the warm masculine figure beside her, the warm idea that maybe this was last fall, that time had not passed and she was in bed with Dean like she'd wanted to be since the first time she'd seen him.

"Angel," he whispered.

He'd called her that then. It only confirmed her muddled thinking that this was real and that maybe the dream was all that came after. That it was perfectly fine for her to turn into him now, that their naked bellies would meet, that her small breasts and tight nipples would poke against the hard, hot wall of his chest, that his erection would poke at that sensitive skin along the inside of her thigh.

Marlys ran her hands through his hair and brought his head down for a kiss. It burned her mouth, burst like liquid fire in her veins, a jolt to her system that didn't shake her into logic—but into longing.

His tongue thrust hard inside her mouth and she moaned as she took him deeply. His hands slid down her back to her behind and he cupped her in his palms, tilting her so that his penis dragged through the curls at the apex of her thighs.

More heat flashed over her skin.

He moved her again, and she parted her legs so that the smooth head of his erection dragged against her clitoris.

She arched into the little kiss of sex-to-sex and they both groaned.

"Do you want me?" he murmured.

"Yes. *Yes*." Of course she wanted him! She'd always wanted him, and in this fuguelike state she couldn't recall why she couldn't have him. "I love you," she said, because there couldn't be a reason not to say that either.

His next kiss was tender, but his hands turned urgent. They slid to her breasts, cupping them and rubbing against their taut centers. She whimpered.

His lips slid down her neck and along her collarbone. "I love you, too," he said, his mouth moving over her heart.

She shivered, trembling at the dual sensations of the reverent echo of his words and the heat of his tongue as it circled a tingling nipple. She squirmed, her legs restless, and he pushed a knee against her sex, letting her ride the rounded base there as he played at her breasts, kissing and tonguing her nipples until she was digging her nails into his hard shoulders.

"Please, Dean. Please."

He shifted, letting a little air into their heated nest of sheets and blankets, so she snuggled down to root against the wall of his chest until she found one tight point. He gave a satisfying groan and she sucked at it harder, flexing her fingers in his skin like a cat. Then she let one hand drift toward his waist.

Ah. He'd moved to grab a condom, she guessed, because his stiff penis was covered and ready to go. She pushed him on his back and climbed on top, kissing his mouth as she guided him toward the wet and throbbing place where she wanted him.

"Take it easy, angel," he said, his hand stroking her hip. "Go slow."

Eager to please him, she followed directions, letting him slide inside her one thick inch at a time. She threw her head back and arched as their bellies once again met. It was a tight fit, a delicious fit, and she rocked against him as her inner muscles became accustomed to his girth and length.

He found her mouth, and held it to his with his palm against the back of her head. Then rocking wasn't good enough anymore and she had to slide, up and down, clenching and relaxing, following the rhythm that he set with his tongue. She was getting closer, and her movements turned frantic as she could feel the same tension infusing Dean's body.

His hips lifted toward hers, and he was no longer the object of her lust but the fuel to her fire. His hand slid between their bodies and as he jerked upward, his fingers tweaked the throbbing bud of her clitoris, sending her into orgasm.

Only as her after-shivers died off did she open her eyes. It was Dean beneath her. Dean in her bed. Dean and no dream. Her gaze jerked to the window, and the sycamore there was budding with spring leaves, not silvery bare as it had been in autumn.

Tears stung her eyes again. Oh, God. What had she done? Bad Marlys, she thought. Bad Marlys strikes again.

A frown placed a line between his dark eyebrows. "No. I can see what you're thinking and nothing's wrong with this."

He didn't know how wrong. He didn't know how disgusted he'd be with himself—and her—when he found out the truth. She lifted up on her elbows. "Dean . . ."

He caught at the necklace swinging between their bodies. It was the pendant she'd been wearing since he left. "What's wrong was me," he said, his fingers curling into a fist around the tear. "I was wrong to think I could take your tears away. But I can help you carry them." With that, he lifted the pendant over her head and then dropped it over his. The silver tear gleamed against his golden skin and two of her wet ones plopped right down beside it.

How could she tell this man he'd just made the biggest mistake of his life? More tears fell. She pressed her nose with the back of her hand. "But . . . but what can I do for you?"

He reached over to her bedside table, where she saw the condom wrapper and his open wallet. He slid something free of the leather. It was that ragged card she'd seen him holding the day she'd discovered he was back in Malibu. The Ms. M card. "You already did something for me, Marlys. You saved my life."

Fifteen

As Gabe pushed through the door of Malibu & Ewe, he noticed two things, that Cassandra was with a customer and that the customer was looking at him with distinct suspicion. Shit, apparently just another of his admirers.

Hitching the shelving he carried under his arm higher, he ignored both women as he slid the non-soy, extra-shot latté that Cassandra would swear never touched her lips beside the cash register. Then he stomped to the back room, aware of the customer's disapproval tailing him the entire way.

He dumped his red toolbox on a counter and propped the lumber against it. Then he surveyed the area above the countertop where he was planning to add shelving in order to free up some of the cluttered flat space. He'd strapped on his tool belt and had his tape measure in hand when Cassandra invaded the small room.

Her perfume arrived first, a scent fresh and feminine and

that now he smelled on his skin in the mornings. It filled his lungs at night as he breathed her in, his face buried in those luxurious waves of her hair. He played with the stuff as she drifted off to sleep, combing it lightly then wrapping a fistful in his fingers as he closed his eyes and followed her to dreamland.

He'd been sleeping like a baby, his nightmares distant, his conscience quiet, but after this morning's visit from Noah and Jay, his mood was anything but tranquil. With a quick glance he could tell she knew he was out-of-sorts. There was a frown between her eyebrows and she had her full lips pursed in worry.

He groaned, and reached out an arm to draw her close. "Your mouth drives me crazy," he said, kissing her as if it had been days instead of hours since he'd last tasted her. There was the faintest hint of coffee on her tongue and he smiled inside, glad he'd brought the latté though he'd never admit to buying it for her just as she'd never admit to drinking it.

The next kiss turned hotter, and as he slanted his head for the perfect fit, she curled her fingers in the low-slung tool belt to keep her balance. His dick reacted to the proximity of her slender fingers and, groaning again, he pushed her away. "Unless you want to do it on this countertop, Froot Loop, you better keep your distance."

She licked her bottom lip, her blue eyes dazed in a way that never failed to give an extra yank on his libido. "I-I think I want to do it on the countertop," she said.

He squeezed shut his eyes. The thing was, the almost-thirty-year-old virgin was a woman determined to make up for lost time. She wanted to do it everywhere, any way and any time that he suggested it. Not that he was complaining, but if one of them didn't keep some control they were bound to be caught in a compromising position. The night before he'd thrown out the playful dare that she try to get him hard as he drove them both home from a grocery store run. She'd gotten that wide-eyed, dazzled-by-desire look that invariably took him under.

Next thing he knew, he was driving with one hand while the other stroked her hair as she slid her tongue along his suddenly erect flesh. "I win," she'd whispered, then sucked the throbbing head into her wet mouth. He owed her payback for that, but damned if he would play tit for tat during business hours. All he needed was for her sisters to walk in on them. It seemed as if they already considered him just one notch above depraved.

"Gabe . . ."

He placed a finger over her lips and she sucked it inside. With a yelp, he jerked it from her greedy mouth, heat shooting down his spine and goosing his cock. "And to think you look so innocent," he muttered. "Maybe the enforcers should be knocking on *your* doorstep."

The dazed look in her eyes evaporated. "Enforcers? What are you talking about?"

He probably shouldn't have said that. So he turned his back on her and applied himself to the task of putting up those shelves. "Measure twice, cut once," he murmured, to explain why he wasn't looking at her. Then he tossed out the really important piece of info. "I'm having a dinner party Friday night. Your sisters will be there. I hope you can make it."

There was a heavy pause. "What are you doing?" she asked.

"Creating some more storage space for you," he answered. "I noticed this countertop was crowded and I thought I could help with that."

She grabbed him by the back of the tool belt and yanked him around to face her.

"Hey . . ." he protested.

Cassandra stared him down, desire gone, determination sparking in her blue eyes. "What are you doing?"

He sighed. "The truth? I'm throwing a party where I plan to shut up every damn person who's been looking at me like I'm a womanizing version of Vlad the Impaler."

"Oh." A little smile played around Cassandra's enchanting mouth. "Is that why Nikki gifted me with a rope of garlic yesterday?"

"It will be silver crosses and wooden stakes next." He folded his arms over his chest. "Christ, Cassandra, what have you been telling your sisters? Because they sent Noah and Jay over to the fish market this morning to buy cups of coffee and administer not-so-veiled threats."

"I haven't told them anything!"

"Yeah? Well maybe it's Carver who sensed the way the wind was blowing the night the Tucker brothers were here. I invited him, too, by the way. I want them all to see that you're with me of your own free will and that I'm not some kind of damn danger to you."

"But . . . Well, first, you don't know how to cook."

He turned back to his toolbox. "I can buy ready-made kabobs at the deli and anything else I need. And you won't be surprised to learn I know the location of the liquor aisle."

Though he hadn't felt the compulsion to drink—or forget—since Cassandra had joined him in his bed. He pawed through his tools looking for a pencil. "Now, get back to work so I can get up these shelves."

She didn't obey. As a matter of fact, she didn't move and the silence between them grew long until she finally said, "I didn't expect you to do all this for me."

He swallowed his sigh. He wished he could say he'd do anything for her, but they both knew that would be a flat-out lie.

By Friday night, however, he was still determined to ease everyone's fears. Though that didn't mean he wasn't above looking incompetent in the kitchen—actually, he pretty much was—so it ended up that professional chef Nikki volunteered to de-bag the salad and also jazz it up a little. Cassandra and Juliet stayed behind to keep her company while he and the men went outside with beers and salsa and chips to study the intricacies of the stainless steel barbecue sitting on the patio courtyard.

"Yo, all," Carver Shields said, slipping out the French doors to join the male half of the party. "Sorry we're late. I left Oomfaa gossiping in the kitchen. Nice digs."

"Thanks," Gabe replied, then decided to take the bull by the horns. "Later I'll give you the tour, though it'll cost extra to see the dungeon where I work at keeping Cassandra compliant. Thumbscrews don't come cheap, you know."

The three men sent a guilty look around their small circle. Gabe shook his head, refusing to take it as it hot-potatoed his way. "Listen, if you think she's unhappy—"

"She's not unhappy," Carver interjected. "That doesn't mean *I'm* happy, but . . ."

"But I don't give a shit about your feelings, Shields," Gabe said. "And I suspect Cassandra would like you all to realize that she knows her own mind. She's been taking care of herself for quite some time. So that's why I don't get how you seem so sure I'm doing something *to* her instead of *with* her."

The men passed around another look. It was Jay who spoke this time. "Cassandra's strong, you're right. And so damn generous. What Nikki's gotten out of their relationship . . . what *we've* gotten out of Nikki discovering a sister to love and trust . . ."

Noah stepped in. "Of course Cassandra can take care of herself. But she has more than herself to rely on now. We're here for her and that's part of what she went looking for when she sought out her biological siblings."

"I know that," Gabe said, running his hands through his hair in frustration. "I've known her for two damn years. Longer than her sisters have known her. And I know her better than you do, Carver." He avoided glancing at that fucking tattoo on the other man's arm.

Though it seemed as if the drummer might have seen through that, because a grin broke over his face. "Yeah. Maybe."

Gabe didn't feel the least bit like smiling, because the problem was, six months ago, hell, a month ago, he would have been right with these guys in being absolutely certain he was no damn good for her.

But he wasn't walking away now. Not yet.

He was offering her something, wasn't he? They'd always been friends, and there was still that. But now, instead of sniping at each other to relieve the sexual tension, they had more pleasurable methods. Was that illegal? And she wasn't complaining, was she?

Still, as intimacy with Cassandra felt so damn right, there was an edge of disquiet that kept slicing into his consciousness. Maybe it was just his usual grim temperament trying to horn in on his current contentment. Maybe it was something else.

Carver's next question didn't help matters. "They find those kids who started the fire at Cassandra's?"

"No. I haven't seen them around. Maybe they've moved on to prank elsewhere."

Noah frowned. "Didn't you have a problem at the beach house recently, Jay?"

"Yeah. Someone broke the lock on an outside door and got into the garage. Nik has a new fridge in there, locked, too, that she uses for work. That lock was jimmied, too, and she lost a bunch of expensive gourmet stuff."

"Someone catered their own party?"

"No." Jay shook his head. "That's what was odd. They just left the door open and it all spoiled."

"We had a couple of attempted break-ins when we were in Kauai," Noah said. "The security company caught wind of them and sent a car out, but they didn't see anything. Once Dean moved into the guesthouse, there wasn't another problem."

"Weird," Carver said.

Weird, Gabe agreed, disquiet skittering down the back of his spine. He frowned, wondering if inviting the group over had been one big, bad idea. He'd decided on the party so he could ease everyone's fears, but now the one feeling spooked, damn it all, was him.

If the phone call hadn't reached Cassandra during Gabe's party, when she was in his kitchen and surrounded by her sisters and Oomfaa, all discussing the details of her upcoming thirtieth birthday bash, she might have made different choices.

She might have found her way to confessing to Nikki and

Juliet that she'd attempted contacting their biological father, Dr. Frank Tucker, and that she'd subsequently met his two adopted sons, Patrick and Reed.

She might have hurried on to say she was sorry for going behind their backs and suggested that if they still weren't in agreement about a face-to-face with the man then she wouldn't pursue the matter further. She would have promised to rescind that invitation she'd sent to him.

But when Gabe handed her his phone, she was unprepared for the identity of the person on the other end of the line. She was unprepared for anyone to find her at all, even though she'd used her telephone company's service and forwarded any after-hours calls made to the Malibu & Ewe number to that of the closest landline where she could be reached. After the fire, it had seemed like a good idea, particularly since cell service in the area was so damn spotty.

But it was *him*, Dr. Frank Tucker. He was back in the States and wanted to meet her. With her sisters gazing at her with mild curiosity, she'd been swamped with guilt, leading her to a quick conversation and quick acquiescence to the man's request so Nikki and Juliet wouldn't discover what she'd done without their knowledge.

Then, hanging up, she was swamped by another crashing wave of shame. Because if she was honest with herself, given a do-over, she wouldn't do anything differently. Both her sisters had been raised by men who they'd known and considered father figures. Juliet had adored her dad; Nikki not so much, but neither had quite the same gaping hole in her identity that Cassandra had sensed all her life.

So, the next morning she started a silent, early roll out of her bed, intent on getting this day, with its scheduled secret meeting, started. A large hand clamped around her wrist, leaving her with just a leg extending from the covers.

"You had a restless night," Gabe said.

Making a face, she turned to look at him. His dark eyes were alert and he looked as handsome as a man could with dark whiskers peppering his face and a cat wrapped around his head.

As if suddenly sensing Moosewood's presence, Gabe grimaced, and used his free hand to lift the slumbering cat. It hung in his grip, completely unconcerned about its fate as it slowly opened its ochre eyes. Gabe frowned. "I don't like cats," he said to Moosewood. "I especially don't like cats who like me."

He deposited the lump of sleepy feline onto the middle of the bed, and from there it leaped onto Gabe's chest to circle, purring. "That's it," Cassandra's lover groused. "We're never sleeping over here again."

Amused, she shook her head at him. After they'd cleaned up his kitchen after the party the night before, it had been his idea, after all, to come over and crawl into her bed. It was obvious to her—though unspoken—that he didn't feel right about leaving the cats on their own every night. "What happened to my prickly, morose neighbor?" she murmured.

He'd heard her. "Now I'm your prickly, morose, horny neighbor," he said, and yanked her over him with such speed that Moosewood was forced to leap off the bed. "Your prickly, morose, horny neighbor who stood up to your legion of fans last night and lived to tell about it."

She wiggled against him. Maybe she should have been mad at last night's guests for worrying she didn't know her own mind. And would some other woman have been annoyed that her lover thought he should be the one to address it with them?

Maybe. But she loved each one of them only the more for caring that much. Even Gabe, she decided, leaning down to kiss his scratchy, whiskered chin. Not *love* love him of course, but love him in the way that you could love a neighbor and a friend who also just happened to be the guy who knew exactly how to get you off.

She wiggled more, a little ashamed of her own crude thought. But then his hand slid under her oversized T-shirt and tickled her ribs on the way to covering her breast. She sucked in a breath as he thumbed her hardening nipple and when she told him what she wanted to do next, she decided his grin made it clear that a little crude was A-okay.

Afterward, he brushed her hair off her face. "What's up for today, Froot Loop?"

Smiling, she closed her eyes, enjoying the casual intimacy of the moment.

"Froot Loop?" Gabe kissed her nose.

She smiled at that, too, because it was such a sweet gesture, and for two years she'd seen Gabe in dozens of moods: desperate, grim, detached, drunk, but never sweet. Never until they'd come together in bed had she ever thought he had sweet in him.

"Hmm?" she asked.

"I want you to be careful, okay?"

Her eyes flew open. Did he know . . . had he guessed? She'd decided not to tell even Gabe about her scheduled meeting. He'd probably understand, but this was her decision, her need to fulfill. Her father.

She swallowed. "Careful about what?"

"Nothing in particular. Just . . . keep your eyes open."

It was an easy promise to make. Keeping her eyes open,

learning what and all she could about the man who'd fathered her was her prime goal of the day.

There was a small café on the premises of the medical building that housed Dr. Frank Tucker's plastic surgery offices. He'd suggested they meet there, and because she'd been eager to get off the phone and eager to put no obstacle in the way of finally coming face-to-face with him, she'd agreed.

It was early, before his office hours, and the parking lot was nearly empty. As she pushed her way through the glass door and saw the seated figure of a tall, silver-haired man, her stomach jittered and her hands felt too empty. She should have brought her knitting, she thought. Or maybe Gabe after all.

The man looked around, caught sight of her, and rose to his feet. Gray slacks, black belt that matched black shoes, a pale blue shirt and a blue and green tie that echoed his blue and green eyes, the mirror of both Nikki's and Juliet's. Cassandra had to force her feet to cross the tiled floor.

Her heart pounded as they stared at each other.

He held out his hand. "Cassandra."

"Yes." The shake was businesslike. Noncommittal. A disappointment.

Which was ridiculous, really. What did she expect? This distinguished, handsome man didn't know her.

"Have a seat," he said, gesturing to the chair across from his own. There was a cup of coffee waiting for her there.

"I like mine black," he said, picking up his own cup. "You?"

Stupid to feel it was like a test. "Sure. Yes."

No. Never. The only coffee that crossed her lips was the steamed-milk kind that Gabe pretended to leave at the shop by mistake. Just thinking of him steadied her a little and she wrapped her fingers around the ceramic cup to hide their shaking. "Was your return trip to the States smooth?"

It went on for several minutes like that. The most banal of banal conversations, when what she wanted to ask was what had motivated him to be a sperm donor, how the fact that he had children he'd never met had affected his life, if . . .

If he'd watched a lonely little girl sit on a swing at a public park and wondered if she was missing the dad she didn't know.

Finally, they exhausted generalities and they both offered a little bit more. He mentioned his wife, who had died of a kidney ailment seven years before. She told him about her fascination with yarn and all things textile as well as the shop she had in Malibu.

He mused, "Besides needles, I'm trying to think of some correlation between plastic surgery and knitting."

She tried thinking, too—how could stitching a wound be like creating a sweater?—but after a few minutes they both gave up and laughed. The laughter was good, she supposed, though now she felt as if she'd failed the exam's Part B as well.

He asked to be reminded how old she was. "Twenty-nine." It was the perfect opportunity to bring up the birthday party and ask if he planned to attend, but the words stuck on her tongue.

Another awkward silence passed. "The other two," her father said. "Nicole and Julie."

"Nikki and Juliet," Cassandra corrected on a whisper, guilt tasting as bitter as the coffee as she thought of her sisters. It wasn't right to bring them into this conversation. She didn't have their permission to speak of them. "But I don't think . . ." she started, reluctance clear in her voice.

"What can you tell me about them?" their biological father pressed anyway.

Because he was already bored with her? The swift thought made the back of her neck flame. She was wicked, she thought, curling her fingers into her hands and pressing her nails into her palms. Wicked, because jealousy of Nikki and Juliet shot through her like a burning knife. He'd like them better.

Maybe he'd even love them.

She cleared her throat, trying to swallow the ugly thought. It roiled in her belly and she was angry at her childishness. Ashamed of her neediness.

"I'm really not comfortable speaking about Nikki and Juliet," she finally said.

After a moment, he nodded. Cassandra blew out a silent breath and relaxed a little. Her father understood. Maybe her father understood *her.*

"My secretary saved those tabloids from last fall and I looked at the photos of you girls," he said.

She knew the ones he meant. She'd shown them to Gabe not long ago. There'd been color photographs of the three donor sibling sisters.

"Those other two each have one blue and one green eye, like me," he continued.

"Yes."

His gaze narrowed on her face. "As a matter of fact, they both look a lot like me—much more than you do."

Maybe. To be polite, she nodded.

His eyes traveled over her with a clinical detachment. "How certain are you about your research? And how reliable are that clinic's records, I wonder." He took another sip of coffee. "Are you really sure that you're my daughter?"

Are you really sure that you're my daughter?

She couldn't hear how she responded to that, not with the high ringing sound in her ears. Once she was on her feet, she supposed she gave him some excuse about needing to get back to the yarn shop. She didn't remember it, or really anything, except that as she beat a hasty retreat from the café that she pushed past Patrick and Reed Tucker. If one of them said anything to her, she didn't hear that either.

The traffic from Beverly Hills to Malibu snarled, just like her tangled thoughts. Not his daughter? Cassandra thought. *Not his daughter?* If she wasn't, then Nikki and Juliet weren't her sisters. *They both look a lot like me—much more than you do.*

Meaning not only no father.

But no family either.

That high whine in her ears broke, and the well of quiet in her head was even worse. What now?

What now was that she was on her own again. What now was that she couldn't share her doubt and pain with Nikki and Juliet when she'd kept the meeting with their father a secret. What now was that the uncertainty and disappointment were hers to bear, all by herself.

Meaning she was more alone than ever.

Sixteen

We cannot destroy kindred: our chains stretch a little sometimes, but they never break.

—MARQUISE DE SÉVIGNÉ

"Look," Marlys said, trailing Dean across the dark parking lot toward Malibu & Ewe, lit brightly because it was Knitters' Night. "They don't like me. They're never going to like me."

He had her hand in his and he squeezed her fingers yet kept on going, even as her reluctance stretched to the length of both their arms. "I thought you said you needed some knitting help."

"I don't need help," she said quickly. She'd asked for his help and look at the serious consequences. *I love yous* and bodily fluids exchanged. Hearts trembling on the threshold of being broken. Hers, anyway. It was his illusions that were sure to shatter and whatever sweet feelings he had for her would spoil and sour.

Dean glanced back at her, his feet slowing. "When I told you I was going out for beers with Noah and the other guys, you said you'd spend time at the yarn shop."

Yes, she'd said that, and yes, she even had the bag with

her project in it under her arm. She'd agreed to come because she had no spine when it came to Dean. Since that afternoon in her bed she hadn't wanted to refuse him anything. They'd shared meals, saw movies, found a startling compatibility. Their instant sexual chemistry hadn't been a shiny object to fake them out. So here she was, accompanying him to the knitting shop where she was certain to encounter her evil stepmother and the woman's wicked half-sisters.

The mean one would probably take one look at her and this time throw her out of the place. Maybe that would be the trigger Marlys needed to tell Dean the truth.

So far, she'd not come close to confessing about Phil, because she'd told herself that facing her feelings about her father was enough confrontation for the time being. Selfish Marlys had convinced herself she could enjoy a short time with the man she loved without ruining it with truth and honesty.

Except the lack of truth and honesty was worrying at her like Blackie worried one of his rawhide bones. Every time she caught a glimpse of that tear pendant that Dean continued to wear for her, guilt throbbed in her chest.

He reeled her in with a tug on her hand. His tender kiss didn't melt her apprehension, but it made it even harder for her to refuse him. "C'mon," he said, starting forward again. "They're not that bad."

Behind his back, she rolled her eyes. It wasn't their badness, but hers that was an issue. He was so nice he couldn't fathom that she wasn't nice. He was so good that her being so not good just wouldn't sink in. His friends saw her clearly though, and they wouldn't let her forget how they felt about her. "I'm telling you," she tried one more time. "They're not my tribe."

The one she hadn't had since her army brat days. "They don't like me," she added. "I won't fit in."

He pulled her close again. "*I* like you. You fit in with *me*."

Inside her, guilt pounded like truth, demanding to get out. She rubbed at her shoulder and then at her thigh with her free hand, wishing she could spend another hour in the shower, because the longer she held off telling Dean what she'd done, the dirtier she felt.

The bells on the front door of the shop rang out as they entered, a similar jangle to the sound of those at Marlys's boutique. Heads turned as Dean drew her over the threshold. Six heads, three couples.

Her nerves jittered and before anyone could say anything—like "Beat it" or "Get the hell out"—Marlys curled her top lip in a cynical scowl. "How sweet," she said, addressing the room. "Everyone all paired up."

Nikki and Jay sat on a couch, his arm snuggling her close.

Both looking tan and rested, Juliet and Noah stood by a table where a selection of refreshments was laid out.

Cassandra had put the cash register between herself and everyone else in the room, though Gabe was hovering nearby, a frown on his face as his gaze returned to the woman with the rippling hair and Bunny breasts. "Froot Loop," he said, ignoring the newcomers. "What's the matter? You've not been acting like yourself . . ."

Her eyes on Marlys, Nikki tried rising to her feet as Jay's hand tightened on her shoulder. "Cookie," he warned.

Marlys pinned on a flirtatious smile. "Hey, Jay. Long time no see. I remember our night together with pleasure."

Amusement gleamed in his eyes as he saw Nikki's face flush with anger. "Marlys. As I remember it, our one date ended early because there wasn't a spark on either side. Zero fireworks."

"You're right." Sighing, Marlys shot Dean a silent apology for the play on Jay she'd tried as a poke at Nikki. "Dudsville."

The man she loved winked, confident that the two of them together were the Fourth of July.

Nikki settled back on the cushions, looking as if she'd swallowed her "humph." Jay laughed and nuzzled her temple. "I didn't bed them all, Cookie. I keep telling you that."

Noah didn't even try faking a welcome as he walked forward. "Don't think you can stir things up here, Marlys. Leave your troublemaking at the door, or . . ."

His head turned as Juliet drew up beside him and put her hand on his arm. As always, she looked elegant with her golden hair falling to her shoulders and with just a trace of coral lipstick on her mouth. Whatever message she gave her new husband from her blue and green eyes he apparently understood, because he sighed, then looked back at Dean. "You told me you were with her, Dino, but I didn't want to believe it. I hope you keep a whip and chair handy."

Juliet grimaced. "Noah—"

"She could have cost me what I value most in the world. I'm not forgetting that." He shook his head. "Dean should know she has no heart."

"I think she has a very big heart," Juliet countered. She switched her attention from Noah to Marlys and there was sympathy written across her face. "Last fall she was hurting."

And Marlys remembered Dean saying to her then: *It's other people that you use to take out your pain. You hurt other people so you don't have to feel a goddamned thing.* But he didn't remember the moment. He didn't remember why he'd said it to her and he didn't remember what she'd done.

The guilt of it kept pounding inside of her though, demanding to be set free. It was hard to hear Juliet over the incessant *bam bam bam bam*.

"Her father," Juliet was saying. "She loved her fa—"

"Don't," Marlys burst out. "Don't say it." She broke away from Dean in retreat. Her heels hit the glass of the front door.

Compassion softened Juliet's face. "Oh, Marlys. You do have a big heart and you did love your father very much."

But she hadn't!

That was the truth of it. She'd wanted him to stay nearby and act like a father instead of a soldier—*You'll be fine*—and when he hadn't, her love had shriveled and died. All her big heart had been carrying inside it these many years was disappointment and bitterness and a profound fear of loving.

Loving didn't work out so well for her.

Her hand reached blindly for the handle of the door.

"Don't go, angel," Dean said.

Her fingers slipped on the metal knob and the knitting she'd been holding under her arm slipped, too. She clamped her elbow against her side, the needles digging into her ribs, reminding her of what she'd brought with her. The seed of an idea, plus restless hours, plus the sense of impending doom she'd experienced since her first shared night with Dean had grown into something that was nearly complete.

Almost as finished as her brief blissful interlude with the man she loved.

It was time for them both to be done.

Swallowing hard, she stepped toward the center area of the shop. Her gaze skipped from Nikki to Juliet to Cassandra. The shop owner looked as if she were in another world, her gaze distant. It was Gabe who noticed Marlys's attention.

"Yo, Froot Loop."

She started, her head jerking toward the man. He nodded at Marlys. "Looks like you have a customer."

"Oh." She blinked, and it was clear that she'd registered nothing of the past few minutes. "Marlys. How are you?"

Marlys clutched her cloth bag to her chest and glanced back at the men. Dean had already crossed to Noah, and Jay was joining them. She reached inside her bag. "I need help with this." Her needles and the length of knitting plopped onto the countertop.

In college, she'd picked up the hobby. For a brief time she'd had a roommate—two weeks into the semester the girl had moved to her sorority house—who had taught Marlys the rudiments. Over the years since, she'd made things here and there, mittens, a few purses. Once she'd even attempted a hat in a Fair Aisle motif. She'd never knitted for anyone but herself.

For this, she'd selected a yarn that was a softened black and silver combination, a choice matching Dean's dark hair and light eyes. Her hand inside her bag again, she rummaged around. "The sleeves are done, but I'm having a little trouble with the rest. Could you help me bind off—"

"No!"

Marlys jumped, surprised by the sudden appearance of Nikki at her elbow and the vehemence in the woman's voice. "What?"

"Um . . ." Juliet was beside her now as well, and she fingered the soft fabric of the almost-finished sweater. "This isn't for Blackie, is it?"

"Are you nuts?" Marlys wrinkled her nose. "Can you imagine my dog standing still long enough for me to get him into a sweater?" Plus, though he could be a pain in the ass, her canine deserved *some* dignity.

"So." Nikki spoke softer now. "This is for . . . for . . ."

Marlys glanced over her shoulder. It was a surprise for Dean. Because he'd been a surprise in her life, a surprise as soft and warm as the garment she'd made for him. Though she hoped it would last a lot longer than their doomed relationship.

"It *is* for Dean," Nikki concluded, looking as if the idea made her sick to her stomach.

Marlys ignored the other woman's distaste and clung stubbornly to her task. "Yes. And to finish it, I just need a little help binding off."

Nikki's gaze shifted to Juliet, and on to Cassandra. Then she shrugged. "I'm afraid we can't let you do that."

"What? I know you're the mean one, but—"

"The mean one?" Nikki's jaw dropped. Cassandra made a sound like a cough, though it was Juliet who flat-out laughed.

Nikki narrowed her eyes at her sister. "Am I the mean one?"

"Of course you're the mean one," Juliet said. Her finger moved around their little circle. "I'm beautiful, Cassandra's talented, and you're mean."

The affront on Nikki's face surprised a laugh out of Marlys. The other woman shot her a glance. "She's meaner," she said defensively, pointing.

Marlys laughed again. "I *am* meaner." Then they all were laughing and she thought, *This is what it could be like.* She could have girlfriends, be part of a tribe, be part of this group with their sisterhood and their shared jokes and the sexy men in their lives.

But her sexy man was just the truth away from leaving

her. Her fingers tightened on the sweater sleeve in her grasp and she looked down at it, blinking away stupid, useless tears. "Now," she said. "About the sweater . . ."

"We can't let you finish it." Cassandra whisked it off the countertop and inspected her stitches. "But nice work."

Marlys was half-flattered, half-frustrated. "I don't get—"

"It's the curse," Nikki explained. "And just to show that I'm not all that mean, I'm going to be the one to tell you about it."

"Yes," Cassandra continued. "If you start making your boyfriend a sweater—"

"*I'm* the one who gets to tell," Nikki protested. Then she turned to Marlys. "If you make your boyfriend a sweater, it's common knowledge he'll break up with you before you bind it off."

Marlys blinked. "You don't really believe that." She looked around the small circle of women and had to change the tone of her voice. "You really believe that."

Juliet shrugged. "Better safe than sorry. Nikki didn't attempt a sweater for Jay until she was wearing an engagement ring."

"*Attempt* being the operative word," the woman in question grumbled.

Cassandra reached out to pat her sister's hand. "Next time you'll get it right. Bring it into the shop tomorrow and we'll frog it together."

"Unravel it," Juliet translated for Marlys.

She shrugged that information off. "The curse doesn't apply to me. He's not my boyfriend, so I can finish the sweater."

Juliet's eyebrows rose. "But you love him."

"Yeah, yeah, yeah," Marlys muttered, impatient with the details. "But that's all about to go away."

"Um, why?" Nikki asked.

"Because . . ." She hesitated. "Because I . . ." The words stuck in her throat. It would be better to force them out, she thought. Get used to hearing them said aloud, get used to saying them aloud, because as soon as the damn sweater was finished she was going to tell Dean. *I slept with Pharmaceutical Phil the very afternoon I agreed to sleep with you.* "Last fall, I was worried about myself . . . or worried about Dean, or . . . Okay, I was worried about what would happen if there was an us and so I—"

"Angel." Dean's hand clamped onto her shoulder. "Don't."

Puzzled, she turned to look into his face. There was so much love in his eyes that she had to start blinking again as he cupped her cheek in his palm. "I have to tell you," she whispered, figuring the moment might as well be now. "I have to tell you that I so screwed this up when I screwed—"

Dean silenced her with a kiss.

She broke away. No. No. "Let me finish."

"No, Marlys. I—"

"Dean!" Noah's voice from across the room. "Hey, Dino, catch!"

When he didn't look away from Marlys's face, a heavy ball of yarn flew through the air, bumping Dean on the head, right over his new scar. He swayed back, his hand going to his hairline.

She clutched at his arms to steady him, then spun to confront the men. "Watch it!" she shot out, angered by their carelessness. "Do you want him to lose the rest of his memory?"

Noah's eyebrows flew up. "What? *Lose his memory*?"

"Memory?" Juliet echoed.

Jay rubbed a hand over his chin, a smile lurking on the

corners of his mouth. "Um, yeah, you forget to tell us something, Dean?"

Puzzled, Marlys swung back to look at the injured man. "I don't understand—"

"Marlys . . ." He lifted his arms, dropped them. "I lied."

"What?"

"I lied about losing my memory."

"What?"

"Not completely. I *did* lose those few months when I was in Afghanistan. I don't remember much of being there at all. But Malibu . . ."

She just stared at him.

"I remember everything about Malibu."

Meaning he remembered about Phil.

Marlys backed away, her spine hitting the edge of the countertop. "No." No, he wouldn't do that. Her mind continued working. He wouldn't have lied to her.

Why would he do such a thing?

It had given them a second chance.

"I came back here because I couldn't stop thinking about you." He shoved his hands in his pockets, took them out, buried them deep again. "I could have died, Marlys. When I was lying in my hospital bed I kept looking at that business card and I decided there was no sense squandering what we might have. Especially when I thought I understood what was going through that convoluted brain of yours."

Hospital bed . . . what we might have . . .

"So when you'd presumed I'd forgotten meeting you . . ."

"You lied," she finished for him.

He nodded. "I lied."

Thus allowing them those sweet, sweet times skin to skin without her worrying about his memory of that episode with Phil.

She stared up at him, nonplussed. Did this mean he really loved her? Did he love her despite knowing all she'd done? How could that be?

"I'm so bad," she whispered, still confused.

He took her in his arms. "No. You're defensive and stubborn and funny and brash and from the moment I met you, I knew you were mine."

Her mind reeled. "And you're so, so . . . good."

His smile kicked up. "Not that good. I lied. I'd cheat and steal for you, too, angel."

She had to laugh a little at herself, her mind still playing catch-up. In recent days he'd taken to calling her "angel," the name he'd used last fall, and she hadn't even caught on. What a bonehead.

What a bonehead.

Yet in his arms, knowing what he'd done so they could be together, she was a brave bonehead. With her forefinger, she touched the tear he wore around his neck. He *was* helping her. He was giving her strength, by carrying that. Enough strength to forgive herself for what had happened before, enough strength to face her fears of the future, enough strength to believe that this lying, cheating, stealing man could love her forever.

"And I'll brave a curse, too," she declared, throwing caution to the wind. She was loved. This man had shown he was more than worthy of her trust in that. She reached toward the women. "Give me the sweater."

She got a marriage proposal instead.

After Marlys and Dean left, Juliet and Cassandra shooed the other men off on their beer-and-billiards evening so that Nikki could have her obviously impending little cry before the knitters arrived in the store. Juliet pulled tissues from the box and handed them over to Nikki as she blotted her face and wiped her nose.

She flopped onto one of the couches and Juliet sat beside her. Cassandra remained standing, her gaze running over the two sisters. The same long legs. Hair within the same color range, though Nikki's was a streaky gold and brown and Juliet's a more subtle caramel. Eyes exactly the same color, one bright blue, the other bright green.

Like Dr. Frank Tucker's eyes.

Unlike her own.

She fingered her own medium brown hair and avoided her reflection in the two mirrors that were set up in separate corners of the shop. Determined to get away from her unhappy thoughts, she wandered to the windows and caught sight of Noah driving off in his truck. Jay followed in his Porsche.

"I really have to get control of my sentimental streak," Nikki said, sniffing. "Hope to God it goes away before I walk down the aisle."

"Focus on your mean streak instead, little sister," Juliet teased.

Nikki flung a damp tissue at her. "Look at you. Marlys caused you a boatload of grief and you're happy for her."

"I am," Juliet admitted. "I'm like you now. I want everyone to find their man."

Cassandra felt both pairs of matching eyes turn to her, so she bustled over to fuss with the items on the refreshment table. So not going into that conversation. They should know as well as she did that Gabe was just her man of the moment, not the kind of man that Juliet was talking about.

There was the sound of Nikki sighing. "And guess what

else? I'm inspired by all these true confessions," she said. "I think we should tell one another something we've been keeping secret."

Cassandra whipped her head to stare at her sister. Did Nikki guess? Had she somehow found out that Cassandra had made a visit to their father? Her cheeks heated. She didn't want them to know about it, and more, she didn't want them to know the doubts the doctor had put in her mind.

Are you really sure that you're my daughter?

Juliet propped her feet on the coffee table and crossed her ankles. "Is this like Truth or Dare?"

"Nope," Nikki said. "This is all Truth. Because I have something I'm just dying to get off my chest."

Despite herself, Cassandra wandered closer to the two women on the couch. "Spill," she commanded, settling on one of the upholstered arms.

Nikki made a big play of looking right, then left, then lowered her voice to a conspiratorial whisper. "You know how Jay and I are writing our own wedding vows?"

Juliet and Cassandra nodded.

"I'm paying someone to do mine for me."

Juliet's blue and green eyes became blue and green saucers. "You can find someone who'll do that?"

Nikki waved her hand. "Easy-peasy. Think about it. When was the last time you went to the movie theater and saw a good romantic comedy? And those ridiculous ones where the loser guy gets the super-sexy knockout don't count."

"There's been a dearth," Cassandra acknowledged.

"Which means there's a lot of clever female screenwriters just around the corner in Hollywood looking to pick up some extra work." She blew an airy breath on her fingernails and then polished them against her shirt. "The man will sink to his knees."

Juliet was frowning. "I think that's a violation."

"Of what?"

"Wedding . . . couple . . . love etiquette. I don't know," Juliet said.

"Oh, please," Nikki answered. "It's self-preservation. Jay's a professional writer himself. It's only fair I get some professional help."

Juliet wasn't buying it. "I think that if you said you're going to write your own vows then you have to write your own vows."

Nikki shot Cassandra a glance. "Goody Two-shoes," they said together.

Juliet straightened on the cushions. "You take that back."

They shook their heads.

Her frown turned fiercer. "Oh, yeah? Well I'll tell you what's not goody-goody. I sent a wedding announcement and a phenomenal, romantic photo of Noah and me to the newspaper in his hometown. There's a certain high school principal and his spawn of a daughter that I'm hoping will experience a very sharp slap of shoulda-woulda-coulda."

"Nice," Nikki said, all admiration. "Maybe you can start being the mean one."

Cassandra laughed, and slid off the arm of the couch onto the cushions beside Nikki. The younger woman put her head on her shoulder, a rare, though increasingly frequent sign of affection. Cassandra wanted to cry. This is what she'd been seeking all her life. Family. Family sharing smiles and laughter and secrets.

There'd been no need to extract elaborate promises of

keeping the confidences just shared. Each would never betray a sister.

Or who they thought was a sister.

It swamped Cassandra again, the terrible thought that she'd found them just to lose them. The questions could be easily answered, she supposed. She could confess right now and tomorrow order those kits that required a simple cheek swab to determine DNA.

As if Nikki could read her mind, she lifted her head and scooted away a bit so she had room to pivot and face Cassandra. "Now you, Froot Loop."

"What?" she said, stalling.

"What's the truth you've been hiding?"

Cassandra jumped up. "Look at the time. People will be here any minute."

Nikki caught her arm. "Oh, no. You won't get away that easily. Juliet and I spilled our guts."

"But . . . but . . ."

"Something's eating at you," Nikki said. "Don't bother to deny it."

She cast about for something. "Edward's been leaving me messages again."

"Oh, stop talking about that twit. You've been handling his messages and what all without a flutter for months."

"It's something else," Juliet said quietly.

Looking into their faces, she realized they'd likely engineered this moment. It was what sisters did. They'd finagle a way to get the quiet one to talk. A few months back, she and Nikki had done the very same to Juliet.

Nikki gave her arm a little shake. "You can tell us. What's at the bottom of your heart, Froot Loop? What's at the very bottom of your heart?"

At the very bottom of her heart? At the very bottom of her heart was this frightening, terrifying, terrible truth. She opened her mouth and heard it tumble out, just as the bells on the door to the shop rang.

"I'm afraid I'm in love with Gabe."

The shock on the other women's faces startled her. Was it that surprising? But then she noticed they were looking not *at* her, but beyond her. Her insides freezing, she snuck a peek over her shoulder.

Gabe was standing inside the shop, wearing his usual inscrutable expression. Meaning it was impossible to tell whether he'd overheard her deepest, scariest, very-bottom-of-her-heart secret.

Seventeen

Sunday morning, Gabe pulled up outside Cassandra's house,
and she slipped into his car even before he'd turned off the
ignition. He tried not to react as she leaned across his car's
console to stroke her palm against his just-shaven jaw.
"Smooth," she said. The kiss she pressed to his chin was
casual. "And it looks as if you just combed your hair, too.
Gabe, I'm flattered."

Her teasing eased the knot in his gut that had been
tightening since Tuesday night. He slanted her a grin. "I'm
trying to keep up with Jay."

She laughed. It was careless as well, and he relaxed
further. "I think he gets manicures. Are you prepared to go
so far?"

"Depends. What do you charge?" he asked.

"You can't afford me," she said, sticking her cute nose
in the air. "Accept that."

He didn't stop himself from reaching over and tweak-
ing it between his forefinger and thumb. What an idiot he'd

been, worrying about whatever it was he'd overheard—
obviously wrongly he realized now—at the knitting shop.
Cassandra could never be in love with him. She was too
smart and too familiar with his demons.

If he had believed she'd fallen, he wouldn't have risked
spending any more time with her, no matter how tempting
she was every time he looked at her. Today she was wearing a sweater she had surely made. It hugged her breasts
and was the exact color of her blue eyes. Her long legs were
encased in jeans and she had on high-heeled, suede boots
that looked like butter and appeared almost as soft as her
skin. He regretted that he'd lost out on the chance of having those long limbs wrapped around his hips for the last
few nights.

She'd given him a reason to keep them in separate beds
since Knitters' Night. Working overtime on stuff for her
upcoming birthday party. He hadn't questioned her closely,
uneasy about what he'd hoped he hadn't heard, but now just
looking at her made him keenly regret those hours apart.

He took a breath instead of crassly trying to persuade
her back into her house. Only a stupid man suggested sex
right off the bat. To cool his libido, he thought of her nosy
cats. "How's the menagerie?" he asked.

"Pining for you."

He shot a look at her, but decided he'd imagined the
note of true emotion in her voice. "We'll bring them home
some salmon from brunch."

Yeah, he'd actually asked her out. His last date had
been a hundred years ago and it probably involved a pitcher
of beer and some soggy pretzels. He would have felt like
an ass now, dating after a century's hiatus, except that it
was Cassandra sitting beside him and his world was right
again.

"Bed's been too empty," he heard himself say. "I've missed you."

"You've seen me every day."

Lattés. He had to bring her lattés. And he'd finished the shelving in her back room. But the yarn shop had been full of customers every time he'd arrived and it seemed to him they'd both been relieved by the buffer. But they were alone now, and he threaded his hand through her luxurious hair and pulled her close with it for a kiss.

Yeah. "Maybe I need to say hello to the cats after all," he murmured against her mouth.

She softened, and he drew his mouth toward her ear. "Baby . . ." he murmured, grateful as hell they were back to their new normal, in each other's arms. "How about I buy you lunch instead?"

Her lips curved. "Well—"

His cell phone rang. Jerking back from her mouth, he cursed and fished in his pocket. "*Now* it chooses to find some reception." Glancing at the readout, he groaned. "Property management call."

But maybe one that wouldn't ruin their plans for the day. He would have passed it on to a service, but the request for repair was simple and from one of Cassandra's friends. He started his car. "Let's go fix Oomfaa's garbage disposal."

One of the Most Famous Actresses in America leased a house he owned in the infamous Malibu Colony—the original oceanfront development that Hollywood stars of the 1920s had settled. Oomfaa had been in this house for something like six months without a problem. This one didn't look serious in the least, Gabe thought, as he played with the switch on the kitchen's granite backsplash.

Cassandra and Oomfaa were indulging in mimosas.

"Carver's coming over," the actress told them, her smile luminous. Without all the movie magic, freckles dusted her nose and cheeks. Gabe thought she was prettier with them.

He was crouched on the floor to reach under her kitchen sink when the attack came. The front door opened, and a spatter of feet and high-pitched voices assaulted him. In an instant, he was brought back to Maddie's fourth birthday. Lynn had read that the guest list at a child's party should be the number of the child's age plus one. Tossing that advice to the wind, they'd invited twelve little girls to the house for the afternoon.

These were only three children, he noted, even as instinct urged he climb under the sink altogether. A trio of the female gender: seven, five, and three, he guessed, each of them in pink and glitter and ruffles, all that froufrou stuff that he knew some little girls, like his own, were born to love.

Carver followed the posse in, a baby wrapped in more pink in his arms. On top of the child's head fountained a feathery, Pebbles ponytail. The other man caught sight of Gabe, frozen on the floor.

"My nieces," he explained. Fisted in his free hand were white paper bags reeking of fast-food breakfast items. "Four of 'em, can you believe it? I'm giving my sister and brother-in-law a much-deserved morning off."

Gabe wanted off. Out.

Yeah, he'd seen kids around, of course. You couldn't avoid them. But you could stay out of their way and you could stay out of places that packed tiny toys with every meal. There'd been a basketful of them in Maddie's sunny bedroom, because it was their father-daughter weekend ritual, a walk to the park so Mom could sleep in, followed by the short drive to the Golden Arches.

Now the smell of maple syrup made him ache, remembering sticky little girl kisses.

"You okay, man?" Carter asked.

"Yeah." He couldn't turn around and look at that baby again.

He hadn't thought much about the kid issue when he was a young man and even a young married man. Busy building his career and his portfolio, he hadn't noticed their friends joining the diaper set, but Lynn had. And when she'd brought up having a child—well, even though he thought they were too young or he was too busy or perhaps not ready because the idea didn't goose a single warm thought out of him—he hadn't said a word. You went to college, you worked, you married, you had kids. The natural order of things.

Unlike burying your young wife.

Unlike deciding on the epitaph for your daughter's headstone.

"Can I help?" Carter again.

Gabe risked a glance over his shoulder. The drummer had divested himself of food bags and from the sound of things the little girls were having a breakfast of champions in the nearby alcove, but that baby was still on the man's hip. He was hunkered down and the child stared at Gabe while she gummed a piece of toasted English muffin.

He couldn't look away from her. It had been like that when they'd put Maddie in his arms minutes after her birth. Up to that point he'd been neutral on the whole project. Just another agenda item. But then they'd put this living, squirming, warm bundle of person against his chest. She'd stared up at him from unblinking eyes, as if she saw everything about him in that first look.

Had she known then that he would fail her?

This baby studied him in the same way. Then, with a four-toothed grin, she held out her scrap of muffin to him.

Gabe stood so fast he slammed his hip into the countertop. Grunting at the pain, he pivoted for the front door. "I need something from the car," he said.

Outside, he breathed in air. Salty, crisp Malibu air. He'd never expected it to cure him, when he'd taken up residence here, but sometimes he thought he was better: when he was trading insults with the vegetarian next door, when they put up wallpaper or painted new shelves, when he wrapped himself around her at night.

And then sometimes, like now, he knew he would never be whole.

The ash that was the residue of his heart sickened his soul. Eventually, it would darken everyone he touched. And now, the knowledge of that opened the ever-present hole at his feet. There was a bottle of vodka wrapped in a rag in his trunk. He could take it out, slug down a mouthful or two. More.

Such an easy slide into that dark place.

But not right now, he told himself. Not with Cassandra in the house as well as Oomfaa and Carver. Not with children around. He could keep it together. He *would* keep it together.

He made himself return to the house. The garbage disposal was grinding merrily and Carver wore a warrior's grin. "Who said I was just another pretty face?" he said, sending a triumphant look at the two women still overseeing breakfast. Gabe followed his gaze.

Cassandra was holding Pebbles.

The sight struck him like an ax to the chest. He couldn't breathe as he took in the softened lines of her face, the little back-and-forth rock of her body as she murmured to the baby, her cheek against the child's temple. The baby's head was snuggled into Cassandra's neck and one small fist was tangled in her hair that tumbled over her generous breasts.

Gabe knew the wonder of her silky hair and that bountiful softness. He closed his eyes as pain shredded whatever soft parts he had left inside him.

"She'll make a great mother, eh?" Carver asked.

"What?" He opened his eyes again.

"Cassandra, a great mother," the other man said, elbowing Gabe with the arm illustrated with that naked lady tattoo.

It usually pissed him off, but now he stared down at the ink instead of looking at the woman who was so like it.

"A wonderful mother," he agreed, and he knew without a doubt that it was what she wanted for herself.

Of course it was. Family was her thing. Her lonely child, outcast upbringing had pushed her to pursue every biological tie. She loved her sisters and would revel in the role of aunt, if that came about, but she had to want the tighter bonds of her very own children.

Which was the last thing he had to offer her.

So their "new normal" was only postponing the real inevitable. They couldn't be together. They shouldn't be together.

Every moment he took from her only took her away from the man she needed to find, the one who would give her babies. Every moment he took from her only took her away from those she'd be with for the rest of her life.

At the shrill peal of the phone, Cassandra jolted awake. She stared into the dark, heart pounding with that familiar where-is-Gabe fear, until she remembered he was beside her. As the ring sounded again, she sat up and glanced over at his side of the bed.

It was empty.

He was gone.

She snatched up the phone. "Yes?"

It was routine, the finding of clothes, keys, the drive to the Beach Shack. She peered into Gabe's car as she jogged toward the bar's doorway, noting the empty bottle of vodka on the passenger seat.

Mr. Mueller was waiting for her. "I'm sorry, Cassandra. I only came in a short time ago to close up or else I would have called you sooner."

"Sooner" Gabe had been beside her in bed. They'd spent the day together—a late brunch, an afternoon with the newspaper and the three cats, a shared dinner. When Edward had called, Gabe had happened to pick up the receiver for her and she thought his intimidating growl might have put the other man off for good. When she'd teased him about his caveman phone manners, he'd chased her into the bedroom and they'd wrestled until lust had been declared the winner.

There'd been two condom wrappers tossed on the table on his side of the bed when she'd fallen asleep. And after that he must have snuck out on her.

"Where is he?" she asked, glancing around the small place. A woman was huddled on a stool at the dim end of the bar, but there didn't seem to be anyone else drowning their sorrows.

"He took off," the bartender said. "Was drinking with her when I came in"—he indicated the lone figure with a cocked thumb—"but when I reached for the phone, he stumbled out."

Yet he wasn't in his car or loitering in the parking lot

either. Squaring her shoulders, she forced herself toward the woman nursing the last of a beer. "Hey," she said, then had to clear her throat and start over. "I'm a friend of Gabe's. Might you know where he went?"

Bleary eyes swung her way. Platinum, teased hair was pinned in a messy updo and her bangs tangled with black-as-black eyelashes. "I do his hair," the woman said. "He called me and asked to come in for a trim."

Cassandra pressed a fist beneath her breasts and tried to focus on the matter at hand. But it hurt bad, it hurt right there below her heart, to think that he'd left her bed for another woman. His barber, Sammy. For a "trim." Yeah, right.

"I have a styling chair on one side of my duplex." She blinked and then seemed to really see Cassandra. "You could come in. I could cut your hair in a bob."

"No, thanks. I've seen what you do to Gabe."

"Don't blame me for that," the other woman said. "When he gets a hankering for a haircut, he lets me go at it with scissors, and then he takes the clippers and finishes the job himself. Always looks like hell."

"So I'm looking for a refugee from the underworld." Cassandra sighed. "Do you know if he called himself a cab?"

The woman shrugged. "He called himself a selfish son of a bitch and then he walked out."

What could she do but start for home? If Gabe had any sense, he would have climbed into a taxi and headed back to their canyon. He'd probably beat her there.

Rain started to fall as she pulled out of the bar's parking lot. The back end of the car fishtailed, a side effect of Southern California's almost perpetual sunshine. During the long dry spells, oil built up on the roads, only to rise as it rained, turning asphalt into dangerous slicks.

People who said Californians didn't know how to drive in the rain had never tried driving on a greased surface. She kept her speed slow, but the cars sharing the four-lane Pacific Coast Highway weren't always as cautious. As one rushed by her, throwing up a rooster tail of wet that landed on her windshield, she was blinded for the instant it took for her to edge up the action of her wipers.

When they cleared the deluge, she saw him. Gabe. Walking in the middle of the highway. Where there were no wide turn lanes and no concrete dividers.

Terror clamped like a skeletal hand around her throat. Her mind raced as she checked her rearview mirror. Clear.

Up ahead, though, coming from the opposite direction, another car approached him. He kept walking, head down, and it laid on the horn as it passed. He didn't flinch.

She swallowed a shriek, but kept moving, slowing as she came abreast of him. Clammy sweat broke over her skin as she flipped on her hazard lights. Her finger punched the window opener.

Cold raindrops fell on her cheeks. "Gabe!" she shouted. "Gabe, get in the car."

He kept walking.

She checked her rearview mirror again, and edged her car forward. "Gabe!"

His head came around. In the glare of headlights off the wet asphalt, his face glowed like a ghost's. He blinked, as if he didn't recognize her.

This wasn't the time to make introductions. Gritting her teeth, she pulled the car closer to him, put it in PARK and set the brake, then jumped out. Fueled by a potent mix of fear and anger, she dragged him to the passenger side and stuffed him inside. Then she ran around and got behind the wheel.

"I'm going to kill you," she said, as she accelerated, taking them back up to a safe and sane speed. "I'm going to . . . going to . . ." And then she humiliated herself by breaking into choking sobs that sounded loud and pitiful and desperately worried because that killing is what she was afraid of most. That Gabe was once again contemplating killing himself.

"Cassandra." His hand awkwardly patted her thigh.

"Don't touch me." She hunched away and tried wiping her face on her wet shoulder. Then she glanced over at him, taking in the drenched state of his clothes. "God damn it, Gabe," she said. "What were you thinking?"

"I was thinking about Maddie," he said. If he was drunk, it was only the slightest of slurs in his voice. "I've been thinking about Maddie all day."

"Oh, Gabe."

"I loved her, Froot Loop. I was a good father, I think. Not great. Too busy. But I tried to let her know how special she was to me." He closed his eyes. "I miss her so much."

Fresh tears fell, warm over Cassandra's cold face. At Oomfaa's that morning, she'd noted his tension around the children, but he'd seemed to pull himself together. He certainly hadn't mentioned any mental anguish to her. But all day, as they ate together, played together, made love, running through his head like a cold, secret spring, had been thoughts of his daughter.

His wife, too, she guessed.

Gabe's ghosts.

Indefatigable. Undefeatable. At least it seemed that way to her right now. Maybe in the morning she could imagine some way to rescue Gabe from the clutches of his memories and his pain.

She pulled into their driveway and then parked in front

of her house. Weary and frozen to the bone, she headed for her door. Gabe didn't follow. He trudged up the drive toward his place, head bent, his posture the same as it had been as he'd walked the line on the highway.

Lost in thought.

Or just plain lost—at least to her.

Eighteen

Friends are God's apologies for relatives.

—HUGH KINGSMILL

Under dreary skies and dripping rain, Cassandra opened Malibu & Ewe. In the quiet time before the shop's business hours, she went over her checklist for her birthday party the next day. Celebration was the last thing she had in mind, but the invitations had been sent, the food and beverages bought. She had no clue if Dr. Frank Tucker would show up.

She'd still not confessed to Nikki and Juliet about contacting him. She'd not confessed to them she wasn't certain they were her sisters, either.

All her important secrets were still safe from the relevant parties. After finding Gabe in the rain last night, she was only gladder that he didn't know her feelings for him. A safe heart equaled a whole heart.

The bells on the door rang out and she walked into the main section of the store to find Juliet. "I didn't expect you back at work so soon, did I?" she asked, surprised.

"I'm home from my honeymoon and all unpacked. Noah's

returned to his office. So I thought you might need a backup today." Her blue and green eyes took a slow, considering pass over Cassandra.

"You heard something," she said flatly. "People are talking."

Juliet lifted her hands. "It's Malibu. Someone called Jay and then Nikki called me."

Cassandra turned away from the other woman's probing gaze. "Well, I'll be glad to have the help today. There's a group coming through on a yarn crawl and we're one of their first stops."

"That's all you're going to say?"

Eyebrows raised, she turned back. "Uh . . . can I make you some tea?"

"Yuck, no," Juliet replied, sounding just like Nikki. "I mean, aren't you going to tell me about last night?"

She shook her head. Not this time. "Let it go, Juliet."

Whatever she might have responded was lost in a flurry of activity as the first couple of customers of the day arrived. Umbrellas had to be propped open to dry, rain exclaimed over, worry expressed about what Mother Nature had next in store for beautiful but unpredictable Malibu.

"We tarped our entire backyard," a woman said. "We don't want it to start sliding. The moment I heard them predicting a slow-moving storm, we got out all the plastic sheets we've been storing since last year."

Juliet looked over at Cassandra with a little alarm and she remembered the other woman had only moved to this particular eco-system just a few months before.

"It's the slow movers that scare those built on bluffs," she explained. "Enough rain over a long period of time saturates the ground and causes it to shift. But even a small amount of precipitation can make burnt-out areas precarious."

"And if it turns out to be a hard rain, we worry about flash floods and debris flows," the woman who tarped added.

"It's not just about sunscreen anymore, Toto," Juliet murmured.

Cassandra patted her on the shoulder as she passed. "You're good, up where you are. Nikki and Jay will be fine at the beach house."

"How about you?" Juliet asked. "You and Gabe are in that canyon."

"Hay bales and sandbags for us," she said. "To channel potential water and debris. If it's an issue, Gabe will take care of it."

If his hangover would let him, she added to herself. But that thought didn't worry her. If he was lying in bed and nursing a headache, she at least knew where he was.

The group on their yarn crawl arrived next. Despite the crummy weather, they were cheerful and enthusiastic and Cassandra helped who she could, though most of them were content to nose around the shop on their own or plop down on the couches and work on their project du jour.

"Let's forget the rest of the LYSs on our list," one woman suggested. "The traffic will be a bear."

They entered into a debate about the idea of abandoning their little yarn shop tour when the bells on the door rang out again. Digging through a bin at the rear of the store, Cassandra knew something was up when their discussion petered into silence.

"Gabe." Juliet's voice, full of . . . shock?

Her heart pounding, Cassandra turned. Oh. Oh, God.

In the drama and the deluge of the night before, his new cut hadn't registered. There was a quarter-inch of black hair left, so short that the bones of his skull and the lean angles of his face were highlighted. Along with the greenish, morning-after pallor of his face, and the whiskers he hadn't bothered to shave, he looked like a walking corpse.

Nikki breezed in the door behind him, took a look, then did a double take. "Eek," she said. "Casting call for the new zombie movie?"

Gabe didn't flicker an eyelash. "Cassandra, can we talk a minute?"

No, her instincts answered for her. But she didn't get a chance to express them before Gabe had her by the elbow and was hustling her into the shop's back room.

There, she pulled free from his grasp and backed up against the now-less-cluttered countertop. "What's going on?"

He rubbed his hand against the back of his neck. "First, uh, thanks for the ride home last night."

"Do you need help collecting your car at the Beach Shack?"

"No." Annoyance crossed his face. "I don't just come to see you when I need something." When he rubbed his neck again, she felt his weariness.

I was thinking about Maddie, she heard him say in her head, his voice raw. *I've been thinking about Maddie all day.*

No. She'd fall to pieces if she let her mind go in that direction. For once, she had to hold her emotions close and tight. Stiffening her spine, she steeled her voice, too. "So what's the second reason you're here?"

"I'm going away today."

She stared at him. Going away? She'd expected the apology. She'd anticipated moodiness, a grim attitude, a return to his prickly distance. For God's sake, she'd seen him walking down the highway last night as if it didn't matter whether he lived or died!

But going away?

"I don't know when I'll be back," he continued. "I didn't want you to wonder."

"Wonder . . . what?" She was still waiting for the words to sink in.

He shrugged, then looked away. "I don't know. Where to send the rent checks."

An inappropriate laugh bubbled up from her belly. "The rent checks?"

He glanced up, glanced down. "Yeah."

"We've been friends for two years and you think I'd be wondering about *the rent checks*?"

More than friends. She thought of his mouth on her throat, her breasts, of his hard palm stroking over her hips and down her thighs. She thought of how he slept curled around her at night, the fingers of one hand twisted in her hair and the other nestled between her thighs as if they were each the power charge the other needed. "For God's sake, Gabe."

His hands came out in a placating gesture. "No need to get emotional."

"I can see that." Another laugh bubbled from some deep, bitter place. "It would be so inconvenient."

Then she couldn't get away from him fast enough. Her footsteps sounded loud against the hardwood as she hurried from the back room.

"Hey . . ." he said, but she ignored him, rushing into the main area to take her place behind the cash register. Now there was something solid between herself and the man who strode in her wake, frustration wafting off him like brimstone.

"Say good-bye to Gabe," she told Juliet and Nikki, ignoring the other customers in the shop. "He's going away indefinitely."

"Before your birthday party tomorrow?" Juliet asked, looking between the two of them.

She threw up a hand. "Before the rent checks are due. Imagine that."

Gabe's frown was fierce. "Jesus, Froot Loop . . ."

"Sorry." She made a face and threw a look at her sisters. "I'm not supposed to get emotional."

Bristling, Nikki glared at Gabe then marched over to Cassandra's side. "I'm going to kill him."

"Don't bother," she muttered. "I bet he's got that covered."

"What the hell is that supposed to mean?" Gabe demanded.

Too late, she remembered she was keeping her feelings close to her chest. He'd warned her not to let them out, and as much as she'd hated to hear him say it, it was exactly the caution she should heed. For her dignity. For her secrets.

"Never mind," she said, turning her attention to a stack of receipts.

Gabe wasn't having it. He bellied up to the counter and reached across to grab her chin, lifting it so their gazes met. "Explain yourself."

"You don't want me to say. I don't need to say."

His fingers tightened.

She grabbed his wrist and forced it away from her face, shaking with everything she didn't want to feel. "I don't have to tell you that you've been daring that death wish inside of yourself for as long as I've known you."

"Death wish," he muttered. "I don't know what you're talking about."

"Gabe, I caught you with a noose. You still have a hose

hooked up to the exhaust of that very embodiment of a death wish that you call your classic Thunderbird."

"You're overreacting. I was just playing with that rope. And that car thing was months ago. It's just that I haven't needed that hose again."

"You were walking in the middle of the dark, rainy highway last night, Gabe. *Last night*."

He pressed the heels of his palms to his eyes. "I can't do this."

"Yeah. Run away. That's been working out so well for you." She couldn't help the sharp edge to her voice. "Or you could try facing your feelings this time. See if that helps."

His hands dropped, and he stared at her from bloodshot eyes. "This is coming from *you*?"

She waved her fingers. "Don't try to make this about me."

"Why not? Because you're always so excellent at expressing your emotions? Facing *your* feelings?"

She frowned, knowing it was his own pain that was causing him to turn on her. "Well, I am."

"Did you tell your mother you wanted her home for your thirtieth birthday? Or let's go back further. Did you ever tell her that you didn't want to be Judith and Cassandra but Mom and daughter?"

Okay, it always surprised her to find out that he'd been listening all this time. But it ticked her off, too. She sucked in a quick breath. "Gabe—"

"If it's so easy to lay it all on the line, then let's see you do it, Froot Loop. Let's have you spill every one of your home truths. Like, why don't you tell your sisters you contacted your father and met with those adopted sons of his?"

Nikki sucked in a sharp breath. Cassandra shot a look at Juliet, but she was harder to read.

"Did you?" the other woman asked, her voice quiet.

"Yes." Cassandra turned her attention to Gabe. "Happy now?" Then she swung back to her sisters, determined to get it all out. "And I met with him, too. Dr. Frank Tucker. And he . . . and he . . . well, he accepts the two of you, but he has doubts whether our DNAs would match. He's not sure I'm your sister."

"What?" Nikki and Juliet said together.

"Oh, God," Gabe muttered, his hand over his eyes. "Oh, my God. I am such an asshole."

"You won't get an argument from over here," Cassandra said. There was a high-pitched ringing in her ears. "But if you want me to lay it all out . . . there's just one thing, okay? One last thing."

"Don't—" he started.

She talked right over him. "I'm in love with you, Gabe. No surprise, I'm sure, but if you're going away, you can go ahead and take that with you."

"Oh, Froot Loop. *Cassandra*." The fight had all gone out of him. "It's no good. You can't . . ."

"Don't try to tell me how I feel. At least give me credit for knowing myself." And herself was all she'd ever had.

"Look," he said, his voice tight. "You know I can't marry again. And I never want another child. But you deserve those things. It's why I have to leave."

She heard herself laugh. "Don't try to say you're going away for me. We both know you too well for that."

Nikki crowded closer to Cassandra. "Shall I throw him out now?"

Gabe's gaze didn't leave hers. "She has more to say."

"You're right, I do." Cassandra gripped the edge of the counter until her knuckles whitened. "Your friend Sammy said you called yourself a selfish SOB last night. Well, you're right about that as well. You only think of yourself."

"Cassandra—"

"Otherwise you'd know how it's made me feel to find you half-dead from alcohol. You'd think how horrible it would be for me to see you return from one of your dawn-to-dusk kayak voyages with that look of disappointment on your face."

"Cassandra . . ."

The sting of the tears in her eyes was nothing compared to the wrenching pain in her chest. "I'm sorry that you feel guilty for not being a perfect husband and for not having the perfect marriage. I ache for you that you miss Maddie so much. But none of that means you shouldn't have realized how you hurt me, Gabe. How you hurt me when you expressed such unmitigated relief that we hadn't created a child."

"Cassandra." It was Juliet who said her name now, Juliet who touched her with a hand meant to comfort.

She kept her focus on the tight-lipped man across the counter. "I get that we'll have nothing, be nothing, make nothing together, Gabe. But would it really have been such a terrible disaster?"

He pushed his hands through his nonexistent hair. "This isn't what I wanted."

"I get that, too." She turned away from him. "Because you're too much of a damn coward to live again."

When silence was his only reply, she managed to get out the only two words left to be said. "Good-bye, Gabe."

Hearing his feet stride for the exit, she forced herself to look back. Seeing it would be believing it. He stilled, his hand an inch from the door's plate glass, and she watched raindrops roll down its surface. He turned his head and caught her gaze.

His voice was raw. "But if I could, Cassandra, I would want my life to be with you."

"It's my party," Cassandra Riley told her companions as she wiped a tear from her cheek with the back of her hand. "I'll cry if I want to."

The pair on her couch didn't look up, and the one near the overstuffed chair in her living room continued toying with a small ball of soft yarn. It was left over from the dress Cassandra had made to wear to the celebration-that-wasn't, and she fingered the mohair-nylon-wool of the crocheted skirt wishing the April sky would take its cue from the blue color. Stanching another tear, she pressed her nose to the sliding glass door that led to her backyard. Beyond the small pool with its graceful, arching footbridge, the green of the surrounding banana trees, sword ferns, and tropical shrubs looked lush against the dark storm clouds.

The rain hadn't let up.

And neither had Cassandra's low mood.

Thirty years old, she thought, feeling more wetness drip off her jaw, and she was all dressed up with no place to go.

That wasn't strictly true. Three miles away on the Pacific Coast Highway, at her little yarn shop, Malibu & Ewe, the ingredients for a birthday bash were ready and waiting. But a spring deluge had hit overnight and before her landline phone connection had died she'd been informed that the road at the end of her secluded lane was washed out. The narrow driveway beyond her place led to only one other residence.

She wouldn't be partying over there, even if the owner

would let her through the doors. Even if he was inside his bat cave.

Though they'd been lovers for four weeks, he'd dumped her yesterday, hard. She suspected that following their public scene he'd immediately headed someplace where he could indulge in another of his self-destructive benders without anyone's interference.

"That means we're alone, kids," she said over her shoulder. "Isolated."

All she'd never wanted by thirty.

She'd made contact with her donor sibling sisters because she wanted the family ties her sperm-inseminated, single mother had always eschewed. Cassandra had forged a real relationship with Nikki and Juliet now, but there was trouble on that front, too.

So here she was, all by herself again. Lonely.

The rain picked up, drumming harder against the roof and all three "kids" jumped. She'd taken them in last year during a torrential storm and they probably remembered what it was like to be wet and muddy and barely clinging to life.

She couldn't blame the cats for being spooked. Besides being brokenhearted, Cassandra felt a little twitchy herself. She wiggled her toes in her warm down slippers and rubbed her arms to smooth away her chills. Dark was approaching, the weather wasn't abating, and with the road gone already, she had to be on the lookout for more evidence of mud slides.

Blinking back another round of self-pity, she scrutinized her backyard once more. At the rear was the first of the narrow flights of steps that led to the other house farther up the Malibu canyon. A creek ran through the northern end of the property, very picturesque, but if its banks overflowed, then water would come gushing down those stairs, just like—

Oh, God.

Just like it was doing right now.

She stared at the widening wash of muddy runoff tumbling Slinky-like down the cement steps. This wasn't good.

This wasn't supposed to happen on her birthday.

Or ever, for that matter.

Thumping sounds from the direction of her front porch caused her head to jerk around. Floodwaters behind her and what—who was on her porch? Her heart slammed against her chest. The cats jumped to their feet and rushed toward the front door.

Surely only one person could get them moving with such haste. They loved him, though he pretended not to care.

Could it be . . . ?

She crossed the room, almost beating the kids in the impromptu footrace. Their tails swished impatiently as she grasped the doorknob, then twisted and pulled.

In the deepening dusk, the visitor was just a dark figure in a sodden raincoat, a wide-brimmed safari-style hat shadowing his face and leaking water at the edges like she'd been leaking tears a few minutes before.

Cassandra's heart smacked in an erratic, painful rhythm against her breastbone. Yesterday he'd walked away from her and she'd doubted if she'd ever see him again.

The figure pushed aside the open edges of his long coat. The sleeve slid up, reminding her of the bandage he'd wound around his cut wrist just a few weeks before. She knew the skin was healed there now.

His hand appeared pale against the blackness of his clothes. She saw the gleam of something metallic shoved into the waistband of dark jeans.

Oh, God.

She'd known he was in a bleak mood yesterday.

I was thinking about Maddie. I've been thinking about Maddie all day.

But even after the many times she'd rescued him off barroom floors, even after the numerous occasions he'd gone missing for days at a stretch, even after the skydiving and the hang gliding and the dangerous ocean voyages, not to mention that walk down the middle of a dark, rainy highway just two nights before, her mind couldn't fathom . . .

"Gabe?" she whispered, her gaze lifting to the face beneath the hat's brim. "A gun?"

With one hand he took it from his waistband, with the other he pushed her into the living room. Cassandra stumbled back, surprise locked in her throat along with her breath. The front door slammed and he pushed off his hat. It hit the floor with a plop, causing Ed to skitter away.

She gaped, tears shocked away. "Reed?"

The dreadlocked man didn't smile. "Your 'sort-of brother,' isn't that what you said? That was your mistake. Trying to insert yourself into other people's families."

Nineteen

In every conceivable manner, the family is link to
our past, bridge to our future.

—ALEX HALEY

Could this be happening? Cassandra thought. What was
Reed Tucker doing? "What's going on?"

"I told you," he said, shrugging out of his raincoat one
sleeve at a time. The gun traded hands so that it stayed
trained on her.

A gun was trained on her!

"You shouldn't have tried to horn in on our family."

She put out a hand. "I wasn't trying—"

"You certainly were!" Reed interrupted, his eyes narrowing. Red color flushed his face. "You want Dad's money."

"No, no. I don't want money." Cassandra inched away
from him. "Just . . . information. Connections."

He shook his head, his dreadlocks dancing with the
movement. "I thought that at first, which is why I only did
those little things to bug you, like the idea of you and your
'Malibu Babe' sisters was bugging me."

Her mind scooped up each piece of information, trying

to puzzle them altogether. "The fire in my shop? Nikki's food spoiling?"

"And the rock you ran into," Reed added, then frowned. "That wasn't my best idea. Too unpredictable. But it came to me because I hike the area a lot."

Moosewood and Breathe were twining Cassandra's ankles, emitting anxious meows. She shuffled back, as if reacting to the soft push of their bodies instead of the insistent scream in her head to flee.

She was going to do that, as soon as she got a little closer to the sliding glass door behind her back. Her gaze trained on that gun, she retreated another step.

"Look out!" Reed warned, but it was too late.

She'd forgotten about the basket of knitting sitting beside the couch, and her feet tripped over it, tumbling her onto her butt. She went with the fall, letting the momentum roll her toward her goal. When she felt cold glass against her spine, she scrambled to her feet, using the door handle to pull herself up. Then she froze there, her hands wrapped around the handle at the small of her back, her focus fixed on Reed and the gun.

"You warned me about the basket," she said. "You don't really want to hurt me."

"Like hell I do." He glared at her. "Don't be like Dad and Patrick—they always underestimate me. They don't think my recycling business will ever amount to anything."

"It's a great idea," she said quickly. "Especially when the world is going greener every day."

"Yeah, yeah," he said, waving his gun-free hand. "But just in case, I don't want to be written out of Dad's will, or even see it split five ways."

"Oh, I'm sure your father wouldn't—"

"You want him to. That's why you sent him that invitation to your birthday party and had coffee with him. That's when I realized I had to stop with the fun and games and kill you. All three of you."

Her fingers tightened on the handle of the door as she realized he was serious. He might look like a laid-back surfer dude, someone more into ganja than guns, but she was sure now that it was murder, not marijuana on his mind.

And though that gun in his hand looked about as big as a cannon to her right now, she couldn't wait another minute.

On a breath, she shoved open the door and ducked, plunging into the rain and muck that was her back patio. The crack of the gun, the clap of thunder? She didn't know; she only ran as fast as her slippers would take her, zigzagging like all those self-defense documentaries prescribed as she headed for the steps leading to Gabe's. It was her only way out.

She grabbed the railing and started pulling herself up the steep stairs, allowing herself a quick glance back, only to see Reed slide in the mud and tumble into her pool to his waist. Adrenaline allowed her another burst of speed, even as she saw him scramble from the water, the gun still in his grasp.

Her leg muscles burned as she tried to take advantage of his stumble. From the corner of her eye, she saw the cats racing beside her and could only guess that their animal instincts were in line with hers. Reed Tucker meant business. He meant to kill her.

Reaching the sloping lawn that led to Gabe's compound, she slid on the slick grass, tipping forward. She caught her fall with her palms and pushed off, her gaze catching on the flick of a tail racing in the direction of the closest solid structure—the smaller of two stand-alone stucco garages that housed Gabe's vehicles. Her legs churning, she took off in the direction of its narrow side door.

Get inside. Turn the lock. Pray he looks for you elsewhere.

Her wet hand slipped on the metal knob. She tried again, trying to swallow her panicked, whimpering breaths. The handle turned, she pushed it open. Two cats raced over her feet as she stepped inside.

A force wrenched the knob from her hand. She leaped into the dim interior as the metal door crashed against the inside wall and Reed Tucker filled the entry. It was almost dark outside, and even darker inside the 15×20 building, but Reed found the light switches.

The overhead fluorescent tubes flickered then blazed to life as Cassandra shuffled back until her thighs hit the side of the classic Thunderbird that Gabe had restored—the replica of the vehicle in which his wife and daughter had died.

How fitting, Cassandra thought, trying to clamp down on her hysteria. This car was going to be the last stand of another woman who loved him.

Gabe cursed himself for not leaving the day before as he'd intended. Now with the damn rain coming down and the road at the end of the lane washed out, he was stuck only one hundred yards from where Cassandra lived.

And with her birthday gift in his pocket.

There were a dozen ways to deal with it. Forget about it—she likely didn't want a present from him. Or mail it to her anyway, and imagine her overarming it off the balcony of Malibu & Ewe and into the ocean. Or take it to her place and leave it by the back door.

He figured she'd made it out of the canyon in time to get to her party at the yarn shop, though she'd have to stay the night with either Nikki or Juliet. When she returned to her house, though, he'd be gone and she'd find the box he'd left behind.

Maybe it would convey all that he couldn't.

She was precious. Sparkling. Valuable and enduring. He hated that he'd hurt her and regretted like hell that she'd witnessed him flirting with his own death so many times.

Cassandra had been right about him—except he wasn't cowardly. That would have been making the easy choice to stay with her, allowing her to shower her love on the shell of a man he'd become.

But before he left, he could make sure she got his gift.

He shoved his hand in his pocket, his fingertips finding his wallet instead. Setting his jaw, he forced himself to draw it out. There were other people he owed. He opened the leather. Flipped to the photos. Sweet Maddie. Lynn. For the first time since her death, he steeled himself to meet her eyes.

There was no accusation in them, he realized. It was just Lynn's warm gaze, smiling in the happiness of that moment with their daughter. Those two were still together, weren't they?

Oh, God, he thought, as the truth hit him. Of the three of them, the only one who was lost, really, was him.

He ran his thumb over their faces. "I'm sorry," he whispered, because like Cassandra, they probably expected better of him, too. It just wasn't in him, though.

The heart of him was gone.

Reseating his wallet beside the small gift, he jogged to the door that led to the most direct route to Cassandra's place. Christ, the rain was coming down in sheets. Mailing the gift from wherever was his first stop on the road seemed like a better idea now. Then he squinted, peering into the dusk and the drenching rain. What the hell was Ed doing wandering about?

The cat looked miserable and about five pounds lighter with his fluffy, black and white hair plastered to his body. Gabe cracked open the door. "Ed!" he called out. "Come in. You look like hell."

Instead of running for the offered shelter, Ed sat in a puddle and stared at Gabe. He ran his hand over his stubbled hair. "Okay, I look like hell, too, but have enough sense to get in out of the rain."

Ed didn't move.

"Fine then," Gabe muttered, and moved to close the door. But his conscience pricked at him, and then a sense of real alarm. Cassandra wouldn't have let the cat out in a storm.

Without another thought, he stepped out, rain immediately wetting his clothes. Ed turned and scampered off, and Gabe jogged to keep up. "Lassie ain't got nothin' on you," he muttered, as Ed looked over his shoulder and then picked up speed. "This better be good, cat."

Ed led him straight to the smaller of his two garages. Seeing the light spilling out from the open side door, Gabe hurried to it, only to come up short when he saw a pale Cassandra pasted against the Thunderbird. What the hell?

Reed Tucker held a long, hand-knitted scarf in one hand and a gun in the other. At Gabe's appearance in the doorway, the gun's barrel instantly shifted, including both him and Cassandra in target range.

Those facts came at him in a rush. Supposition soon

followed. The fire. And what else? What else was this bastard capable of? "Don't hurt her," Gabe told the man through clenched teeth.

"I'm not going to hurt her," Reed answered matter-of-factly. "I'm going to kill her."

Gabe surged into the room. Reed's arm jerked toward him, then back to Cassandra. Halting, Gabe held his arms wide. "Choose me instead. For three years I've been hoping to die."

Cassandra made a little sound. Distress. Fear. Gabe didn't look away from Reed, but softened his voice. "Take it easy, Froot Loop. Take it easy."

"It's gonna be easy," Reed said. Then he leaped, grasping Cassandra and yanking her back against his chest. He still held the scarf, and now the gun was closer to her frightened face. "Cassandra and I were just discussing how easy."

Gabe looked at her. "He saw the hose in the exhaust pipe," she explained, her voice strained. "And how you threaded it through the window."

Shit. He didn't like where this was heading.

"So we're going to put your little setup to good use, my friend," Reed said, smiling. "Death by carbon monoxide poisoning. It was going to be a solo suicide, but with you, this will look even better. Some sort of lover's thing, right?"

"Everyone knows Gabe doesn't love me," Cassandra said quickly. "So just let him go."

Oh, Froot Loop.

Generous, open-hearted Cassandra. She deserved someone whole and unshadowed, and instead she was facing this moment with him. The ash inside his chest was swirling, rising, choking him. He couldn't breathe.

He couldn't bear to think of Cassandra not breathing.

Cassandra not breathing. *Cassandra!*

The thick cinders suddenly stopped their twisting spin. They fell, settling back into his chest, their shape and size the semblance of a heart.

And then it beat, whole and steady.

Determined.

His eyes on her, he took a sure step forward.

Reed jabbed the gun into Cassandra's temple, forcing Gabe to halt again. "So you *both* think I'm stupid, just like Dad and Patrick. How do you suppose that would work out, huh? Me letting either one of you go?"

Jerking his head, he indicated the car. "Dude. Get in."

Cassandra felt the tension throbbing throughout Gabe's body, even though they were each in a bucket seat with a leather bolster between them. The convertible top was up but Reed had been unable to get the power windows to rise.

In a dry voice, Gabe offered to help, but Reed had declined to untie the knots he'd used to bind their hands together and then to the steering wheel. "No worries," he said, sounding cheerful. "The garage looks airtight. It will only take you a little longer to drift off."

Then he made another check of the knots that bound them tight. "You make this scarf?" he'd asked Cassandra.

"Yes," she said. It matched the hat she'd made Gabe and Reed had found it hanging on a hook on the wall.

"It came in real handy. I'll get rid of it after the two of you are gone." Reaching through the passenger window, he turned the key in the ignition. The engine roared to life. "Bye, folks!" he said gaily, and then he was gone. The door slammed behind him.

"Shit, shit, shit," Gabe cursed, struggling against the bonds of the scarf.

"No," she whispered fiercely. "Stop. Stop moving."

"Damn it, Froot Loop." Frustration filled his voice. "I'm not letting this happen."

"We're *not* going to let this happen," she said, turning her wrists gently, trying to shift one of the scarf's knots. "It's not going to happen."

He seemed to sense her seriousness, his tension changing tenor. "What? What don't I know?"

Her heart was thrumming in hummingbird panic, but it was another creature altogether on her mind. "We're going to take a little trip to the frog pond."

"What the hell?"

"Rip-it, rip-it," she said, as she bent her head to the end of the scarf she'd managed to twist toward her mouth. "We're going to unravel the scarf."

"Unravel . . . ?" She felt his surprise, and then his comprehension. "You can loosen the knots by undoing the stitches. I didn't think about that."

She spit some fiber from the tip of her tongue. "Lucky for us, Reed didn't think about that either."

"What should I do?"

"Hold still unless you can reach an end." She bent back to her work.

Gabe was forced to rely on her efforts and after another few minutes, she could sense his renewed impatience. The exhaust was sweetening the air in the garage and she had to lift her head to cough.

"Damn it, damn *me*," he said, letting his head fall back. "Cassandra, I don't know if we'll have enough time."

"We'll have enough time. At least, the carbon monoxide isn't going to kill us."

His gaze jerked her way. "How do you know?"

She yanked free another row of the scarf with her teeth and then took a shallow breath. "When I caught on to your setup out here, one night I came back and punched some holes in the walls along the foundation. From the outside they're covered by the oleander bushes. Inside, well, you never noticed I rearranged a few cardboard boxes here and there."

"So we have some ventilation." He was silent a moment as she hurried to unravel more rows with her teeth. "God, I love you, Cassandra," he finally said.

She didn't bother looking up or responding, figuring she understood the spirit of his words. There was another matter anyway. "When we get out of these knots though . . . how we get away from Reed is all on you."

His plan was simple. Once free of their bindings, he helped her silently climb out of the car. Then he pressed her against the wall, positioning her so she'd be behind the door once it opened. He caught her mouth in a hard kiss, then crossed to the car and turned off the ignition. The engine died. With luck, Reed would think they had, too.

"He'll think the car ran out of gas," he whispered, hurrying to the opposite side of the door. "Just stay put and stay quiet."

With the Thunderbird no longer rumbling, the garage was too silent. Surely Reed would be able to hear her heart pounding, even over the persistent drumming of the rain. Despite her efforts at cross-ventilating the building, her head was spinning and the urge to cough welled up in her throat. She clapped her hands over her mouth and felt the fine tremor in her fingers.

She didn't want to die.

She'd never wanted Gabe to die.

"I love you, Cassandra," she thought she heard him say again, then the door creaked open. A figure stepped inside.

Gabe's fist struck Reed's jaw.

The younger man fell, half-in and half-out of the doorway. The door swinging shut caught his ribs. He grunted, his lax fingers twitching to contract around the gun that had landed on the floor beside him. Gabe scooped it up, then pointed the barrel at their assailant. Relief didn't make a dent in the mix of adrenaline and carbon monoxide coursing through Cassandra's system.

"Cassandra, do you know where I stashed that noose?" Gabe asked, his voice tight. "I think we've found a better use for the rope."

Twenty

The bond that links your true family is not one of
blood, but of respect and joy in each other's life.

—RICHARD BACH

After a tense night guarding their prisoner, at dawn Cassandra laced up her hiking boots. She struggled into a slicker,
listened to another round of Gabe's admonitions, and then
mouthed a number of promises, some of which made little
sense.

She didn't need to see a doctor and she wasn't going to
hole up with one of her sisters after making contact with the
sheriff. As it happened, once they heard her story, the authorities kept her at the station in Calabasas until Gabe and
Reed could be collected. He must have called Nikki and
Juliet on his way in—maybe the sheriffs had some secret
cell reception—because the other two women, along with
Noah and Jay, arrived just minutes before the man who had
saved her life.

He raised his eyebrows when she expressed the senti-
ment in the hallway at the station. "We'll discuss who rescued who later, Froot Loop."

"I'm too tired," she said. Neither one of them had slept

the night before while they watched over Reed, suffering through his ranting and his too-seldom sullen silences. "All I want to do is go home and sleep."

It was past noon when Noah drove them back up the canyon. The road had been cleared of mud and debris, but there were leaves and downed branches all over their narrow lane. When they came to her place, Noah kept his foot pressed to the gas.

"Wait, wait," she protested from the backseat.

Noah exchanged a look with the man on his right.

"You stay with me for now, Froot Loop," Gabe said, his voice adamant.

"No." Tears pricked the corners of her eyes.

"Please."

Noah glanced over his shoulder. "Otherwise I'll have to take you back to Juliet," he added. "And she told me to tell you that on this issue you can count on her being 'the mean one.' She said you'd understand that."

She understood *them*. They were still determined to behave as if they were her sisters, even though that was no longer a certainty. DNA testing, she reminded herself, putting it on her mental list, right after sleep and some time to allow the shock to wear off. That day that Gabe had left the shop—was it only forty-eight hours ago?—she'd apologized to Nikki and Juliet and put forth her plan for genetic testing. They hadn't exactly agreed.

Maybe it was best to forget that anyway. Perhaps she should break contact and sever ties with the other two. After all, Reed Tucker had planned on killing the three of them in order to protect his inheritance. A plan she'd set in motion by her selfish desire to find herself a family had backfired with near-fatal results.

It would be better for everyone if she remained alone.

Gabe seemed to understand that. Few words were exchanged between them as he ushered her into one of the spacious guest rooms with an attached bath. Her plan was a long shower, but she was so exhausted she settled for a short one. Then she braided her wet hair, wrapped herself in a terry robe hanging on the back of the bathroom door, and fell into bed and into sleep.

She awoke, heart pounding and disoriented.

"It's okay, baby." Gabe's voice. "You're safe."

Her eyes flew open to find him sitting in the upholstered chair near the bed. In jeans and a T-shirt, his feet bare, he looked as if he'd been there awhile. She could tell from the light outside the window that it was closing on dusk again.

"Nothing could get to you," he said. "I watched over you while you slept."

She struggled to sit up, gripping the lapels of the robe together. "You should have slept yourself. I'm fine."

Leaning forward, he took a glass of water off the bedside table and handed it to her. "I had to make sure of that."

She shot him a look, but his face wore one of those inscrutable Gabe expressions that told her he was deep in his interior world. *Not your puzzle, Cassandra*, she reminded herself. *Soon he'll be taking himself away and all his moods with him.*

Her hands seemed to be trembling again, so she carefully put the glass down. Beside it on the little table sat a small package wrapped with a mangled bow.

Gabe noticed the direction of her gaze. "It was in my pocket when I set out in the rain last night. For you. Happy belated birthday."

Oh. Yeah. She'd forgotten all about that. With trepidation, she eyed the gift. "Am I supposed to open it?"

He shifted in the chair. "Up to you. I . . ." Hesitating, he forked a hand through his nonexistent hair. "I hope you like it. It's, uh, organic."

Eyebrows raised, she took it in her hand, holding the small package on the shelf of her palm. "You bought me an organic present? How enlightened of you, Gabe."

Shrugging, he leaned forward in his chair with his elbows on his knees and his dark, watchful eyes on her.

The ribbon fell away. The lid of the small box lifted on a hinge. Set in white velvet was a pair of diamond earrings. Sparkling, platinum-set, hefty-sized diamond stud earrings.

Her mouth dried. She'd expected something made at a craft fair, maybe. A gift certificate to the local farmer's market folded into quarters.

He slumped back in his chair. "Boring, huh? Conventional."

"Organic," she whispered, touching one with a fingertip. Gemstones and precious metal. But she didn't understand. Diamond earrings weren't a gift you bought for a neighbor or a friend. You bought them for a woman. A lover. And surely not one you planned on leaving.

"I picked them up a couple of weeks ago."

Ah. When they *were* lovers. When he wasn't leaving. Before he'd decided he didn't want her anymore. She pasted on a smile. "Thank you. I'll treasure them. They'll always remind me of you."

"Cassandra . . ."

"A birthday gift and a good-bye gift," she continued, deciding it was imperative she let him know she understood. "That's how I'll think of them."

He groaned. "*Cassandra.*" In a breath, he launched himself out of the chair and was in the bed, over her, his body's weight on her, his hands warm as they cupped her face. He kissed her mouth, her nose, her chin. "My heart almost crumbled all over again when he put that gun against your head."

She knew what he meant. No matter the separation to come, they'd shared a past that included those terrifying moments. Her hand stroked his short hair. "Mine shredded when he pointed it at you."

His mouth pressed more kisses to her cheeks, her throat, and then her mouth again. "Let me heal it, baby. Let me put it back together for you."

Oh.

"Let me show you how glad I am that we're alive."

Oh. Even through the covers she could feel the heavy bulge of his sex.

He was offering one last chance for intimacy with him. More of that good-bye, she supposed, as well as a celebration. But . . .

With his next kiss, logic, sense, self-preservation flew out the window. She couldn't say no. She wouldn't. They *were* alive, after all.

"Cassandra?" He looked into her eyes.

"Yes."

The air chilled her suddenly hot skin as he pushed the covers off and drew open her robe. He rubbed his smooth cheek against her breast, and she held his head close, perversely missing the usual rasp of his whiskers. But then his lips found her nipple and it stiffened as it always did in the heat of his mouth and against the flickering tease of his tongue. She arched, and he cupped the other breast in his palm, thumbing the nipple to a matching peak.

He drew her robe away from her bare body and tossed it over the side of the bed. Then he rolled, bringing her over him so that he could run his big palms over her back and along her bottom. His hands squeezed and she gasped, her thighs parting so he could press his jean-covered leg against the warm, already wet place between hers.

She squirmed, loving the knowing pressure, but wanting more. Her hands pushed at the hem of his T-shirt and he jerked it off in one movement. Closing her eyes, she inhaled his clean scent, then indulged herself, retelling him her deepest secrets by tracing them with her tongue on the muscled expanse of his chest.

I love you.

I'll always love you.

He shuddered, and buried his hands in her hair. "Witch," he murmured. "Take me into your body," he said, his hips lifting against hers. "I'll make it so good for you. I'll make it so right."

She smiled against his skin and thought about telling him that she didn't expect his promises, that no one had ever given any to her, but that was just too much talk. So instead her hand wandered down the rippled muscles of his belly. The skin there twitched when she reached the button of his fly.

Groaning, he rolled again, leaving her splayed beneath him as he drew off his jeans. Then he rose over her, and took the backs of her knees in his palms. As he sank into the mattress, he lifted her legs and opened her. His expression softened and his eyes glittered as he looked down on the swollen wetness of her sex. It throbbed under the heat of his gaze and she saw his nostrils flare and his chest rise and fall in heavy breaths. "You're so pretty. So pretty and so ready for me."

He dipped his head and drew his tongue from the sensitive button at the top of her cleft to the warm lower well where he lingered, tasting her. She cried out as his tongue painted her with pleasure until she pulled at his arms, asking to be filled by him.

He didn't acquiesce, not until she was sure she wasn't breathing, when there was no oxygen pumping through her body, but only desire. His hips pushed her thighs wide. His erection nudged at the melting entrance to her body.

"Do you know what we're doing, sweetheart?"

"Hm?" Her eyes closed, she lifted her hips, trying to take him in, but he held back, asked her again.

"Do you know what this is?"

She lifted her lashes, looking into his face, knowing there was some message there. Her trembling fingers played over his lips and he nipped at them, sending another jolt of desire through her already jangled system.

"Cassandra, do you know what I'm trying to tell you?"

"Tell me?" She couldn't think. "Good-bye?"

His eyes closed. "No, sweetheart." Then they flared open. "Or yes. Yes. It *is* good-bye. Good-bye past." He fitted himself to the notch in her body and pushed in. "And hello us, Cassandra." He slid deep.

Her body swallowed every naked inch.

Her heart seized. Her eyes flared wide. *Every naked inch.*

"Shall I pull out?" He ducked his head so his serious, dark, dark gaze met hers. "Is that what you want?"

She shook her head, tears stinging her eyes. "Do you know what you're doing?"

"I know I love you. I've loved you for nearly two years. I've probably been in love with you for that long, too. But even though you gave me a lecture the other day that pulled the wool from my eyes . . ."

His silly pun brought a tremulous smile to her lips.

". . . I couldn't move on until I was faced with another potential tragedy."

He kissed her mouth, still buried deep and unmoving, even as her inner muscles undulated against his thick flesh. "Not until I saw you with death just a bullet away. I couldn't bear the idea of losing you. Of losing all the possibilities of a life we could have together. Of a life we might *make* together."

Her heart felt too big for her chest. She touched Gabe's face, touching his brows, his chin, his beloved lips.

They moved under her fingers. "Will you be my future, Cassandra? Will you be my friend, my wife, the mother of my children? Will you be my family?"

Emotion rippled through her. Did she need to answer? He knew what it would be because he knew her so well. *Be my family.*

The man was always listening.

"I love you, Gabe," she whispered, then she took a deep breath. "Make me a baby."

He grinned, looking younger than she'd ever seen. Happy. "For that, as many as you'd like."

Cassandra firmed her grip on the key to Malibu & Ewe and forced herself to ignore her roiling stomach and fit it into the lock. Gabe had his hand on her shoulder and the warmth of his touch eased some of her nerves. She was keenly aware of the envelope in her other hand, and she worried that her sweaty palm might obscure the information that it contained.

Or maybe that would be a good thing.

She and Nikki and Juliet had sent their DNA tests away. A simple cheek swab and from there a laboratory had done the work. It was supposed to take a couple of weeks, but Jay, who seemed to know everybody in the world, was able to make a call and cut the wait time in half.

They all had received the results and were meeting at the knitting shop today—a semineutral location—to open them together.

"Froot Loop?" Gabe said, running his hand along her hair. "You okay?"

She hadn't moved.

He turned her in his arms and tilted up her chin so their gazes met. "Cassandra, sweetheart. No matter what happens, no matter what that piece of paper says, it doesn't change anything I feel for you. Or anything about our future plans. You know that, right?"

She managed a smile. "I know that."

His kiss was soft and sweet as his hand brushed her lower belly. "If there's a baby in there, we don't want it upset by you worrying."

"There might not be a baby in there. Have you thought about that?"

"Yeah." He grinned. "I've thought about what a hardship it will be for us to keep trying to get one planted."

" 'Planted'?" She pushed at his shoulder. "Eew."

His arms pulled her closer and he pressed his cheek to hers. "Like a garden, sweetheart," he whispered. "Our very own spring flower."

Her heart rolled in her chest and she had to bury her face in his shoulder to keep the tears at bay. "I'm getting as bad as Nikki," she told Gabe, when she dared look up again. "Crying all the time."

She didn't let herself think it was baby hormones, not yet.

"Speaking of Nikki . . ." he murmured, nodding toward the Malibu & Ewe entry.

The reason they were at the shop swamped her again. Today she'd find out whether or not the two women she felt so close to were in fact her sisters. Taking a breath, she moved out of Gabe's arms and turned back to the door.

"No cowards here," she murmured, putting the key in the lock and giving it a turn.

"Not anymore," Gabe agreed.

She threw him a smile over her shoulder. Her brave guy, willing to start again after so much pain. She'd make sure he never regretted it. Still looking at him, she pushed open the door.

"Surprise!"

The many-voiced shout had Cassandra's head whipping around. The lights in the shop blazed on, revealing dozens and dozens of smiling people. A HAPPY BIRTHDAY! banner was strung up in the middle of the space and there were tables of food and buckets filled with ice and beverages.

Tears started in her eyes again. Blindly reaching back, she found Gabe's hand and drew him to her. "You did this."

He grinned. "I did this."

"With a little help," Nikki said, coming out of the crowd with Juliet by her side. They each grabbed one of Cassandra's arms and drew her into the midst of the party.

"But . . . but . . ." She looked down at the envelope in her hand.

Nikki grabbed it and tossed it on the counter by the cash register. "We'll get to that later. Now it's party time."

What could she do but celebrate? Most of the Chamber of Commerce was there and several from the city government. Other Malibuites she'd known all her life. The regular Tuesday Night Knitters were doing most of the hostessing work, plying people with little sandwiches and items from the fruit and vegetable trays.

Gabe appointed himself beverage patrol and he was wandering around passing out beers and topping off champagne glasses. He handed her a plastic flute full of sparkling bubbles. "A sip or two won't hurt our flower," he said.

Nikki and Juliet cast her identical round-eyed looks at that, but she pretended not to notice, instead turning to the ringing telephone on the counter. She snatched it up and had to put her hand over her other ear to hear the voice on the other end.

"Happy belated birthday!" It was her mother.

Cassandra smiled. "How did you know I'd be here?"

"Gabe and I have been in contact."

She sent him a look over the heads of the crowd. He caught her eye, and gave her another one of those carefree smiles that thrilled her. "He's thrown me a wonderful party."

"I know. And I really tried to see if I could make it back, but there just wasn't enough time."

So her guy had been applying a little pressure. She shook her head. "That's okay, Judith."

"I'm just so glad you're safe, Cassie." Her voice thickened. "That young man . . . that Reed Tucker . . ."

"He's locked up. He won't be hurting anyone ever again." From what they'd heard through Noah's contacts at the D.A.'s office, Reed's father was putting pressure on him to take a plea deal that would keep him safely away forever.

Her gaze caught on a pair of newcomers entering the shop. Gabe greeted them with noticeable affection and she narrowed her eyes as he drew them through the partyers in her direction. "I have to go now, Judith," she said. "Let's talk soon."

"We will," her mother promised. "Gabe knows how to reach me."

And then he was standing in front of her, beside a tall, gray-haired man and a much smaller woman who seemed to be blinking away tears. That crying thing must be contagious.

"Cassandra." Even Gabe sounded a little emotional as he gestured between her and the unknown pair. "These are my parents, Rosemary and Brock."

Oh. *Oh*.

The older man, so like Gabe, shook her hand, then held her to him for a brief, hard hug. His mom didn't bother with the handshake. She drew Cassandra against her, clasping her in an embrace that communicated how much she'd loved and missed her son. "Thank you," she said. "Thank you for bringing my boy back to me."

They were both sniffing as they turned to Gabe. "You've been busy," Cassandra said to him, accepting the tissue his mother pulled from her purse.

"Making up for lost time." He put an arm around each parent. "They're going to spend a few days with us here in Malibu."

She sniffed again. "I know what you're doing."

"You always have."

He was giving her family. In every way that he could.

"And guess what?" he said. "Dad's a vegetarian now."

"No!"

Brock Kincaid nodded. "Yep. For my heart. The old ticker has to be able to keep up with the grandkids."

She shot a look at Gabe. He shrugged, an "I didn't tell them" in his eyes.

Gabe's mom intercepted their unspoken communication. "We always have to have hope," Rosemary said.

Cassandra wasn't sure that's what she was feeling as the

party wound down and the shop emptied. Gabe took his parents to his house to get them situated and promised to be back for her shortly. Jay and Noah, bless their hearts, took it upon themselves to be the cleanup crew, and One of the Most Famous Actresses in America was helping them, along with the drummer from the heavy metal rock band Mercy. Carver grumbled something about being conscripted into service or else Gabe was going to drag him to a local parlor to make some painful changes to his favorite tat.

Cassandra had yet to figure out what that was all about. But she let it go as she and her sisters settled in the chairs on the shop's balcony. The tide was in, and they were suspended over the Pacific as the warm sun sank lower. They each held an envelope in their lap.

Cassandra's two sisters exchanged glances. Her stomach fluttered with more nerves. "Well?" she asked, when they didn't speak up. "It's obvious you have something to say."

"We went to see Dr. Frank Tucker," Juliet said quietly.

"Oh."

"I didn't like him much," Nikki added.

"You don't like anybody much," Cassandra pointed out. "At least not at the beginning."

The younger woman made a face. "Okay, true, but I'm starting to get tired of being the mean one."

"Let's leave that to Marlys," Juliet suggested. "Gabe invited her and Dean today, you know. But they were off to Las Vegas."

"Sealing the deal?" Nikki asked.

"Sealing the deal." Juliet nodded.

Cassandra fingered the envelope in her lap. "Speaking of seals—"

"We asked him why he decided to make contact with his donor offspring," Nikki interrupted. "With us."

Cassandra shifted in her chair. They were back to Dr. Tucker, not exactly her favorite subject. "And?"

Juliet looked down. "He said it was because his two sons didn't look anything like him. His wife couldn't have children, so they adopted, but he really wanted kids who resembled him."

"Oh." Cassandra didn't know what to say to that.

"I think it's the plastic surgery angle," Nikki said. "He's all about the surface stuff."

They went quiet. All about the surface stuff, Cassandra thought. Her hand crept over her belly. If she and Gabe had their spring flower, she couldn't imagine it would matter who he or she resembled. And if they found out she couldn't get pregnant, she was certain that she and Gabe would consider adoption.

All about the surface stuff.

Her hand tightened on the envelope in her lap. "Let's not open them," she blurted out.

Nikki and Juliet turned to her. "What?" they said together.

"I don't need to know what the results are. Do you?"

Nikki blinked. "This was all your idea, Froot Loop. Juliet and I never wanted to waste our time with this. We never doubted you're our sister."

"Then let's not look at them." Cassandra gripped the envelope. "Let's just . . . just . . . rip them into pieces and throw them out to sea."

Smiling, Juliet stood up. "Sounds good to me."

"Me, too." Nikki jumped to her feet.

Cassandra joined them at the rail of the balcony. "I love you guys." The threat of tears was at the back of her throat and in the corners of her eyes again. "You know, we did it. We knit together a family."

Nikki groaned. "Corny."

Juliet made the first tear in her envelope. "It's her birthday party so she can be as corny as she wants."

"Yeah, but—" Nikki started.

Juliet shot her a look. "I thought you didn't want to be the mean one anymore. Get ripping."

And so they did, all three of them tearing their envelopes into little pieces that they tossed over the railing where they caught the breeze like confetti. Another celebration.

When the paper had blown away on the ocean breeze, they sat down on the chairs again, Juliet, then Cassandra, then Nikki.

"Wow," Cassandra said. "I can't believe how free I feel."

They listened to the waves wash in and out against the bluff below them. Then Nikki spoke up in a small voice. "I have a confession to make."

Frowning, Cassandra looked over. "Another one? What is it?"

"I peeked." She said it quickly. "I looked at the results before I brought them here."

"Me, too," Juliet said.

Cassandra straightened her spine and whipped her head in her older sister's direction. "But . . . but you're Goody Two-shoes."

She shrugged. "Not always."

After a moment, Cassandra flopped back in her chair. "I looked, too."

No she hadn't. But it didn't matter, did it? They'd decided to be sisters. They'd decided to be family.

Her sisters were smiling at her. Maybe they guessed she was lying. Maybe their smiles meant they were pleased they were biological sisters or maybe their smiles meant they were pleased that even though they weren't, Cassandra was happy.

"Froot Loop?"

She turned to see Gabe in the doorway. Now she smiled, her heart swelling. She held out her hand to him, his touch the anchor her life needed.

She was no longer rootless or alone. With friendship and love in her life, there wasn't any room for loneliness, only possibilities.

Epilogue

A baby is God's opinion that life should go on.

—CARL SANDBURG

Playing in the Malibu sand under the hot summer sun, seven-year-old Riley Rosemary Kincaid decided this was the best day of her life. "I'm never going to forget it," she said, looking over at her mommy, who was lying under the shade of an umbrella.

"That's nice, baby," her mother murmured, her eyes closed.

Riley scratched her skin where the tag of her bikini bottoms—*Hand Knit By Mommy*—rubbed. The swimsuit was the best, too. Her mother had finished it last night. It was as yellow as her older cousin Annabelle's long blond hair, and the ties of the top had little crocheted pink flowers attached to the ends. When her other girl cousin, Aunt Nikki and Uncle Jay's daughter, Serena, had seen it, she'd begged her mom to make her one just like it.

Never going to happen. Aunt Nikki was stuck forever at the knitting scarves stage.

Riley glanced around for Serena now but didn't see

her. She looked toward the steps leading into Serena's house and figured the other girl was inside, pestering her mother about recipes as she prepared lunch. Serena was nine years old and already working on her second cookbook.

A trickle of sweat ran down Riley's temple and she stared at the cool ocean just a short distance away. Glancing over at her dozing mother, she rose slowly to her feet.

"Don't even think about it," her mom warned, her lashes still resting on her cheeks. "You don't go into the water without Daddy."

Riley frowned. How did she *do* that? With a flounce, she plopped back to the sand and turned her gaze on ten-year-old Annabelle, the daughter of Aunt Juliet and Uncle Noah. The oldest girl cousin, she sat like a princess on one corner of the blanket and drew a comb through her length of beautiful hair. Riley frowned deeper and tugged on the ends of the stuff she'd chopped off herself last week. Her father had choked the first time he'd seen what she'd done, but her mother had only sighed and reminded him that artists found canvases everywhere.

He'd made her promise never to get a tattoo or pierce anything but her earlobes, and then he'd taken her to the store and bought her new paints and brushes. He was so easy.

"Hey, shrimp," a boy's voice called out. "Think quick." A Nerf football bounced off the top of Riley's head.

She glared up at her brother Simon. He was just a few months older than Annabelle and the exact same age, of course, as his twin, Scott. A whole group of boys surrounded her: Simon and Scott; her other brother, eight-year-old Kyle; Annabelle's younger brother Adam; and Serena's brother

Mitch. With a grin, Mitch tossed the volleyball he carried at her, and she barely batted it away before it hit her nose. What a dummy.

"Are you okay?" Someone else kneeled down beside her. His black eyebrows came together over his dark brown eyes. Luis Santos. He was also ten, and much nicer than her brothers or her cousins. Annabelle thought so, too, Riley could tell, because she sat up a little straighter and tucked her comb under her hip. Luis didn't notice the other girl though; he was still looking at Riley.

She smiled at him. "I'm fine, Luis." He lived just one house away from Serena and Mitch in a little cottage that was painted a pale turquoise. Garlands of shells and starfish were hung like curtains over the windows. Riley loved it there, because it was so colorful and smelled of the sweet blossoms from the plumeria plants that Luis's dad had everywhere.

"Who wants to go swimming?" another voice boomed out.

Riley forgot all about blossoms and shells and even Luis as the man she loved most in the world approached. "Daddy!" She jumped to her feet and ran toward him. He swung her up in his arms and smacked a kiss on her cheek, his dark whiskers already a little rough.

"How are you, Mommy Froot Loop?" he called over her head.

Riley's mother smiled sleepily. "Incubating just fine, Gabe, thank you very much."

Her mom was pregnant again, her belly as big as a beach ball. It was another male baby her parents said, but Riley didn't mind. That would leave the three girl cousins in charge of all the boys, just as it should be.

She scrambled around to grasp Daddy's shoulders so he could cart her, piggyback-style, into the water. He loped toward it, the boys trailing behind. His feet splashed into the surf, but Riley was still high and dry. He turned his head to look at her. "Happy, honey?"

"Happy, Daddy."

He smiled, shaking his head a little. "Those blue and green eyes."

Riley had them, just like her aunts Nikki and Juliet. None of the other kids did, which she was secretly pretty pleased about. Artists didn't want to be like everyone else.

Her father strode deeper into the water and Riley looked back toward shore. The other adults in her family were gathered around the blanket, her aunts Nikki and Juliet and her uncles Jay and Noah. Luis's parents, Shana and Jorge, were there, too. Serena was sitting with Annabelle now, and they were playing with a baby. It had to be Marlys and Dean's new one, because those two grown-ups were herding their other kids toward the group.

Riley's mom had gotten up though, and was standing at the edge of the water watching as they waded. She ran her hand over the sarong-covered bulge of her belly. Riley waved to her. Then she waved to the dark-haired little girl standing nearby. She was wearing pink tights and flat pink slippers. Riley saw her every once in a while, sometimes at the beach, sometimes at home. She was always smiling. The ballet girl waved back now, then pirouetted off down the sand.

Cold water splashed Riley's legs as her daddy went deeper into the ocean. She squealed just a little and held him tighter. His back was warm and solid and she rested her cheek on his shoulder for a moment, then peered over it to look out at the endless water. She was never going to forget this moment, this day . . .

Oh, who was she kidding? She *would* forget today, she knew it, but only because there were a bazillion others just as perfect waiting on the horizon.

Who knew knitting could be so sexy?

Don't miss the first two books in the
romantic, lighthearted series featuring
the Southern California beachside
knitting store, Malibu & Ewe.

BY *USA TODAY* BESTSELLING AUTHOR

CHRISTIE RIDGWAY

How to Knit a Wild Bikini

&

Unravel Me

M402AS0309